PRAISE FOR WINIFRED ELZE

HERE, KITTY, KITTY

"Clever, entertaining."
—*Publishers Weekly*

"This tale of suspense is not just another kitty ditty . . .
The plot develops, quickly building to a satisfying . . .
conclusion."
—*West Coast Review of Books, Arts & Entertainment*

"Entertaining."
—*Locus*

THE CHANGELING GARDEN

"A quick, engrossing read . . . Imaginative."
—*Publishers Weekly*

"For readers who like scares served up with a more subtle
flavor than that of Anne Rice or Stephen King."
—*Library Journal*

"A marriage of *The Secret Garden* and *Rosemary's Baby*."
—*Kirkus Reviews*

St. Martin's Paperbacks Titles
by Winifred Elze

THE CHANGELING GARDEN
HERE, KITTY, KITTY

NNIE'S BOOK ST...
PEN 7 DAYS - 10 AM...
70 SOUTH MAIN ST...
RUTLAND, V...
775-...

Here, Kitty, Kitty

WINIFRED ELZE

St. Martin's Paperbacks

NOTE: If you purchased this book without a cover you should be aware that this book is stolen property. It was reported as "unsold and destroyed" to the publisher, and neither the author nor the publisher has received any payment for this "stripped book."

HERE, KITTY, KITTY

Copyright © 1996 by Winifred Elze.

All rights reserved. No part of this book may be used or reproduced in any manner whatsoever without written permission except in the case of brief quotations embodied in critical articles or reviews. For information address A Wyatt Book for St. Martin's Press, 175 Fifth Avenue, New York, N.Y. 10010.

Library of Congress Catalog Card Number: 96-6986

ISBN: 0-312-96317-3

Printed in the United States of America

A Wyatt Book for St. Martin's Press hardcover edition/July 1996
St. Martin's Paperbacks edition/October 1997

St. Martin's Paperbacks are published by St. Martin's Press, 175 Fifth Avenue, New York, NY 10010.

10 9 8 7 6 5 4 3 2 1

chapter 1

Billie had been missing when they locked up for the night. When a cat's cry awakened Emma at first light she smiled, pleased that Billie was all right, and pulled the covers tighter under her chin. A second cry, more pitiful than the first, made her sit up and swing her legs out into the cold morning air. She walked to the window and looked out, expecting to see Billie looking up at her from the deck below.

The deck was empty. Puzzled, Emma pushed her hair out of her face. The cry came again, and she looked at the garden, the lawn, the shore. Where . . . ?

Another mew, and Emma located the sound across the water. She must be on Ten-acre Island.

"Oh, Billie, how did you get out there?" Emma muttered. It wasn't as though she could stow away in somebody's boat: nobody went out there anymore.

Wondering if she could get her husband to go after the cat, she looked at the bed. Max slept soundly, his high-bridged nose in profile against the pillow, his mouth slightly open, revealing the one crooked incisor that kept his teeth from being perfect. She pulled jeans and a sweatshirt over her summer pajamas, slipped her feet into boating sneakers, and went downstairs.

The grass was silvery with dew, and Emma felt the bottoms of her jeans grow wet against her ankles as she walked to the shore. Before getting into the rowboat, she paused to look for Billie's position on the island's shore. She could just make out the small figure of her cat sitting on a log that had one end on the island, the other in the water. Billie saw her. She stood, tail aloft, and gave a more hopeful cry.

"I'll be right there, Billie," Emma said, untying the rowboat from their small dock.

The water was perfectly still, and wisps of mist rose from it toward a lavender-grey sky tinged with pink in the east. The island, too, was still, and night lay on the cedar trees. She didn't want to go to the island, and could feel apprehension constricting her chest at the thought of stepping onto it.

Billie cried again, moved back and forth on the log the way cats do when they're looking to jump.

Emma got into the boat and rowed toward her cat. The oarlocks creaked as she pulled the oars against the water. Ripples spread behind her passage, then faded to stillness. Billie's cry was getting closer, and she hoped the cat would be cooperative for once and not make her get on shore.

She pulled up near the log and shifted the oars into the boat. Billie greeted her with a rough and noisy purring, and Emma was able to lift her from the log without much trouble as the boat glided by. The purring stopped momentarily while Billie was suspended over the water, but resumed as soon as she was safely in the boat.

"How did you get out here?" Emma asked, stroking Billie's head and back. The cat wasn't wet at all. If she'd swum out, it had been hours ago.

Billie rubbed against Emma enthusiastically, apparently wanting to be petted everywhere at once. Suddenly she stopped and looked over Emma's shoulder. Billie crouched, arching her back and growling. Emma turned quickly to see the problem.

The forward momentum of the boat was carrying them along the margin of the island, toward a low outcropping of rock where rusted metal rings had once moored boats. No boats were there now, but a huge deer stood on the rock.

It was the largest deer Emma had ever seen. It was drinking from the lake, but raised its head to watch them pass. The boat drifted quite close to the rock, and Emma saw water dripping from its bearded chin. A round chin, the muzzle making a perfect circle. Its coat was shaggy brown, and thick, a coat for cold weather. Its hooves, inches from her, were so large she didn't think she could encompass them with both hands. Its chest was broader than a horse's, and when she looked up, she saw it regarding her with a mildly curious gaze.

Its antlers were not those of a deer or a moose, but they were big. The rowboat was directly under it, and the antlers extended beyond both ends of the boat. The sun came up then, behind it, a dazzle of light through the knobby, branching black shadow of its antlers.

It turned and moved off. The rowboat drifted farther out into the lake as Emma watched the deer lower its bulk into the water and swim toward the forest preserve on the far shore, only its antlered head raised high above the surface.

"Hey, hey, watch where you're going!" Charles Flewellen's voice cut through the silence.

Emma jumped, turned, scrambled for her oars and got control of her boat just in time to keep it from colliding with Charles' boat. He sat as he had every fine morning since his retirement: fishing creel in hand, filament stretching into the water. He wore a plaid wool shirt, worn through at the elbows, and a shapeless hat with fishing lures stuck in the band. Below the hat he was all elbows and angles, and his knees poked above the sides of the rowboat.

"What are you doing out here so early?" Charles asked.

"Did you see that deer?"

"What deer?"

She looked toward the far shore. It was pulling itself out of the water. "That one."

He glanced over. "They do swim."

"It's huge," Emma said. "Look how big it is next to those trees."

"Saplings," Charles said. "I told you, you lose perspective out here."

The deer disappeared into the forest.

"No," Emma said. "I mean, it's huge. Its antlers . . ." She did some quick mental arithmetic involving the length of the rowboat. "Its antlers are at least nine feet wide," she said quietly, trying to take it in herself.

Charles laughed.

"I mean it. I didn't know they got that big."

"They don't."

"But . . . didn't you see it? It was standing on the rock on the island, drinking water."

Charles chuckled. "Do you take your cat fishing every morning?"

4

Emma looked at Billie, who was seated in the rear of the boat and peering intently into the water. Her tail twitched. A school of little brown fish darted toward the front of the boat, and Billie's gaze followed them.

"This wasn't exactly a deer," Emma said. "It was bigger boned, more like a moose. Only it was bigger than a moose, too."

"On the island, you said?" Charles' rod bent, and he reeled in his line. A trout made a glittering, wriggling arc into his boat.

"Yes."

"Everything has to do with that island."

"What do you mean?"

Charles detached the fish from his line and dropped it into his basket. "You're letting your emotions about the island color your perceptions of it, Emma. It's just an ordinary island except for what happened to your father out there."

"You mean, you think I'm making this up?"

"No, not exactly. But I think your imagination's making you exaggerate a tad."

Emma thumped the oars back into the locks and gave the right oar a strong, sudden pull. The boat turned. Startled, Billie dug her claws into the seat. "I am not exaggerating," Emma said. "Why don't we go look for hoofprints?"

"Thought you said it was on the rock. Won't be any hoofprints on the rock."

Emma thought there would be prints in the interior, but she didn't want to go into the interior. Saying anything about that would only make things worse. "You're just so blinded by your own preconceptions, you can't see what's in front of you." She pulled on the oars, but jerkily, and they

5

popped out of the locks. She fumbled them back into place to the background noise of Charles' laughter.

"Wait, wait, don't go away mad," Charles said. "Here: take a trout back for breakfast." He wrapped a fish in newspaper and handed it to her.

"Thank you," Emma said through clenched teeth. Charles laughed again. Emma decided she was tired of his laugh.

Billie instantly sniffed the paper, poking her nose between the folds.

"That's not your breakfast," Emma said, holding it up and wondering how she was going to row home and keep Billie away from the trout.

"Here," Charles said. "Here's some bait fish for you." He threw a couple into the boat and Billie pounced on them.

Emma set the trout on the seat beside her and rowed toward home.

"Friends?" Charles called after her.

"Of course," she shouted back. "But I still saw what I saw."

The boat glided past the island, and the loudest sounds were Billie's chewing and the oars slapping the water. Sloppy rowing style, Emma knew, and tried to calm down. Birds trilled on shore, calling to each other.

How had Billie gotten onto the island? She hated water. Emma had seen her up to her elbows hunting frogs and fish, but if she fell in that always put an end to it. She just wanted out.

Maybe she'd fallen in and grabbed onto a log or something and it drifted out to the island. But what current would it drift on?

Emma supposed she'd never know. It was just one of those mysterious situations cats get into.

The mist was rising more quickly now, and soon would all be gone. The sun was bright on the water, the sky without clouds. Today was going to be a scorcher, she could tell.

She looked across the open expanse of lake, past the island to the far shore with its thick growth of trees down to the waterline. Did the forest hide herds of giant deer? Or was Charles right? Was her imagination compounding them out of grief and fear?

She thought of the deer on the rock.

She had seen what she had seen.

Billie was finishing the last bites of fish when the boat bumped against the shore. The motion jarred her balance, and she dropped the fins. They were too sharp, anyway. She jumped onto the seat and licked the fish smell off her whiskers.

Her person left the boat and walked toward home. After a few steps, she turned toward Billie and crooned a signal to come.

Billie followed across the wet grass. With each step, she shook her paw to get the annoying water off. The woman went ahead.

A feathered thing fluttered onto the grass and Billie paused. The bird inspected the ground, pecked. Billie crouched, and the muscles of her back twitched, then the tip of her tail. She eased forward. The bird hopped. Belly to the ground, ears flat, Billie inched toward it.

The air suddenly went out of Billie's lungs as a hand lifted her from the ground. A sound of feathers was in her ears as the bird flew off. Billie found herself in her person's arms. She regretted missing the bird, but was glad to be off the wet grass. She purred and stretched herself over the woman's shoulder.

As they continued toward the house, Billie sniffed the air. There was a trace of the deer from otherside, but all the remaining smells were of home. The deep red light was gone from the island. The doorway her person's father had made to otherside was closed.

chapter 2

Emma carried Billie up the stairs to the deck.
When they reached the top step, the glass door
to the kitchen slid open. There was Max, checking
the morning and probably looking for her. He wore his
Mummenschanz T-shirt and jeans, and his hair was wet from
the shower. A drop of water fell from his hair, already fighting to regain its wiry curl, and slid along his jawline. He held
a steaming mug in his hand.

"I made coffee," he said, sounding relieved to see her.
He smiled, and the trace of anxiety left his eyes.

Billie jumped onto the deck and went inside.

"Great. I've got a trout for breakfast." Emma kissed him
lightly as she went past him into the kitchen. She wrapped
the fish in plastic and put it in the refrigerator.

"You got up to go fishing?"

"I got up to get Billie." Emma poured herself coffee.
Max had turned on the kitchen TV and it chattered in the
background. "The fish is from Charles. I had to row out . . ."
The sound of Billie scratching in her litterbox came from the
downstairs bathroom. "I can't believe it: she got me up to

9

bring her home so she could use the litterpan. That cat is overcivilized."

Emma brought her coffee out to the deck and sat at the table with Max, the glass door open between them and the kitchen. Inside, overcolored images fluttered on the TV screen: a weather report. They were predicting heat and sunshine.

"I hate deadlines," Max said, then sipped his coffee.

Emma looked across the lake and marveled at how different it was from the grey and misty place of shadows she'd visited a short time ago. Now it was all crayon colors: blue sky, green trees, blue water. Charles rowed by, red shirt, yellow boat. He nodded to them, his hands busy with the oars, and they waved back.

"I saw a deer on the island," Emma said.

"I suppose it swam out," said Max. He set his coffee down and, improvising a picture frame with his hands, scanned the lake. Suddenly he dropped this game and turned to Emma. "Wait a minute. Are you telling me you actually went onto that island?"

"No. I rowed past and rescued the cat. And there was a huge deer standing on that rock at the end and drinking from the lake."

Max put his hand over hers. "I don't like waking up alone."

"Max, you're not listening. This deer was so big, it had feet like hubcaps. The span of its antlers was at least three yards."

Max spluttered, trying not to choke on the mouthful of coffee he was swallowing.

"Its antlers were wider than our rowboat is long, and

the boat is nine feet," Emma said, pulling her hand away from him.

"I guess we're lucky it didn't drink the whole lake." Chuckling, Max shook his head. "Emma, deer don't come that big."

"Fine. Go ahead and laugh. You're as bad as Charles."

"Charles saw it, too?"

"No, and he didn't believe me either."

"But he was out there?"

"I know what I saw," Emma said. She stood, threw what remained of her coffee out in a brown arc that fell into the grass, and went inside.

Max followed, still chuckling. "Now calm down, calm down," he said. He tried to put his arms around her, but she shrugged him off. She took the fish out of the refrigerator. "Here, you can clean it," she said, pushing it toward him.

Max sighed. "It's that island. You see anything to do with it as strange."

Emma cut up an onion, whacking the blade of the cleaver up and down on the cutting board in rapid little strokes that she knew would dull the edge, but she didn't care. "It is strange."

"But it doesn't have things on it that don't exist."

Emma slammed the frying pan onto the stove with enough force that Max winced. "How would you like it if you saw something and nobody would believe you?"

"Happens all the time. It's called imagination. Only I've learned to put it in cartoons and get paid for it. Hey, how come that cat isn't pestering me for this fish?"

Emma was frying the onions, but she glanced over her shoulder. Billie lay stretched out in her basket, her paws twitching, her eyes displaying REM movements beneath the closed lids. "Charles gave her a couple of bait fish."

"Look at her. She's exhausted. You'd think she worked for a living."

"She was out all night. And you're just trying to change the subject."

"Absolutely. I hate a fight before breakfast." He put his arms around her, and this time Emma didn't push him away.

"Billie saw the deer, too. She growled at it," Emma said.

After breakfast, Max went downstairs to his drawing board. Emma showered and dressed, then cleaned up the kitchen. When she vacuumed, Billie awakened and went downstairs stiff-legged with annoyance.

In the late morning, Emma carried a book and the binoculars onto the deck. She sat, the book unread beside her, and studied the island.

A thick growth of cedar crowded the island's shoreline, except for the end to her right, where bare rock glared in the August sun. Seen through the binoculars, the individual trees leaped into focus. The branches bent toward the water and touched their reflections. Emma followed the waterline to the rocky outcropping and the rusted rings attached to the fissured granite. She wanted something unusual to appear, but it all looked stubbornly normal. She picked up her book.

Emma had read a few chapters when a splash caught her attention. She grabbed the binoculars.

A large animal was swimming away from the island, disturbing the rock's reflected image. From what she could see of its body beneath the surface, she estimated its length at five or six feet. Its head rose sleek and wet above the water, and it was doing a standard mammalian dog paddle. It swam in a line that would carry it between the island's rocky out-cropping and the matching rock on the mainland, where Rutledge's house stood.

The animal had an unfamiliar look: a big head, small ears spaced wide apart, dark fur. Maybe it just seemed strange because it was wet. Maybe it was a bear, or even a dog with a big head. But she didn't think so. It looked more like a beaver, but it was too big. Soon it would round the point, and she wouldn't be able to see it.

Emma heard Max's footsteps behind her in the kitchen. When he came up without being called, it meant work wasn't going well. "Max, come here, quick. There's something swimming in the lake."

He joined her on the deck. "What's for lunch?" he said. "I'm starved."

"There's a giant beaver or something swimming in the lake," Emma said. She pointed, but it had disappeared behind the shoreline trees.

Max looked at the empty lake. "Are giant animals going to be a running joke all summer?" he asked.

Max's hair was standing up untidily, a sure sign he'd been running his hands through it. "Frustrating morning?" Emma asked.

In answer, he stretched his arms up over his head and yodeled.

"I wish you wouldn't do that," she said.

"What's the point of living in the country if you can't make a little noise? I'm going to give up cartooning. I'll drive a school bus instead."

Emma, who had heard this before, leaned across the deck rail and tried to see farther up the lake. She caught a whiff of something that distracted her from the animal. "I smell smoke," she said. She raised her binoculars and scanned the trees across the lake in the forest preserve for signs of fire. The line of green abutting the blue sky was nowhere broken by smoke, or made wavery by heat. The same was true of the island, where the dark green cedars stood sentinel, their drooping branches guarding the view to the interior.

"It was a chilly morning," Max said. "Maybe somebody's using their woodstove."

"Not Rutledge. It would be a point of pride with him not to have a fire in August," Emma said, but she looked toward his house anyway. Rutledge would build a good fire, one with very little smoke, so she checked for the wiggily signature of heat above his chimney. There was none.

"That wouldn't stop your sister or her husband," said Max.

"There's no smoke coming from their chimney," Emma said, pointing toward Dana and Bootsy Moore's house. "And I do smell smoke."

Max put his arms around her and sniffed the air. "I smell perfume," he said, nuzzling her neck. "We're not going to have another worrying day, are we? Strange animals, and smoke, all at once."

She pushed him away. "I'm serious. Don't you smell it?"

He frowned at the air. "Maybe somebody's burning trash."

She shook her head. "It's a wood fire."

"My wife, the expert on woodsmoke."

"Bootsy and I came up here every summer with dad when we were kids. When you live in the woods, you learn

14

to pay attention to what woodsmoke smells like. You'd better."

An expression of enlightenment spread over Max's face. "I know. They're burning off paint down at the boatwright's."

Emma considered this, sniffed. "Could be."

"It is. You may know wood, but I know all about paint. Let's eat."

He drew her to him and led her inside. The kitchen was cool and dim, with a lemony-herbal scent from the furniture polish she'd been using that morning. Emma reached into the refrigerator for lettuce and mayonnaise. "I don't know what it was out there," she said, rattling through the gadget drawer for the can opener. "But it was big, maybe six feet long, and furry."

Billie was napping lightly on the windowsill when her ears caught the sound of the refrigerator opening. She raised her head, eyes open but third eyelid still partly in place, and listened. Clatter in the can opener drawer brought her fully alert. She sprang from the windowsill and ran into the kitchen.

Her people were there, uttering their customary chirps and mews. No point in bothering with the larger one: he only fed her when the smaller one wasn't there. The woman held the can opener, anyway, and the whoosh it made was followed by a tantalizing scent. This was something they usually shared with her, pouring the juices into a saucer, and Billie rubbed against the woman's ankles in happy anticipation, stating her claim both to the person and the food she held.

The woman made a sound she used to express a confusing range of emotions, including affection and territorial defense and polite offering, but always somehow directed toward her, so Billie recognized the sound. This time, it meant polite offering: the saucer of fragrant liquid was duly set before her. She lapped contentedly, and purred her appreciation.

Her people sat at the table, eating with their hands as they always did, the larger one making discontented noises, the smaller chirruping lightly to distract him. Billie listened to their cries while she cleaned her face and whiskers, and wondered how he could be unhappy with such a delicious treat before him.

Suddenly she noticed a deep red light outside: The doorway on the island was opening. She ran toward it, forgot about the glass door, hit her nose. She skittered along the polished floor and scrambled onto the deck.

A low red light the color of heat, the smell of blood, spread out from the island's rocky point. Waves rippled through the light, the crests of the waves rising higher and higher, drawing closer together. The light kept folding on itself until it fused into an opening through which she could see ground and the bottoms of shrubs. This was the doorway her person's father had made into otherside. The opening on the island was large, but the openings that rode the crests of the waves grew smaller and smaller as they got farther away from the old man's machine. The one near her house was cat-sized.

Billie heard rustling from otherside that was more than just the wind: it was patterned like a food search. Her whiskers tingled with excitement.

She looked back at her people, who were chattering away, oblivious to what had happened. It puzzled her that her people, who could open refrigerator doors, doors to inside, to outside, to cabinets of food, never saw these doors. When Billie stared at a doorway to otherside, they would stare at her with puzzled expressions on their faces. They would look where she looked, and seem to try to see the doorway, but clearly they never did. The first time Billie returned through a doorway and landed beside the man, he jumped and spilled his drink. Then he blamed Billie.

The old man had never seen the doorway, either, even though he had made it.

Billie returned her attention to otherside. A small rodent came into view, nose twitching with puzzlement. It smelled something it didn't like, probably cat, and scurried away. Billie leaped after it. The doorway closed behind her.

"If this afternoon doesn't go better, I'm going to strangle those kids myself," Max said. With his finger, he drew a frowning face in the condensation on his iced tea glass.

Emma shook her head and clicked her tongue. "And you want to drive a school bus."

"The advantage of fictional kids, especially comic characters, is you can strangle them whenever you want to and not get arrested." With a forkful of tuna and lettuce halfway to his mouth, he stopped and stared at Billie, who had suddenly tried to run through the glass door. She made a frantic effort to get around the door, succeeded and, once outside, promptly sat down. "Your cat is wierd."

"All cats are weird."

"Maybe I ought to give one of the kids in the strip a cat," Max said. He was halfway through his salad. Emma could see he was cheering up.

"Oh? And could you think like a cat?" she said.

He shrugged. "That's easy. They only think one thing:

feed me. The real problem is I've never been able to draw a cat."

Emma stiffened, listening.

"What?" Max said.

"I think I hear a siren."

"First smoke, now sirens. You . . . you're right," he said, as it grew louder.

They hurried out onto the deck. The emergency siren blared, supplemented by the wail of an approaching fire engine. Billows of smoke rose from the lakeshore.

"I told you there was a fire," Emma said.

Max rushed through the kitchen toward the front door.

Wanting to put Billie inside, Emma looked around for her, but the cat was gone. Scared off by the sirens, Emma supposed. Max was already going out the front door, and she hurried after him.

From the steps, Emma could see Bootsy and Dana come to the edge of their lawn, perplexed expressions on their faces. "Where's the fire?" Dana called out. The rough beard he'd been cultivating this summer was newly trimmed and, together with his arched eyebrows, gave him a Mephistophelean look. Bootsy had scissors in her hand and Emma suspected she was responsible.

"On the lakeshore," Max shouted.

Just then, Rutledge Harrison ran from behind Dana's house and across his lawn. Rutledge was pulling on his volunteer firefighter's jacket as he ran. His helmet was already in place. The long, thin face was unsmiling, his concentration locked on the fire in a way that increased Emma's uneasiness.

Dana's perplexity changed to annoyance at the sight of Rutledge crossing his lawn. Emma remembered Dana had been willing enough to agree to Rutledge's right-of-way when he'd wanted to buy the property, but now that he had what he wanted, he was annoyed at having to keep his part of the bargain.

Rutledge ran up the road.

"It must be nearby if he's not taking his car," Emma said.

"He's going toward Nelson's. Runs fast for a guy his age," Max said. "Come on, let's find out what's happening."

chapter 3

Emma and Max hurried along the dirt road behind Rutledge, whose boots kicked up a haze of dust particles. As they passed Rutledge's scuff marks, the dust had begun to sift back down onto the pebbles and ruts in the road.

"It's been a dry summer," Emma said anxiously.

"The town's overdue on oiling the road, is all," Max said, taking her hand in his reassuring grasp.

The woods on either side were shadowy places lavish with ferns. Above layers of interlocked branches, a dazzle of sky caught in the topmost leaves. The sirens' wail grew louder, then cut off. The relative silence unmasked a cicada's drill-like hum.

Closer to the boatwright's, the small rustlings in the forest increased. Squirrels leaped from tree to tree, their path evident in the swaying branches they left behind them. Mice scurried through last year's fallen leaves, and a family of quail picked its way hastily. A raccoon blundered into the road, squinted at Emma, then crashed back into the undergrowth.

"They're running from the fire," Emma said, quickening her pace toward Nelson's. The smell of burning wood grew more acrid.

The fire truck's massive, gleaming presence was a jolt of red among all the green. Two men in firemen's hats and slickers trained the truck's hose on small fires in the woods and brush, while others ran around spotting fires and signaling where to point the hose. Everybody seemed to be shouting orders at everybody else.

Nelson Lang's boatwright's shop, architecturally an airplane hangar with a Victorian porch wrapped around it, stood unharmed. Emma was glad: Nelson had put a lot of work into renovating it when he'd retired from the navy. Beyond the shop a shed blazed, and beside the shed a smaller object had already collapsed into a heap of embers.

Snakes of fire traveled through the dry grass, and sparks rose and floated toward the adjoining woods. They had already ignited a couple of small fires in the dry leaves of the forest floor, and one high in an old squirrel's nest.

The firemen ignored the shed and concentrated on keeping the flames from spreading. The two with the hose were constantly busy, and Nelson, wearing his white naval officer's cap, worked among a group of men digging a strip of bare earth through the grass to keep the fire away from his shop. The others wore firemen's hats with jeans and T-shirts, or slacks and short-sleeved dress shirts, having come from work when the alarm sounded. Walter Tymeson's burly figure stood tall among them, and his hat bore the fire chief's emblem.

"You wait on the porch," Max said. He went over to the men and Walter handed him a shovel.

Lillian, Nelson's wife and bookkeeper, stood on the porch under the "Nelson's Boats" sign. She leaned forward, watching the activity, her perky face lined with anxiety, her thin hands tense on the railing. She wore an A-line skirt, co-ordinated sweater set, and sensible pumps, which meant she considered this one of her working days.

"Lillian," Emma said, walking toward her. "Anything I can do to help?"

Lillian shook her head and her short, frosted curls bounced. "Best leave it to the firemen. They should be able to get it under control.

"What happened?"

"Fool with a heat gun, burning the paint off the bottom of a boat. He set fire to it instead. Those things are perfectly safe if you use them properly."

A teenage boy left the line of diggers and came over to the porch. He seemed more sooty than the others, and his eyes were red-rimmed. His shoulder-length hair was stringy with sweat, and there was a look of discouragement on his face that seemed too old for the smooth cheeks, stubby nose, soft mouth. He plopped himself down on the steps. "Could I have some water?" he asked Lillian.

"Waste of a good boat, not to mention the shed. To-tally unnecessary," Lillian said.

The boy coughed. Lillian's expression hardened, and Emma wondered why. The boy coughed again, at length. Emma made a movement toward the shop: he obviously needed a drink. But Lillian put out a hand to stop her.

"I'll get it," Lillian said grudgingly, and stalked inside.

The boy's coughing subsided. "It's all my fault," he said despondently.

Emma realized this must be the fool with the heat gun. "What happened?" she asked.

Lillian came back with a glass of water, and the boy downed it thirstily. "Thanks, Lillian," he said.

"I hope you appreciate the trouble you caused Nelson," Lillian said. "If you'd paid attention to what you were doing, there's no way this would have happened."

"I was doing fine, until that thing come at me."

Lillian looked at Emma. "Petey here saw a bear, so he dropped a paint stripper turned to high on top of a wooden boat and ran off. Can you believe it?"

"It wasn't a bear. I just said it was as big as a bear. It was this big hairy animal, and it come out of the woods, straight at me."

Lillian snorted. "If it's as big as a bear, and as hairy as a bear, and it comes out of the woods, it is a bear."

"Was it wet?" Emma asked, but Petey didn't seem to catch what she said.

"Thanks for the water," he said to Lillian, setting the glass down. He headed back toward the fire, obviously preferring it to Lillian's company.

Rutledge and another fireman grabbed axes from the side of the truck and headed into the woods.

"What are they going to do with the axes?" Emma asked.

"They'll pick a narrow place and cut down a few trees to make a break in the woods. It's to keep the fire from leaping from treetop to treetop, if it gets out of control down here. I don't think it will, though."

Dana joined them on the porch. The beard looked better close up, but Emma would bet that when he went back to the university in the fall, his students would be drawing caricatures of him with horns and a tail. "Looks like they have it almost out," he said.

Emma wondered why, if Dana was as anxious to become part of the community as Bootsy seemed to think he was, he hadn't joined the fire company or the rescue squad or even the church choir. She glanced behind him. "Where's Bootsy?"

"Guarding the homestead. She's wetting down the roof with our garden hose."

Lillian snorted.

"I don't think that's going to be necessary," Emma said, waving toward the scene. The shed and boat had diminished to the size of large campfires. The woods held blackened patches, but no flames, no smoke. The lawn was a scorched and sodden mess, and a smell of wet ashes moved across it.

"It seems to be well under control," Dana agreed. "But Bootsy likes to be doing something." He held a pipe, and shifted it from one hand to the other, as though wondering whether etiquette permitted him to light it.

By twos and threes, the men ceased their activity and drifted toward the porch.

"They'll be thirsty," Emma said to Lillian. "Should we get them some water?"

Lillian gave her a knowing look. "They won't be wanting water," she said, as Nelson, his white cap stained with soot, bustled up the steps and into the shop. He came out a moment later with a couple of six-packs in each hand, and gave out beers to everyone. Below his T-shirt sleeve, his tanned arm showed a tattoo of a mermaid. Her tail wiggled as his muscles flexed, distributing the beer.

Max walked toward them, the shovel slung over his shoulder, his smile white in his smoke-stained face. He was chatting with Walter, and he looked small beside the ex–football player. Emma had never seen Walter play, but she had seen the wall of his sporting goods store that was covered with pictures of him from his high school and minor league careers. His shoulders had looked bigger then, and his gut smaller, but maybe it was all the padding they wore.

Max accepted a beer and plopped down on the steps near Emma.

"Thank you all for coming," Nelson said, raising his beer can in a toast. His face was red from heat and exertion, and sweat trickled from under his thick black hair. "Sorry for the carelessness."

"Wasn't your fault, Admiral," Walter said, taking off his helmet and wiping the sweat from his forehead with a big blue bandanna. "I guess every man has one fool working for him." He looked pointedly at Jake Witte, the restaurant owner, but Petey, hovering empty-handed at the edge of the group, seemed to be the one to take the remark to heart.

"Why, Walter, I haven't had a grease fire in months," Jake said, taking his cue from Walter and playing to him. Emma wondered if he'd thrown passes to Walter back in their high school days. He was about the right age, late thirties, early forties.

"Not since you fired Petey," Walter said, and the men looked at the boy and laughed.

The smile stayed in place on Nelson's face, but he didn't join in the laughter. He gave Petey a look of calculated assessment that probably stemmed from twenty years' experience dealing with boys Petey's age. "Hey, Petey," Nelson said, "catch." The boy looked up and Nelson threw him a can of beer. "You did good helping put it out."

Petey smiled, and the smile seemed more natural to his face than the earlier look of dejection. He caught the can and popped it open, spraying himself and the man next to him. Neither of them seemed to mind. "Wouldn't have happened at all if that thing hadn't come at me out of the woods," Petey said.

"Petey claims he was attacked by a bear," said Lillian, who seemed to take a more sour view of midshipmen.

"Bear? Kind of close to houses, for a bear, especially this time of year," said Walter.

"We have a problem behind the restaurant," Jake said, "But that's because we throw out a lot of food. Do you have a bear problem, Nelson?"

Nelson shook his head.

"It wasn't a bear," Petey said. "It was more like a beaver."

Walter guffawed. "You were attacked by a beaver?"

"Was it wet?" Emma asked again, and again was ignored.

"It was a big beaver, big as a bear. Maybe five feet tall. Big as me, anyway."

Nelson kept a straight face. He was the only one who did. "Son, beavers don't come that big," he said.

"This one did," Petey said. "He come at me out of the woods, and he kind of looked at me with one eye, then got a fix on me with the other, and came slavering after me. He had teeth like . . . Well, like I don't know what, but they were big teeth, beaver teeth."

Even Nelson lost it then. "Petey was attacked by a buck-toothed bear."

"It wasn't no bear," Petey shouted. "And if you all had a six-foot beaver coming after you, you wouldn't think it was so funny."

"It's getting bigger," Jake said.

"The beaver that ate Tokyo!" said Walter.

Rutledge and the other fireman were back with their axes. "What's so funny?" the fireman asked. Emma recognized him when he spoke: Howard Connely, who ran the motel.

Nelson had regained control of himself. "Petey says he was attacked by a giant beaver, causing him to drop the paint stripper and accidentally set fire to the boat he was working on."

Rutledge and Howard looked at each other, then back at Nelson. "You're putting us on, right?" said Howard.

"Not me," Nelson said, handing them each a beer. He now had a handful of empty plastic rings. "Lillian, would you mind . . ."

"I can see no more work's going to get done this afternoon," Lillian said, going inside.

"I saw something swimming in the lake," Emma said.

"Was it building a dam?" Walter asked. Emma gave up trying to make the group listen. "If something like that showed up around here, it would be in Emma or Bootsy's backyard."

Emma gave Walter a look she hoped would turn him into stone, or at least shut him up momentarily. But he seemed not to notice.

"You two are back fast," Walter said to Rutledge and Howard.

"We didn't have to do any cutting," Rutledge said. "Somebody's beat us to it: couple of trees were down by the water, maybe not exactly where we'd have cut, but close enough."

"Somebody's been in my woods with a chain saw?" Nelson asked.

"No," said Howard. "Not a chain saw. They'd been chopped."

"Chopped?" said Nelson.

Lillian returned to the porch with a stack of six-packs. She carried them with a practiced air that shed light on her attitude toward midshipmen. Emma helped her set them down.

"Maybe they were gnawed," Walter said, accepting a second can from Lillian. "Maybe Petey's giant beaver did it." He wiped tears of laughter from his eyes and turned to Dana. "What do you say, professor? You're the expert. Are there giant beavers in the Adirondacks?"

Dana seemed surprised to be spoken to. "Not anymore," he said. Emma noticed he'd stowed the pipe in his pocket and was holding the beer can away from his body, the picture of a man who's afraid of spilling beer on his jacket.

It was Walter's turn to be surprised. "Not anymore?"

"So there are giant beavers?" Petey said hopefully.

"There was a giant beaverlike animal who lived in this area," Dana said. "But it's been extinct for ten thousand years."

Everyone laughed as though Dana had come up with the best punch line of the day. Dana beamed with pleasure.

"Petey was scared by the ghost of a beaver," Walter choked out through his laughter.

Nelson raised his beer can. "To the giant beaver of Lake Harrison!" he said. "We are witness to the birth of a legend!"

chapter 4

Billie landed in otherside and missed the rodent by inches. It shrieked and ran into the undergrowth. Billie followed, her concentration sharpened to a pinpoint focus on her prey. They zigzagged through a twiggy growth of birch, paws slipping on last season's leaves, until, at the base of an oak, the rat gave a final swerve and disappeared into a hole among the roots.

Billie sat down to wait. It would have to come out eventually. She noticed a smell of cat urine from the tree, a territorial marking, which she recognized as the signature of one of the great cats. She wondered how far away the sabertooth was, and looked around to make sure she had several avenues of escape should it suddenly appear.

After a time a wiggily nose poked out of the hole and Billie pounced, but not quickly enough to snatch the rodent from its burrow. It squealed and made angry, chattering noises with teeth she knew from experience to be sharp. She retreated and crouched a little way off, peering over the tops of the leaves that surrounded her.

A sound to her right caught her attention: something

large moving through the birches. She sat up and opened her mouth, the better to taste the air. The air itself was less complicated here, without the car smells and polishes, the paints and cooking odors that overlaid the plant and animal smells of home. Identification was easy: mammoth. And coming closer.

Billie leaped at the oak and climbed quickly, pulling herself above the massive bodies on their big feet, out of range of the twisting, curious trunks. Her claws found easy purchase on the coarse bark, and she soon found a limb she considered both safe and comfortable. She sat, tail twitching with excitement, and watched what was happening below.

The mammoths were browsing on grass and birch twigs. They scraped the ground with their long, curved tusks to loosen the young birches, then twisted their trunks around the saplings and pulled them up. Calves toddled beside them and accepted a share of the food the adults gathered. Two of the babies took time out to play, and their long, shaggy hair rippled back from their outthrust trunks as they ran. Against the black of their fur, their budding tusks flashed white.

Billie noticed movement directly beneath her. Unseen by the mammoths, a sabertooth stalked them, using the birch thicket as cover. Billie could see the top of its head and long, tawny back ending in a tailless rump. She crept farther out on her branch, to see better, and stretched her body along it, causing it to sway slightly under her weight.

The leaves at the end of Billie's branch rustled, and the cat below her glanced up, presenting its massive head and the weaponry of its teeth to her view. Billie looked down into round, golden eyes, the pupils round and as deeply black as the lake at night. Even though she knew she was out of reach, she felt the fur along her back bristle in response to this gaze. Then the great cat gave a dismissive twitch of its whiskers and moved on.

It circled the birch thicket in a gliding crouch that brought it to the meadow's edge. The baby mammoths were playing near the adults, running in circles and disturbing a flock of orange-and-black butterflies. A mammoth calf broke away and ran toward the clearing's center, away from the browsing herd.

The sabertooth sprang. The little mammoths shrieked and ran for safety. The cat ran, anticipating their path. It hit the slower one with its paw, a heavy blow to the head, before the adults had even looked up. Then it held the stunned calf with both front paws and ripped its neck open with one blow of its fangs.

The other calf reached the adults just as the herd turned to look at the cat.

The sabertooth stood over the dead calf. It faced the herd and snarled, arching its back and baring all its teeth to show its fangs at their most threatening. Its mouth was blood-smeared, and red drops fell from the tips of its fangs.

The herd stood motionless, poised. Then the largest male lifted his trunk and trumpeted. Suddenly they all ran away across the tundra.

The cat settled down to eat. The twittering of birds, which had stopped during this encounter, started up again. The butterflies fluttered back into the grass.

Billie noticed a figure at the edge of the oak forest: a person, dressed in animal skins. It faded back into the shadows. Billie knew where it came from, had seen its home, and didn't think much of it: it had no refrigerator, no cupboards. She waved her tail in a contemptuous arch.

Billie stood up and stretched each muscle in her body, one at a time, starting with the tips of her paws and working all the way back to a rippling movement of her tail. Then she yawned.

She was hungry. It was time to go home. She climbed back down the tree and looked for a door, recalling places where she had found them before. When one twirled open, she jumped through, checking first for water. This place was much the same as home, the most important difference being that the lake at home was far larger. If there was anything she hated, it was jumping through a doorway from dry land only to plunk into water on the home side.

The fire having been pronounced out, and the beer drunk, the group outside Nelson's went their separate ways. Emma walked toward the road with Max, Rutledge, and Dana. Max and Rutledge, equally soot-streaked and sweaty, had fallen into an easy companionship because of having fought the fire together. Rutledge had his firefighter's jacket under his arm, and dangled his hat from one callused hand. His deeply lined face was bright with life. He laughed at something Max said, then pointed to Max's Mummenschanz T-shirt.

"What is that, a rock group?" Rutledge asked.

Max laughed. "Not even close. It's a theater group. Kind of a cross between mime and puppetry."

Dana walked silently, a little apart, deep in thought. He tripped, pulled his hands out of his pockets to keep his balance, and suddenly looked at the others as though he'd just noticed they were there.

"What do you suppose the boy saw?" Dana asked with eagerness that went beyond idle curiosity.

"Petey?" said Rutledge. "I don't know. I wouldn't call

him a reliable witness, not under the circumstances."

"I saw something, too," Emma said. "It was swimming across the lake."

"But not a six-foot beaver," Max put in hastily, taking a protective stance toward her. "It could be you saw whatever animal frightened Petey, it's even probable you saw it. But you don't know what it was, either."

"Did you? That's very interesting," Dana said. His eyes held a selfless, appealing simplicity.

"Backs Petey up, anyway," said Rutledge. "What do you think it was, Dana?"

Dana looked back at Nelson's and the lake beyond it. "I'd love to know. There's over two million acres of land set aside to be forever wild, starting on the other side of that lake. Could be we don't know everything that's in there."

They reached the dirt road. Emma stood looking toward the gap where the trees had been felled. The firemen had probably been right, it was probably just somebody with an ax. And yet . . . trees had been cut like that on the island last summer. She felt a malaise that would only be dispelled by going there and seeing a perfectly normal bit of woods.

"Bootsy and I would like you all to come for drinks tonight," Dana said, the cocky awkwardness returning to his manner. He stroked his new beard. "You, too, Rutledge."

"I don't know, Dana," Max said. "I'd like to, but I've got this deadline . . . oh shit."

Emma turned and saw that he was looking at his watch.

"Charles and Peggy are coming," Dana said. "Bootsy's feeling down because of its being the anniversary of your father's death. She could use some company. I thought I'd cook something on the grill, keep it simple. If you have to leave early to finish work, it's no problem."

"We'd love to come," Emma said.

Max put his arm around Emma's waist. "Sure we'll come."

Dana nodded glumly. "I'm glad you two moved into the old house."

"Of course they did. I couldn't have strangers living next to me," Rutledge said, punching Dana's arm lightly and breaking the solemn mood. "You're not going to have shish kebabbed liver and chickpea balls again, are you?"

Dana shuddered. "No. We're having hamburgers. I don't guarantee there won't be some gourmet treat coming out of the kitchen, but I'm cooking hamburgers on the grill."

"Isn't that dangerous?" Emma asked. "You don't know what Bootsy might be mixing into the chopped meat, to make them more interesting."

"I give you my word," said Dana, bristling with helpless frustration, as many people did when talking about Bootsy. "I told her she has to consider the tastes of the people she's cooking for, and to save the sophisticated dishes for her friends from the university. Also I made her scrub all that chickpea crap off the grill last time, and I told her if she didn't leave the barbecuing up to me, she was going to have to clean the grill every time. She did a good job on it, I'll give her that."

Emma's mind drifted off toward the puzzle of those cut trees again. It didn't add up. Beavers made sense in one way, but they were hardly fierce animals.

"Emma? Honey?" said Max. The three men were standing expectantly a little way up the road. Max stood a little closer than the other two, his thumbs hooked into his jeans, his head tilted to one side and a little frown of concentration between his eyes. She'd noticed the line didn't go away anymore when he stopped frowning. "Are you coming?" he asked.

"Not just yet. I want to go look at those trees that were cut down."

"Why?"

She shrugged. "Curiosity."

"Might not be such a good idea," Rutledge said, deadpan. "That beaver might still be around."

"He has a point," Dana said. "I mean, not about the beaver, but if there's a bear in those woods, you shouldn't be wandering around alone."

"A bear?" said Emma. "Please. After the fire and all the commotion this afternoon? No self-respecting bear is within miles of this place. I'll see you later." She went toward the clearing. Within minutes, Max had caught up to her and was walking beside her. "You really don't have to come," she said.

"Yes, I do." Max pointed to the "Nelson's Boats" sign. "Do many people call him 'Admiral'?"

"The wags do. The nickname's inevitable, don't you think?"

"Does he like it?"

"He tolerates it. Lillian calls him Nelson, though, I noticed." Emma stopped on the weedy shoulder near the area where the trees had been felled. "What about your deadline? Shouldn't you be home working?"

Max threw his arms in the air but, mercifully, didn't yodel. "Of course. This is classic avoidance behavior."

They stepped onto what had been a section of woodland. Straggly undergrowth was all around: spindly saplings and leggy plants that looked puny in the sudden, full daylight.

"If I don't get an inspiration soon, I may have to base my drawing on the newly discovered great beaver of Lake Harrison," Max said.

When he was stuck for an idea, he had a habit of throwing words against her like a ball against a handball court. Emma tuned out Max's chatter and looked at the tree stumps. Three of them were either gnawed or chopped, and too thick to be the work of an average beaver. She searched the ground for pawprints, scratch marks, anything, but saw only a large clump of fern flattened as though something heavy had rested on it. She sat on it herself and gazed out across the bright lake. The smell of crushed fern enveloped her. Between the time she saw the animal, and the time Petey did, it wouldn't have been able to gnaw down one tree, let alone three.

"Emma? Emma!"

Max's voice startled her. Of course he'd been talking, and she hadn't been listening. "What?"

"You tell me," he said, all playfulness gone from his face.

"Nothing."

"Don't give me that. You've got that closed-up look; you had it on the road, too. Why else do you think I came along?"

"It's all right, Max."

"No, it's not all right."

Emma lay back on the ferns and stared out into the cloudless, cloudless sky.

"Emma, nothing happened here. No one was killed. It doesn't do any good to think back to something you can't change, something you never could have changed."

"I'm not so sure about the last part," Emma said.

"I am. Come back with me now." Max held his hand out. Emma took it and he pulled her up, then hugged her tight. He smelled of smoke and sweat, and she wrinkled her nose but didn't pull away because he felt so reassuringly solid.

"Max, are you ever sorry we had to give up the apartment in New York so we could keep Dad's place?"

"No. I love it up here. Besides, this is a much better place to raise the kids we should think about having before we get too old."

"I'm not old! You're the one who's thirty."

"And still too poor for you to be able to quit your job." He held her at arm's length and looked searchingly into her face. "Are you ever sorry you married me?"

She smiled. "Never."

"That's better!" he said. He took her hand and they walked toward home.

chapter 5

Billie emerged from otherside onto the rocks that jutted out into the lake just beyond her territory. Her brother, who lived there, lay drowsing in the sunshine. She stood aside politely, in case he wanted to go through the doorway, but he only half opened his eyes to look at her, yawned, and stretched. Pudding was a big, round-headed tom with a lazy nature, and probably would have come fully awake only if she'd come back with her jaws clamped on that rat she'd missed catching. She looked at his fat, defenseless belly with its tuft of white fur and had a good mind to whack him. She strode toward him.

He rolled over, gazed at her with a benign expression, and purred. Like her, Pudding had thick fur, but unlike her tasteful white, his coat was a clownish ginger color, impractical for stalking. His purr was an invitation to enjoy the sunshine, the warm rocks. She sat and licked her paws clean of the smells of otherside, rubbed them off her ears and whiskers. Her brother's face, she noticed, was less than tidy, so she grabbed him and gave him a thorough cleaning, growling at him to be still when he protested.

When he was free of smells to her satisfaction, she rested her chest and forepaws on his pillowy shape. Pudding closed his eyes and resumed purring, but Billie was just hungry enough to stay alert despite the soporific effect of the sun. She looked at the rocks and water and far shore, and watched doors wink open and shut with the same quick rhythm as the choppy little waves twinkling in the sunlight. The doors opened only briefly, but she could have pounced on most of them if she'd had a mind to. She wouldn't pounce on the waves, which splattered nasty and wet on her paws, and couldn't be caught.

She noticed a red shimmer through the island trees, and tensed. Her brother caught her elbow in the ribs, and grunted, then curled up and rolled onto his side.

Billie stared across the lake. The big door on the island was open; the little doors were caused by breaking wavelets of its energy. She opened her mouth and tasted a faint smell of otherside on the air. She wondered what had come through. Curiosity drew her to the island, but she couldn't get directly to the door, with all that inconvenient water in between. To investigate, she would have to open a door on this shore, go to otherside, and walk a long way. And she'd missed the rat: hunger called her home.

Her stomach won. She bounded over her brother and ran home.

When she got to the top of the outside stairs, she was disappointed to find no one in the food room. She pawed at the glass, knowing it slid to the side somehow, but unable to get it to move. She sat and called to her people to come.

Emma and Max came through the front door and separated, Max going upstairs to shower, Emma heading for the kitchen. Once there, Emma saw Billie sitting on the patio, crying and looking pitiful. She opened the door and Billie bounded in.

"Hi, Sweets," Emma said. "Hungry?"

Billie stopped and went rigid. Slowly her back arched, her ears flattened, the fur on her back and tail rose.

"Billie, honey, what's the matter?" Emma asked, reaching out to soothe her cat.

Billie hissed and struck out.

Emma cried out in pain. Blood welled from the top of her hand and dripped onto the floor. "What's the matter with you?" she said, but Billie was under the cupboard.

Emma ran cold water over her hand, then turned the faucet off. The blood welled and flowed again, and the top of her hand was puffy. "Damn cat must have nicked a vein," she muttered. It hurt like hell, too. She grabbed the dish towel, loaded it with ice, and held it against the scratch. In a little while, the bleeding stopped.

Billie was still hiding.

Whatever was the matter with that cat? She'd never done anything like that before.

"Billie?" Emma tossed the towel into the sink and crouched down to look under the cupboard. Billie's eyes shone round and frightened in the darkness back against the wall. "Billie? What's wrong?"

Billie growled.

"Did something happen to you? Do you have an abscess or something?" Emma asked, remembering a cat she'd had in her childhood, a tom who used to get into fights and have hidden wounds under his thick fur. She'd be petting him, and he'd be purring away, then suddenly he'd bite. It was always to let her know she'd touched him where it hurt. But she hadn't touched Billie at all.

Billie's eyes looked less frightened, and she'd stopped growling. Emma stifled an impulse to reach toward the cat; her hand was still sore from the last time. Instead, she got up and opened the refrigerator.

A whiskered nose poked out from under the cupboard.

"There might be something in here for a good cat. A cat who apologizes," Emma said, taking a slice of boiled ham out of the meat drawer and dangling it about two feet above the floor.

Billie came out, gaze intent on the ham. She cried, then circled Emma's legs, rubbing against them.

"All right, you're forgiven," Emma lowered the ham into reach and Billie snatched it. She ate hungrily, with a husky purr. Emma tentatively stroked the cat's back, but elicited no reaction and couldn't find anything wrong with her.

Max came in wearing fresh jeans and T-shirt, his hair still wet and tousled from the shower. "What's going on?" he asked, looking at the drops of blood on the floor, the bloody towel in the sink.

"Cat scratch."

"She scratches you, so naturally you reward her with ham."

"I wanted her to come out from under the cupboard. She seemed terrified of something."

Max inspected her hand. "That looks unpleasant. You'd better put something on it."

"I will. And you'd better get to work. I'll call you when it's time to go next door for dinner." She pushed him gently toward the stairs.

"I hate cartooning! I never want to see another draw-ing board as long as I live," he said as he went downstairs to his studio.

Billie was cleaning her whiskers.

"Feeling better now?" Emma asked.

Billie purred.

Hungry, Billie waited outside the kitchen door. At last her person came and slid the door open, but when Billie jumped inside she was immediately assailed by the scent of a large an-imal from otherside. Her muscles tensed, her heart beat faster. Her person reached for her and the smell of otherside flowed from the woman. Fear overwhelmed Billie's under-standing. She struck out, then fled to the cavelike safety be-neath the cupboard.

She heard her person moving about, running water. Nothing attacked Billie, and her heartbeat slowed.

The woman presented her face in the opening and war-bled in soothing, nonthreatening tones. But her smell was wrong, her smell was from otherside. Billie growled.

Her person went to the refrigerator, held out an offer-ing to her. Billie put her nose outside the entrance to her hid-ing place and sniffed. Meat, and that animal smell, but also the smells of home.

She went over to her person. Yes, the hands smelled right, but the legs were disgusting. The legs smelled of crushed fern and the great beavers that lived otherside. Her person must have rolled in this smell. Billie rubbed against the legs, marking them with her own scent. When they were again familiar, she accepted the food offering.

When she finished eating, she sat and cleaned her

whiskers. How had this animal smell gotten here? Did it have anything to do with the door on the island? She purred, her belly full, but more and more she wondered what was going on. Tonight she would hunt answers.

chapter 6

"I'm very lucky," Max said. "I get to do the work I love, and get paid for it, too. Almost doesn't seem right to take the money."

Emma reflected on the difference a serviceable idea always made in his attitude toward cartooning. He looked rested now, serene, fashionable almost in his oatmeal cotton sweater and summer tan. The hand that now held the stem of a wineglass with studied negligence looked as though drawings just flowed from its long fingers in careless profusion.

Peggy gazed at him with the expression of sympathy bordering on admiration she usually reserved for her most promising students at the middle school where she and Emma both taught. She turned to Emma. "It must be wonderful, having such a confident, creative man around all the time," Peggy said, a smile creasing her plump cheeks.

Emma laughed.

"What?" Max asked with exagerrated innocence.

"Nothing." Emma turned away to hide her smile. Dusk was settling round them, and from Dana and Bootsy's patio she could see a glimmer of lake between the black silhouettes of trees. Farther out, on the promontory, the hunched shape of Rutledge's cabin showed dark against the water.

"So, Emma, I hear you and Petey saw some big animal today?" Peggy asked in what Emma recognized as an attempt to draw her back into the conversation. Peggy leaned slightly forward and pushed one side of her grey pageboy behind her ear. A diamond stud, a silver anniversary present from Charles, glittered on her earlobe.

"I saw something swimming in the lake," Emma said. "From the island."

Peggy touched Emma's arm. "Don't brood about the island, dear. Charles says you're fancying all sorts of things about it."

"Peggy, I'm fine. Really I am."

Max teasingly interrupted. "So what are your plans for the summer, Peggy? Fishing with Charles?"

"Oh, he put you up to that," Peggy said, releasing Emma's arm. "Him and his smelly old fish. No, I just got a little blue jay with a broken leg yesterday, and an injured hawk the day before. I'll be busy rehabilitating birds."

Emma gave Max a brief smile of thanks for changing the subject, then looked across the lawn to the brick barbecue, where, smiling, Charles and Dana and Rutledge stood grouped around a charcoal fire. An oil lamp on Dana's worktable lit their faces from below like boys around a campfire. The light accentuated the arch of Dana's eyebrows, but softened the signs of age in Charles and Rutledge.

"The summer is when I have more time for my birds. It's nice to be able to forget about teaching and spend my day with creatures who don't talk," Peggy said. "I'm thinking of building another flight cage, maybe getting involved in rehabilitating other animals, too, depending on how much energy I have. That's what you need, Emma: some hobby to occupy your mind while school is closed. Something worthwhile."

"Bootsy's been in the kitchen a long time, hasn't she? I'm going to see if she needs help," Emma said, getting up.

"Oh dear. That girl works much too hard at her cooking," Peggy said pointedly as Emma moved off.

Emma found her sister whisking egg whites in a bowl while reading from a cookbook. Her strawberry blond hair was piled in a loose knot on top of her head, and her little heart-shaped face with its pointed chin was filled with concentration. She seemed to be putting the finishing touches on a casserole, or at least something in a casserole dish. The kitchen smelled of browned meat and cinnamon. Bootsy poured the contents of the bowl onto the casserole.

"What's that?" Emma asked, sitting at the kitchen table to watch.

Bootsy flashed a bright smile. "Meringue."

"So it's dessert?"

"Oh no. It's an entree. I think. It's beef, and peaches, and onions with a meringue topping."

Emma sniffed. The message her nose was sending confused her stomach: it didn't know what to expect. "Is it sweet?"

"I expect so. It's got half a cup of sugar in it." Bootsy, clomping in heavy boots, put the casserole in the oven. She was wearing an apron over a wispy floral dress.

"Bootsy, why do you do it? You know not a man out there will eat that."

"I have a low threshold of boredom when it comes to cooking. They can at least try it."

"I don't think anyone will eat this one. Can't you leave your experimental approach to life in the laboratory? Food is supposed to taste good."

Bootsy brushed wisps of hair back from her forehead with an annoyed gesture that called to Emma's mind the saying that you should never trust a skinny cook. Bootsy's figure was definitely in the frail-to-delicate category.

"Somebody thought it tasted good. Somebody liked it enough to print it in a recipe book," Bootsy said. "What happened to your hand?"

"Cat scratch."

"It looks all bruised."

"She flew into a rage. I have no idea why. I guess cats just have brains that are organized differently from ours."

"That's not altogether true," said Bootsy. "They lack the higher functions, but their lower brains are very much like ours. Unfortunately for them. That's why they get used in experiments so often. Their sight's different, though: they can see farther down into the red end of the spectrum, maybe even infrared. How's the wine holding up outside?"

"I didn't notice."

"Probably need another bottle," Bootsy said, taking one from the refrigerator. "So why'd you come in? Was it just to criticize my cooking?"

"Peggy was mothering me."

Bootsy shrugged. "Aren't you used to it by now?" She uncorked the wine and filled two glasses. "You seem down or something." She sat opposite Emma at the kitchen table.

"And you're not? On the anniversary of Dad's death?" Emma said.

Bootsy's head drooped on her thin neck, then rose like a defiant flower. "I keep busy. I do things."

"Like cooking? That explains a lot," Emma said, and they both laughed.

Bootsy sipped her wine. "God, I can't wait for summer to be over."

"I can," said Emma. "Since when don't you like vacation?"

"I like vacation just fine, but Dana drives me crazy. He feels obliged to try to be one of the boys with the locals."

"What's wrong with the locals? You're getting snobbish just because you work at a college."

"Rutledge is always teasing me about my cooking and loves to get a rise out of me. Walter sells hunting supplies and I believe in animal rights. Nelson and Jake want to cut lumber in the woods, and I believe 'Forever Wild' means just that. I spend the whole summer biting my tongue or arguing."

"You've been arguing with Walter and Nelson and Jake every summer since you were nine. That's why they used to call you the mouth. Probably still do. What does Dana have to do with it?"

"He was supposed to take me away from all this. Instead he falls in love with it. Besides, he's my husband. If I can't blame him for things, what do I have him around for?"

"The man's a saint."

"I thought you thought he was a nerd."

"The two aren't mutually exclusive." Emma pulled the cookbook toward her. "What is this, a book of recipes for bored cooks?"

"It's Latin American, actually. There's an interesting one for turkey with chocolate and chili sauce."

Emma looked at the cover, which featured a roast turkey

51

apparently covered in mud. "You're going to be dangerous come Thanksgiving, aren't you?"

A flicker of sadness touched Bootsy's face. "It'll be a year tomorrow," she said. The timer went off.

"I know," Emma said.

"I hope this Thanksgiving is better than last," Bootsy said, taking the casserole out of the oven. The meringue topping was lightly browned. "It's funny not to have Dad carving the turkey. Everything about Thanksgiving and Christmas reminds me he's not there."

"Maybe you're right. Maybe we need a break from tradition." Emma looked at the cover picture of the turkey. "But does it have to be such a drastic one?"

Bootsy dropped her apron over the back of a chair. "You take the wine, I've got the casserole," she said.

It was quite dark out, and everyone had gathered near the barbecue, where Dana had an oil lamp burning. Peggy leaned against Charles, who had his arm around her. Charles had gotten loose-limbed and gangly with age, like a white-haired teenager, while Peggy had grown sleek and plump as the mourning doves that came to her feeder. They looked contented.

"I hope Dana and I are that comfortable together when we're as old as Charles and Peggy," Bootsy said, putting the casserole down. "But we don't seem headed toward it." She lit the lamp on the picnic table and smiled tenderly at Emma through the lamplight. "I always wished I had your hair. It's so smooth and shiny."

"It's brown," said Emma incredulously, setting the wine beside the meringue-topped beef. "Want me to light the torches?"

Bootsy tossed her the matches. Emma struck one and

lit the first of the bamboo sticks topped with wax and a wind-resistant wick. She walked to where the second was stuck into the lawn, down near the bushes edging the lake, and paused to look out across the water. The moon had risen, and its disk floated in sky and water. Starlight softened the sky, and the lake glimmered. All the darkness was muted to shadowy tones, except at the lake's center, where the island's evergreens made it a black void. Emma shuddered and struck a match.

The torch flared into life. Something nearby hissed, and Emma dropped the box of matches. The light was between her and whatever it was, and too close to her eyes, but she thought she caught a flash of white fangs. The bushes rustled with the sound of a large animal hastily departing. Emma smelled its odor, perhaps its breath. It was very like a cat's breath when it spits at you. She picked up the matches and joined the group near the barbecue.

"Are there any big cats around here?" she asked.

"Mine's pretty big. Putting on weight every day, too," Rutledge said.

"No, it wasn't Pudding. Not anything house cat size: bigger. Like a mountain lion or something?"

"Not around here," Dana said, brushing sauce on a steak. "They're extinct in the Adirondacks. Why?"

"Something hissed at me in the bushes down by the lake."

"Probably a raccoon," Charles said. "They hiss."

"No, it was bigger," Emma said. "It got scared when I lit the torch, must have been frightened of the fire. I just got a glimpse of really big teeth."

"Maybe it was Petey's beaver," Rutledge said, and the men laughed.

chapter 7

Billie napped through the afternoon, and when she woke, night had come. She went into the kitchen and pawed at the door, but no one was around to hear her. She called, then padded through the silent house, but her persons were not to be found.

She went into the upstairs bathroom and leaped onto the windowsill, then pushed against the screen. It gave way in the corner, as it always did, and she squeezed through onto the porch roof.

The night smelled of flowers and cut grass and lake water. A raccoon had passed by not long ago, leaving its scent trail in the air. In the garden below, fireflies blinked on and off intriguingly.

Billie jumped onto a branch of the tree that grew beside the porch, and a pair of blue jays cried out a shrill warning. She ignored them and climbed down the trunk, into the garden.

A firefly lit up in front of her, then went out. She waited for it to light again, but when it did, it had moved. She turned her head quickly, but the light went out. She pounced. The firefly glowed inches from her nose, and her paws were empty.

A scent of crushed catnip pulled her attention toward the plant, and she saw her brother sitting there staring at her. Pudding wore a bemused expression. Billie instantly sat and washed her paw, as though that was what she had intended all along.

Pudding turned and looked at the moon. Billie sat beside him. His fur smelled lightly of tobacco smoke, his muzzle and whiskers of the cooked fish he'd had for dinner. She licked the foodsmell off his whiskers, and he batted at her lightly, pulled her down. They wrestled in the catnip, rolling out wonderful scents, then stopped. They sat feeling mellow and looking up into the night.

The moon was round and bright, but crazed with dark lines. Beside it, the most brilliant of the small lights of early evening shone blue-white and steady. Billie could see, above this but in line with it, a smaller red light. She stared at them. Unlike the fireflies, they did not wink into darkness.

Pudding stretched and walked toward the lake's edge, his tail trailing nonchalantly above the ground. A frog broke silence, splashed into the water, and both pairs of feline ears swiveled toward the sound. Pudding crept after the frog, but Billie, although tempted, remained where she was.

She waited for a door. When one opened, she peered through, saw that it led into night under the cover of low branches. She tested the doorway's sides with her whiskers, found them mushy: it was a fading doorway, too weak to stay open long. She leaped through, flicking her tail just in time to keep the tip from getting caught as the doorway closed.

She was under an oak tree whose lowest branches touched the ground. The air was redolent of the slightly acid smell of decaying leaves. Knobby tree roots made a rough and fissured surface, full of hiding places. There was a smell of mouse, but it had passed by too long ago to be of practical importance.

A faint cry piqued Billie's interest. She jumped onto the tree roots and searched for the source of the noise.

The cry came again from the base of the tree. Billie looked down and saw, nestled in a fissure between two roots, a tortie cat nursing a litter of kittens. Two of the kittens were fighting over the same nipple, heads burrowing into their mother's fur, skinny little legs flailing at each other.

The mother's eyes blinked open, suddenly alert. She growled at Billie, who backed away. The tortie relaxed again: a light purring came from the nest.

Billie walked to the edge of the tree's circumference and looked out. A clearing sloped down to the lake on one side and rose toward a mass of rocky land on the other. Over the lake, the same configuration of lights she had seen earlier shone with the moon and were reflected in the water, but the lake itself was smaller.

Landward, there was a different light, earthbound: a cooking fire glowed at the entrance to a shallow cave, and Billie recognized the camp of the people who lived in otherside. Feathers dangled from their hair, and she knew they had no cupboards and no refrigerator. They had no can openers, either, but they were cooking something that smelled interesting. Billie edged closer.

Meat roasted on sticks over the fire. The people sat around the fire's warmth, eating, chirruping, and making that odd barking noise her people made as well. A child dropped a piece of meat and Billie tensed, wondering whether to risk going for it. The hesitation cost her the prize: a rat scooted out of the darkness, grabbed the food from between the child's feet, and ran off.

The child cried. A couple of adults shouted warning tones at the rat, and someone threw a rock, which missed. The rat escaped into the cave, and one of the women sat the child down and handed it another chunk of meat. The woman made angry, trilling noises, dividing her attention between the cave and the men.

Billie went after the rat. Inside the cave, the moonlight was shut out and only traces of firelight penetrated, but Billie's pupils dilated to make it enough.

Rats were everywhere. The one that had grabbed the meat was gulping it down as fast as possible, trying to ward off other rats who wanted a share. Rats scurried along piled-up animal skins and in and out of pottery bowls. They lifted their twitching noses toward the roof, where grain hung out of their reach. Then one saw Billie, and squeaked.

A multitude of beady eyes turned and looked at her. Billie felt the hairs on her back and neck rising, her tail bristling. There were too many of them. She turned sideways and arched her back, bared her teeth. The rats approached. She hissed.

Suddenly a large black tom leaped out of the darkness, howling. He was followed by a grey tabby and a grey cat with white paws. All three attacked the rats, and Billie joined in the frenzy of teeth and claws and shrieks.

All but the four rats the cats had caught fled to their fissures and their crevices.

Suddenly a light appeared at the entrance to the cave, dazzling in the darkness. Billie's pupils quickly narrowed to slits and she saw that a man stood there holding a torch in one hand, a club raised in the other. Billie backed toward the shadows, ready to drop the rat if the man moved toward her, but he only made that barking sound and lowered the club. He shook his head, then clucked his approval before turning his back on the cats and rejoining the group by the fire.

The grey cat, head held high with a rat dangling from her mouth, leaped behind a rock, her white paws flashing. Her disappearance was followed immediately by the excited mews of kittens.

The other two gnawed hungrily. Billie backed toward the entrance with her rat because she wasn't sure how the other cats would feel about her once they'd had time to reflect that she was a stranger. She ate, enjoying the freshness and flavor no canned meat, however good, could quite duplicate. Having had her fill, she left behind the head and tail and that one bitter grey organ no cat will ever eat.

Billie tidied her paws and whiskers, then went to the edge of the firelight and looked at the circle of people. They clapped their hands rhythmically, and one clicked bones together. Another moved his feet in short, hesitant steps, backward and forward, that took him in slow progression around the fire. He wore a downy headpiece with dangling feathers, and in each hand he held a long flight feather. He was ululating, a piercing sound, and she wondered what was wrong with him. Her people made similar cries, and she had never been able to discover what the problem was. He lunged suddenly toward a small child, pointing the feathers at it, and the child shrieked. Everyone made the barking noise, and the man continued his activity, moving farther around the circle.

The adults didn't seem concerned about him, but the children sat openmouthed, staring. Bits of meat dangled from their hands, and it would be easy to go over and slip one free. Billie wasn't hungry at the moment, though the meat smelled good. Slowly, she crept up behind a chubby toddler with a meaty bone held very, very loosely in his hand.

The man added arm movements to his shuffling steps, large sweeping gestures that reminded her of something. She forgot the meat and stared again at the man. He held his arms out wide, and moved his upper body slowly, smoothly. The feathers in his hands made his arms seem longer than they were, more like wings. That's what he was like: a bird, soaring. A large, predatory bird hanging in the air and hunting.

He moved between her and the fire, and suddenly he was black and huge, the fire extending his form with shadows. She saw the front of his headpiece for the first time, saw the big round eyes painted there, and crouched. It was an owl, an enormous owl, hunting.

He lunged forward, pointing the feathers. Billie hissed and jumped back.

The man jumped back, too, and stumbled. He barked. The child who had been between them ran crying to its mother. The man peered at Billie and extended one of his feathers toward her.

Billie hissed again and whacked at the cat-hunting feather.

The man stood up and barked. All the people around the fire barked and rocked back and forth, and she took her opportunity to escape into the woods. She had the distinct feeling her dignity was not being given the consideration it deserved.

It was time to think about going back home. She could

sense the large door she wanted to investigate. She moved over the rocks and scrubby vegetation toward where she felt it would be.

A scent stopped her: peccary. She held still, listening. Yes, several of them, rooting along the ground, grunting, tusks clattering on the rock, their snouts searching for food, for anything that grows or runs or flies. She had no tree nearby to climb. They were between her and the oak. She held still, trusting to their poor eyesight to keep them from seeing her and her own impeccable grooming to keep them from smelling her.

One raised its head and moved on. The others followed, moving toward the oak, keeping outside the firelight. They'd find acorns there, and . . .

Screams erupted from under the oak, grunts and squeals and howls of fury. The kittens! Billie started to run toward them, then hesitated. She was afraid of the peccaries. The people were getting up from the fire, the men picking up their clubs and running toward the tree. Already the screams had stopped, although the grunting noises continued. Billie hoped the mother, at least, had escaped. She turned and walked away.

The doorway was just on the other side of the rock, in a grassy section of land between two outcroppings. It was the largest doorway she'd ever seen. It framed a section of her own lake and stars, and the big rock where the deer had stood. If she went home through this doorway, she would come out on the island. Perhaps she should double back and find a smaller door nearer to her house. Getting off the island was always a problem at home, where the lake was so much larger.

A horrific uproar from the camp decided the question for her: peccary screams this time, and the shouts of men. Billie ran for the doorway, tripping in a large hoofprint before leaping through to safety.

chapter 8

Emma waited for the laughter at Rutledge's beaver reference to die down. She intended to hang on to the subject. Before she could speak, Bootsy came out of the kitchen carrying two baskets of garlic bread.

"Is the steak almost ready? Everything else is," Bootsy said.

Dana scowled. "Almost," he said brusquely.

Rutledge's weather-beaten face expressed amusement. "I thought we were having hamburger," he said.

"Change of plan," said Dana.

"Sit down everybody. We can start on the casserole," said Bootsy.

"Could have sworn you were dead-on determined to cook up some hamburgers tonight, Dana," Rutledge said, moving toward the table.

Emma unfolded her napkin. "I think the hamburger's joined the peaches."

"Is that a fact?" Rutledge beamed at the casserole, but

his expression slowly changed to a mixture of curiosity and apprehension.

Emma stifled a giggle in her napkin.

Charles sat beside her. He cleared his throat and looked out into the gathering darkness. "We have to think about doing something about the lodge," he said.

"You can have the place, Charles," Emma said.

Peggy stared at the casserole, sniffed. "What is that on top, dear?" she asked.

"Meringue," said Bootsy, passing her a serving. "Dana, can't you leave the barbecue long enough to sit down with us?"

"Afraid not. The meat might burn."

"I can't take the place from you, Emma," Charles said. "That wouldn't be fair to you and Bootsy. Your father invested just as much in buying the island as I did, and his share should go to you two."

"I hate that island. I don't want anything to do with it. I'll give it to you, or you can buy us out, or we could just all sell the thing to someone else."

"Now, that's not reasonable. I understand why you feel that way, but it's not reasonable."

Bootsy thumped a portion of casserole in front of Emma and smiled brightly. "Dana's not very adventurous when it comes to food," she said.

Emma was grateful for the interruption. Maybe the casserole wouldn't be too bad. After all, mince pies have meat in them. She teased a little piece out with her fork, tasted it, immediately wished for some discreet way to spit it out. There not being any, she swallowed.

At the other end of the table, Max held his plate up and peered at the meringue. "Good thing you didn't try to barbecue this one. You'd have an even harder time scrubbing this off the grill than you did with the tofu and hamburger."

"Don't be silly, Max," Bootsy said. "I just threw that old grill away and bought a new one."

Rutledge guffawed, and Max joined in. Dana, beside the barbecue, turned his attention pointedly to the steak.

"This isn't a good time to sell," Charles persisted. "The market's terrible."

"I certainly don't want to fix it up and open it. I know that was Dad's plan, and I suppose I should do it for him, but I really can't face it," said Emma.

"Neither can I," said Charles. "I've lost all heart for it."

"Then what is it you want to do?" Emma asked.

Charles sipped his wine. "I have to go out there."

"No."

"I'll be fine. For one thing, all your father's equipment is stored in the lodge and somebody should check on it. For another, I don't think we should let the lodge fall apart. I'm going to see what repairs are needed. Make sure the roof's not leaking, that sort of thing."

"I should return the maser to the university. Could you bring it back from the island?" said Dana.

"Laser?" said Charles.

"Maser. Microwave Amplification by Stimulated Emission of Radiation," said Dana.

"It's similiar to a laser," Bootsy said, "but a laser gives you a burst of high energy. A maser collects and enhances low-level radiation down in the microwave and infrared range. They use them for radio telescopes, things like that. Charles, you're not eating your casserole." Bootsy took a bite of hers and smiled in enjoyment. Emma suspected Bootsy was enjoying people's reactions to the food and not the food itself. Her sister did still have taste buds, didn't she?

Max moved a forkful of beef and peaches from one side of his plate to the other. "Your father was making a radiotelescope? I thought he was experimenting with photography."

"He was," Emma said. "He was using the maser to collect microwave radiation and boost it into the infrared range, where he could photograph it."

"Why?" said Peggy. She took such apparent interest in the subject that she forgot all about the food on her plate.

Emma and Bootsy looked at each other across the table.

"Dad had a theory," Emma said.

"Do you know what de Broglie waves are?" said Bootsy. There was silence around the table.

"Here's how Dad explained it to us. Watch the water," Emma said. She got from the table and walked toward the lake. Water and sky both were deep purple in the lingering twilight. More stars had come out, and from their brilliance and quantity she guessed that the air was clear enough that later she would be able to see the Milky Way. She picked up two pebbles and threw one in. Ripples ringed the point of entry with silvery crests. "See the waves?" She threw in the other pebble. "See how some of the waves from the two pebbles cancel each other out?"

"Those are de Broglie waves?" Rutledge said as Emma returned to her seat.

"No," said Bootsy. "De Broglie waves have to do with atoms. The electrons orbiting an atom move in waves, and if the crest doesn't come in the same place every time the electron orbits, the wave cancels itself out, like the waves in the pond did, and pfft! That orbit's gone. It explains why electrons only move in certain orbits."

"What has this got to do with photography?" Max asked.

"Here's the real food!" Dana said, setting a platter of meat on the center of the table.

"It smells delicious," Peggy said, helping herself.

"There's a lot of information about the past history of the universe stored in background radiation," Bootsy said. "Light traveling from distant stars tells us what the universe used to look like."

"Here comes the fanciful part," said Dana.

"It all sounds fanciful to me," Rutledge said.

Emma noticed that the forks were flashing in the lamplight again, but now they were actually making trips to people's mouths. All but Bootsy's.

"Dad thought there's a lot of information about spacetime stored in radiation, too. Fossilized, in a way," Emma said. "He thought that things that have been in the same place and state for a long time would have information about past space-time encoded in them by the action of the de Broglie waves."

"The rocks out on the island have been there undisturbed since the glaciers left them there. Dad was trying to use the maser to play back some of that information from them, sort of the way we get music from a CD," Bootsy said. "Only he was trying to make infrared photographs of it."

Dana leaned back and laughed.

"The physics department thought enough of the idea to lend him a solid-state ruby maser," Emma said.

"Because I asked them to, and because the thing was made in the sixties. It's practically antique," said Dana.

"I asked them," said Bootsy, "and they were a lot more respectful of the idea than you are."

"Your dad was just a high school physics teacher," Dana said.

"So was Max Planck," said Bootsy. "and where would quantum physics be without Planck's constant?"

Dana threw up his hands. "I should know better than to talk to you two on the subject of your father."

A metallic clatter resounded from the side of the house, and Dana hopped up. "It's that raccoon in the garbage cans again," he said.

"Oh, Dana, sit down and eat, dear," Peggy said. "What harm can it do? The garbage went to the dump today. It'll just rattle around the empty cans."

"There, it's stopped already," said Charles.

There was silence from the side of the house. Dana sat. There was silence around the table. Emma and Bootsy looked at each other. Bootsy's mouth was set in a thin, angry line. Emma didn't think Dana was going to have a comfortable evening after the dinner guests left. It served him right.

"This has been a terrible year for animals getting into the garbage cans," Peggy said.

"Somebody else was complaining about that. Jake Witte, that's who it was," said Max.

"He always complains about animals in his trash," said Charles. "It's all those food scraps from the restaurant."

"Maybe it's the beaver," Emma said. This elicited a mild chuckle round the table. The joke was wearing thin. "No, I'm serious," said Emma. "I think I saw it too."

"Just now, in the bushes?" Charles asked.

"No," said Emma, "this morning. In the lake. I saw something swimming across, something big. I'm not sure what it was."

"Petey's just making this up about a beaver," Max said.

"This could have been a beaver, only it was too big," said Emma.

"Would you think it was a beaver if you hadn't heard about Petey?" Max asked.

"I don't know," Emma said. "I'd like to know whether the animal he saw was wet or dry."

"It was wet," Rutledge said. "I asked him where it came from, and he told me it was wet, so it must have just come out of the lake."

"Then something else felled those trees," Emma said.

"Or it did, before it went for a swim. We don't know how long it's been hanging out in the woods," said Rutledge.

Charles rested his fork on his plate. "It could have been a beaver that you saw. That's entirely possible. Just a normal-sized beaver, I mean. I've seen animals swimming out there, and logs floating, when I've been out fishing, and sometimes they seem an altogether different size from what they really are. It's the lack of perspective, I think, that makes it hard to tell. Nothing nearby to give scale."

"So you saw this thing again in our woods tonight?" Bootsy asked.

"No," said Emma. "Not the same animal. The one in the lake had big teeth, but set close together in the front of its mouth. Like a beaver. But the one tonight had teeth spaced apart, like a cat's fangs, only bigger, oh . . ." she held her hands apart to indicate the size. "About as long as a butcher's knife."

"You've got Petey beat," Max said amid general laughter.

Emma noticed that, although everyone else was laughing, Rutledge remained unsmiling, his lined face thoughtful in the lamplight. She caught his eye and he immediately looked down, busied himself with his food.

After dinner, Dana, Max, and Rutledge drifted into a conversation about football while Peggy and Bootsy cleared the table. Emma moved to help.

"Bootsy and I can bring out the coffee and cake," Peggy said.

Charles poured a little wine into Emma's glass and his own. He set the bottle down, fiddled with the stem of his wineglass, twisting it clockwise, counterclockwise, back again. The light from Bootsy's oil lamps reflected from his glasses but left his face in partial shadow. He looked sad, Emma thought, and reluctant to speak, so she wasn't surprised when he said, "I miss your father."

She put her hand on his arm, and he immediately put his free hand on top of hers, covering it entirely. His hand felt warm, slightly roughened by calluses from fishing.

"I don't remember a time when you two weren't friends." Emma said.

"Oh, since before you were born. When you were a baby, we used to take you fishing with us. You got very excited and tried to tell us whenever there was a fish on the line. If you didn't get my attention fast enough, you'd pull my glasses off. I never could figure out why you thought that would make me see better."

"I'm sorry, that must have been annoying. Did they ever fall in?"

"Not from your hands, no, but Bootsy grabbed a pair once and threw them halfway to Canada. They're still under the lake."

Emma laughed.

Bootsy and Peggy brought out coffee and a chocolate cake which was greeted with enthusiasm because everyone knew it had been baked by Peggy.

Later, during the short walk home, Emma kept to the middle of the road.

"It was a pleasant evening, mostly. I'm glad we went," Max said, putting his arm around her and drawing her to the side.

"Mhmm," said Emma, listening for leaves rustling or branches breaking in the undergrowth. She pulled him back to the center.

"Rutledge says Dana should get a dog," Max said, bringing her to the side.

"Oh? Why?" She put her arm around his waist and dragged him firmly to the center of the road.

"As a garbage disposal. Are we playing some kind of game here?"

"I don't want to walk too close to the woods," Emma said.

"Well, I don't want to get hit by a car," said Max.

"There aren't any cars around. Anyway, we'd see the headlights."

"So here's our lawn. Let's compromise and walk on that."

The grass, in need of cutting, brushed softly against her ankles, a cool touch. In the middle of the lawn, Max stopped and put his arms around her. "Just look at that," he said, gazing into the sky.

Emma leaned against him, finding him pleasantly warm and solid. Overhead, the Milky Way had indeed made an appearance.

"You never see that in the city," Max said.

"Not like this," Emma agreed. The brighter stars managed to shine, but she'd always found the city lights and air dimmed the fainter ones to invisibility. Here were stars uncountable, more and more of them as her eyes grew accustomed to the dark. They were thick and deep, as deep as forever, some intense blue-white, others tinged with gentle yellows and pinks. There were clouds and clusters and nebulae, and dark patches which set off the neighboring brightness.

"All that sky," Max said.

"Yes," said Emma. The rustle of leaves brought her attention back to Earth, and she looked apprehensively at the mass of woodland surrounding them.

"It's just the wind," said Max.

"Let's go in," Emma said hastily. "I'm cold."

chapter 9

In the morning, Emma started the coffee machine and put bacon in the skillet over low heat.

She was surprised when the smell of the bacon didn't bring Billie into the kitchen.

"Max! Have you seen Billie?" she shouted upstairs. "I'm sure she was inside."

Max said something unintelligible, then came out of the bathroom, toothbrush in hand. He was wearing an old pair of ink-stained jeans, but no shirt, and in spite of his summer tan his fair skin looked very white in the half-light at the top of the stairs. "She's pushed the screen out of the window up here again. She was probably out for the night."

"It's dangerous out there. I wish she wouldn't do that."

"So do I. She's ruined that piece of screening."

Emma went into the kitchen and poured herself a mug of coffee. She opened the glass door to the deck and stepped outside just as Charles rowed up to her dock. He had a variety of feathered lures stuck to his fishing cap, which looked as though it had spent the winter crumpled up in his tackle box. She wondered if he'd like a new hat for Christmas. Probably not.

"Look what I found on the island," he said, as Billie jumped from his boat onto the dock. She walked toward the house.

"Thanks, Charles," said Emma. "Do you have any idea how she gets out there?"

Charles shook his head and the little feathers waved. "Swims, I guess."

"She hates the water."

Charles shrugged and rowed toward his own dock, his big jointed, bony arms moving with the same awkward grace as the oars. Max came into the kitchen and turned on the TV, then joined Emma on the deck just as Billie came up the stairs and slipped into the kitchen.

"See? Nothing to worry about," Max said and sipped the coffee he'd brought with him. He'd put on an oversize blue shirt and rolled up the sleeves to keep them from getting stained by his work.

A layer of mist clung to the water, and the island trees rose from it black with dew. "Billie was on the island again," Emma said.

Max turned his back to the lake and leaned against the railing. "Maybe she's got a boat."

"As good an explanation as any I can think of," Emma said.

Max, who was facing the kitchen television, said, "They're talking about Lake Harrison."

Emma turned and saw the TV reporter backed by a picture of the town sign.

Max went inside and grabbed the remote. Emma followed. He turned up the volume in time to hear, ". . . sleepy

74

little hamlet of Lake Harrison. Local restaurant owner Jake Witte was found dead this morning outside his establishment. First on the scene was Walter Tymeson, local fire chief."

The camera cut to a close-up of Walter, visibly upset, his big face filling the TV screen. Somebody shoved a microphone toward his mouth, and he appeared to be wondering what it was doing there.

"What happened here, Mr. Tymeson?" the reporter asked.

"We don't know exactly, but some time in the night Jake . . . Mr. Witte must have gone out back behind the restaurant, and he died there."

"Was Mr. Witte murdered?"

Walter looked like a man who wished he were somewhere else.

"We don't know."

"But you were the first to find the body?"

The corners of Walter's mouth turned down, and his eyes glistened with unshed tears. "I wish I had of been. No, his kid found him."

"Poor Cathy," Emma whispered.

"But there is suspicion of foul play," the reporter went on.

Walter's expression showed he thought he was talking to a crazy person. "The man's throat was ripped out," he said. "He was partly dismembered and eaten. Nobody around here thinks it was a suicide."

The room suddenly went grey and cold for Emma, and there was a noise she couldn't identify. There was no air. She couldn't get in any air, and she realized the noise was her own as she tried to breathe.

Then Max had his arms around her, had hold of her, and he was saying something, but she couldn't take it in. She gasped for air, to get her own words out, and Max's arms were warm around her, and finally she did hear herself say, "Just like Daddy."

She was crying then, and Max held her tight. "I know, I know," he said soothingly. "But Emma. Emma, are you listening? I want you to remember one thing: this did not happen on the island."

Billie heard cries of distress from her person. She came quickly, looking for danger, saw only that the man was trying to comfort the woman. He separated from her and walked quickly over to the cooking place, while she sat on a chair by the kitchen table, her face wet and unhappy-looking.

Billie went over and, standing on her hind legs, put her forepaws on the woman's knee. She looked up into her person's face. There didn't seem to be any injury, or any danger. It was so hard to know what to do for them, what their problem was when they made these mournful sounds. Billie trilled to the woman the way she would to a kitten who needed reassurance.

The woman looked a little more cheerful, and stroked Billie's head and back.

Billie jumped into her person's lap and rubbed her head against the underside of the woman's chin. She was rewarded by having her own chin scratched, and she leaned into it, enjoying the touch. Apparently everything was all right. She settled down on the woman's lap and accepted a crisp and tasty bit of meat from her hand.

Billie dozed, coming only partially awake when the

woman stood up and placed her in her basket. Ordinarily she'd move to someplace else when they had the presumption to move her, but after last night she was too tired to bother. Instead she curled up tight, pulled both paws down over her face, and fell into a deeper sleep.

"It's not too badly burnt," Max said, putting a plate of bacon on the table. He returned to the stove and scrambled some eggs.

"I'm not hungry," Emma said. She gave a slice of the bacon to Billie, who had settled down on her lap. "I think Billie was worried. But she acts the same way when I sing. Maybe she can't tell the difference between singing and crying."

Max set a plate of eggs in front of her. "I have a feeling this day isn't going to get any easier," he said, pouring two fresh mugs of coffee. "Eat." He sat down opposite her.

Emma sipped the coffee. "I should stop by the Wittes' and see if Cathy or her mom needs anything."

"Is Cathy one of your students?"

"Yes. She doesn't like me much."

"A lot of kids come across like that. It just means they don't want the other kids to think they're brownnosers. It doesn't really mean she doesn't like you."

"No, she was friendly enough the beginning of the year, but I had to discipline her." Emma pulled a small piece of egg loose with her fork, held it up, looked at it. "She was defiant about something, I forget exactly what." Emma ate, swallowing with difficulty. She set the fork down.

"Throwing paint, were they?" Max asked.

"No, but it was about a painting. Oh," Emma said, re-membering. She pushed her plate aside. "It was about a painting she did of the lake. There was an animal on the shore and I told her it was too big. The scale was wrong. She got very upset about it."

"What did you do, flunk her?"

"No, no. I gave her the chance to change it, but she wouldn't, so I lowered her grade, I don't know, from a B to a C, something like that." Emma picked up her coffee, noticed her hand was shaking, set the coffee down on the table again. "She was . . ." Emma's voice cracked, and she cleared her throat. "She insisted she had the size right."

"I wouldn't put too much stock in some little sixth grader's artwork," Max said.

"I didn't. But maybe I should have."

"Emma, you really have to stop this."

"I don't know why you think it's good that Jake wasn't killed on the island," Emma said.

"Because you obsess about the island. It's just an island, not some evil place where all the bad things in town happen."

"I wish it were. Because Jake's being killed in town instead of on the island is worse. It means the problem is getting bigger."

"No, it doesn't," said Max. "It just means there's one rogue bear traveling around killing people. That's all it means."

"I'm going to shower," Emma said, getting up and putting Billie in her basket. "Then I'm going into the village." She scraped her bacon and eggs into Billie's dish and put her plate in the sink.

"If you wait 'til this afternoon, I'll come with you," Max offered.

"No, that's all right. You don't even know Cathy. I'll take care of it."

Still seated, Max took her hand and pulled her toward him. He put his arm around her waist. "You sure?"

She ran her hand over his hair, down his stubbly cheek. "I suppose I could put off work," he offered.

"No, don't. You'll just run yourself into deadline problems next week." She pulled away and walked toward the stairs. "I'll be fine. I'm a pro, remember? I deal with kids all the time."

When Billie woke, the kitchen was empty. She yawned, got out of her basket, and stretched, articulating each muscle in turn. She listened to the house: the usual background tickings and hums were present, and from downstairs she heard the creaking and scratching that meant the man was down there. Her other person didn't seem to be around.

She drank some water, checked her food dish. It had bacon in it, and she ate, purring, because this was especially tasty. When she had finished she sat to clean her paws and whiskers.

The sliding glass door was open, letting in a pleasant smell of outside air. There was a throb of deep red light from the island. It shone into the kitchen, and a small door to otherside opened above the kitchen table. She glanced at it. The world seemed to be more crowded with doors lately. She wet her paw and rubbed behind her ear. A rodent twitched its pink nose at the doorway, and she considered chasing it, but she'd just eaten.

The rat fell through. It landed with a squeak on the table, and Billie leaped after it. She pounced before it could get its bearings, and sank her teeth into its neck. It squirmed and gasped, and lay still. She let go and watched it, waiting for it to move. When it didn't, she prodded it with her paw. Nothing.

She hooked the rat with a claw and tossed it into the air. It landed with a plop on the floor, but didn't move. She jumped down and pounced again, batted it across the floor. Not much sport left in it.

She looked at the doorway, but there didn't seem to be any more rodents near it, not just now. How many things had come through that she didn't know about? she wondered. While she watched, the doorway faded and was gone.

It was a nice rat, a handsome golden color striped with brown, and it had a splendidly long pink nose and tail. She wasn't hungry.

She decided to give it to the smaller person, as a present. She sank her teeth into its back and carried it upstairs, holding her head high to keep its weight from dragging on the floor. She went into the bedroom and deposited the rat on the woman's pillow. That should please her.

Billie squeezed through the screen and out onto the roof. She sat in the dappled shade and opened her mouth, tasting the air for signs of otherside.

chapter 10

Emma parked in front of Jake's restaurant.
Traffic was light, as she would expect in the village on a weekday morning. A United Parcel truck sat in front of Walter's sporting goods store, and a few clusters of villagers stood around talking. The maple trees that lined the streets stretched tranquil branches from each side to touch in the middle, and a boy on a bicycle rode along the sidewalk, the red bike flashing brighter whenever he passed through a ray of sunlight that had penetrated the leaves.

There were a few signs that this day was different from others. The driver of the truck had turned its engine off, and Emma thought this was the first time she had seen a United Parcel truck that didn't have its engine running. The villagers stood unusually close to each other and kept glancing toward the restaurant. The local teenagers with nothing to do, who usually hung out on the variety store's front steps, were standing in front of Jake's and looking up the road expectantly for another TV crew to show up.

Emma walked round behind the restaurant to the empty

parking lot. The area where Jake kept his garbage cans was festooned with yellow plastic ribbons that read "POLICE LINE, DO NOT CROSS." She went to the edge of the cordoned-off area and looked at the place where Jake had been killed.

The cans were thrown about, and torn plastic bags spilled spaghetti in tomato sauce, broken bread, wilted salad, onto the ground. Flies made a leisurely inspection of the feast. There were dark red smears on the outsides of some of the cans, and the ground was scuffed up. There was no grass, not even many weeds, probably in part because it was where the cans ordinarily stood, in part because of the shade from low-hanging maple branches that helped screen the cans from view. The dirt was bare and brown, but in the center a black patch glistened. And moved.

Ants. A thick crowd of ants was at work at something that evidently held more attraction for them than restaurant leftovers.

Emma realized they must be eating Jake's blood, cleaning it from the soil. A strong pain gripped her stomach and rose into her throat, nausea hitting an empty stomach, and she stepped back. At her movement, a clatter came from between the garbage cans. Emma turned sharply toward the sound.

A skinny mongrel cringed among the overturned cans and stared up at her fearfully.

"It's okay, fella," Emma said, "I won't hurt you." She took a step backward, keeping her hands at her sides. "You can go ahead and eat. I guess we nearly gave each other heart attacks."

Still watching her, the dog snatched a chunk of veal parmesan from the pile of food and gulped it down. Emma backed toward the farther end of the cordoned area, to give the animal more space.

There were trees here, a dense stand that she thought marked the end of the village. She tried to picture the area in her mind, but seen from above. What was between these trees and the lake? The roads were so twisted that she wasn't sure. Looking in, there was no sign of houses, but these woods could be deceptive. She felt an impulse to go in and explore, but immediately stifled it. The situation must be affecting her judgment: whatever had killed Jake was still in there. A bear that kills people. A bear or something.

Emma turned toward the restaurant. She faced the kitchen entrance, and beside it the flight of covered wooden stairs leading to Jake's family apartment. All the windows on the near side had their blinds drawn.

Emma went up the stairs, past a lingering smell of cooking oil and tomatoes, and knocked on the door. At first there was no answer, but after she knocked a second time, the door opened to the width allowed by the chain. Cathy stood looking up at her, a strip of face and body visible in the opening.

"Cathy? I heard about your dad. I'm so sorry."

"Mrs. Vernon," Cathy said, a flat declarative. "My mom's not home."

"I came to see if there's anything you need."

"She went to the funeral parlor."

"Actually I wanted to talk to you. Could I come in a minute?"

The face, already subdued, became guarded, but Emma counted on its being difficult for Cathy to say no to a teacher.

"I'm not supposed to let any reporters in," Cathy said.

"I'm alone," said Emma. "No reporters."

With clearly reluctant obedience, Cathy undid the chain

and opened the door. Emma saw a solemn-faced child under a mop of dark brown hair. Dark brown eyes, unsmiling, looked up at Emma.

Emma stepped inside. The room was furnished in Montgomery Ward Colonial, with an emphasis on polyurethane finish and bright upholstery, but the perkiness was muted by the drawn window shades. Dust-free and tidy, with silk flowers on a chest against the wall and magazines neatly stacked on the coffee table, the only signs of a disturbance in the household's order were clustered around the telephone: a chair set at a careless angle to the telephone stand, the phone book out and opened, some crumpled sheets of paper and a scattering of pencils.

"Mom was phoning funeral parlors and stuff," Cathy said, following Emma's glance.

"It must be hard on your mother. Does she have someone to help her?"

Cathy nodded. "My uncle."

"Good." They were standing awkwardly just inside the door, Cathy looking small inside an oversize T-shirt. How to begin? "Is it all right if I sit down?" Emma asked.

"Oh, of course," Cathy said, going over to the couch.

Emma sat beside her in the filtered glow that seeped through the window shades. "I want to apologize to you, Cathy."

Cathy looked up, clearly surprised. "What for?"

"Do you remember a picture you made in my class last year? The lakeshore, with an animal standing by some trees?"

The guarded look came back. "Yes."

"And I said the animal was out of scale, that it couldn't be that big?"

Cathy nodded.

"I was wrong."

"You saw it, too?"

"I saw something. It was swimming across the lake. The day before yesterday, that was."

"Are they bears?" Cathy asked.

Emma shook her head. "I don't know."

"Grizzly bears?"

"In the Adirondacks? They shouldn't be. I'm not sure what they are."

"Do you think the thing in the picture killed my father?"

Emma suddenly found the room oppressive: so closed in on itself, so curtained off. She got up, went to the window, and fingered the shade pull. "Do you mind if I open this?" she said, pulling the cord without waiting for an answer.

Sunlight flooded in, and Emma breathed easier at the sight of tree branches and sky. When she turned she saw that Cathy was sitting huddled on the couch, knees drawn up to her chin, arms wrapped around her legs. Her eyes were closed and she was rocking back and forth slightly.

"Cathy?" Emma said.

There was no response.

"Cathy, do you know that my father died last summer?"

Cathy nodded, but kept rocking, kept her eyes closed. Emma sat beside her on the couch again.

"But do you know what happened to him? He was killed by some animal."

Cathy stopped rocking. Her eyes opened in a look of alarm.

"They said it was a bear," Emma went on. "But I'm not so sure. It did the same things to my father as what happened to your father, and bears don't usually . . . It wasn't a typical bear attack. I think they just didn't know what else it could be."

"Maybe it's a monster," Cathy said.

Emma didn't know how to respond to that. But suddenly Cathy was crying, and holding on to Emma with a grip that was painfully tight. Emma got an arm free and stroked Cathy's hair, made reassuring noises until the sobs subsided. At last Cathy drew back and fumbled for tissues in the box beside the couch.

"I'm going to kill it," Cathy said. "I'm going to take my dad's rifle, and I'm going to get silver bullets and put them in, and I'm going to shoot that thing dead."

"Whoa, hold on," Emma said. "There's nothing to say this is anything supernatural."

"I bet it is. My dad knows all about animals, and hunting, and I bet this is a werewolf."

"I wouldn't go that far," Emma said.

"Maybe it's a bigfoot."

Emma felt a headache coming on.

"Or a zombie," Cathy said. "There's a cemetery in those woods, a real old one. Indians might even be buried there."

"Cathy, slow down," Emma said. "Do you still have that picture you painted?"

Cathy frowned. "I throw school stuff out at the end of the year," she said, and Emma's hopes sank. "But my mom usually brings most of it back in."

"Do you know where your mom might have it?" Emma asked.

"Sure." Cathy got up and went over to a deacon's bench, opened it, rummaged through. "These are my paintings," she said, pulling out a rolled-up sheaf of papers. She shoved the silk flowers to one side and unrolled the papers on the coffee table. After discarding the first two on the stack, she said, "Here it is."

They looked at the picture together. Emma recognized the work of a child who had passed that delightful stage of painting what she feels and has moved on to the more painful one of trying to paint what she observes, painful because her level of observation falls outside the range of her technical grasp. It was clearly meant to be the lakeshore, and Cathy had attempted to show trees reflected in the water, but both sets of trees looked the same. The leaves were flat daubs, because she had been trying to paint each one. And the animal staring out at the observer was crudely done, apparently out of scale. Its teeth were too big for a bear, its body too big for a beaver.

Emma thought of Petey's beaver.

"What was it doing when you saw it? Do you remember?"

"It was eating leaves, I think. Chewing on the branches. Then it stopped and stared at me, and I got scared and ran away."

"Could I borrow this?" Emma asked. "I want to show it to somebody. And I want you to promise not to even think about shooting anything until we find out what this is all about. Will you promise?"

"Is that what you saw swimming in the lake?" Cathy said.

Emma put her hand over the lower portion of the animal, so that only the head was visible. "It could be," she said. "It could be."

chapter 11

Billie felt comfortable on the roof. The rough surface was pleasantly scratchy against her belly, and from the edge she had a good view of her yard and trees, of the lake, and even a glimpse of the tall wire mesh trap where the neighboring person kept birds.

When a door opened nearby, she was prepared to dismiss it as too high above the ground, but a closer inspection showed that it led to a tree. The otherside air smelled of sun-warmed resin, and pine cones dangled temptingly just beyond her reach. Billie jumped through and sank her claws into yielding bark. She pulled herself up to a comfortable perch, and the surrounding twigs, thick with pine cones, swayed from her passage. She batted at a pine cone and it bobbed satisfactorily, then fell.

Billie watched it bounce from the needle-covered ground out onto the tundra. A man came into her line of sight. She saw the top of his head, and shoulders, and his outspread arms carrying spears. Several others came up beside and behind him, some carrying spears, some carrying clubs, moving together, their voices silent.

Out on the grassy field, a group of mammoths grazed. They were on the other side of a rock Billie didn't remember having seen before, and that confused her. The camp should be in the woods beyond the clearing. Yes, it was there. A line of smoke showed the cooking fires, and she detected a smell of roasting peccary.

The people spread out, intent on their search, their spears ready in their hands. This puzzled Billie even more. Why were they hunting when they already had food cooking, and the prey wasn't moving in an interesting way, it was just standing there?

The hunters moved onto the tundra and, crouching, advanced slowly toward the mammoths, who gave no sign of knowing the people were there. The wind blew from the plain toward the forest. She caught the grass-eater smell of the mammoths and the grease and dead fur smell of the men. The mammoths couldn't smell the men slouching toward them, but why didn't they hear the grass rustle? Why didn't they see the half-hidden shapes move? Did they think the men were too small to be a danger? Billie thought this was a mistake on the mammoths' part.

The hunters had closed half the distance between them and their prey, when the man nearest the rock suddenly stopped, stood up, and waved his hands and spear. The next man in the line made an abrupt gesture, but the only effect this seemed to have was to make the first man jump up and down. The second man raised his spear and waved it at the first man, who then barked.

The mammoths turned their ears toward the sound.

The rock stood up.

The fur along Billie's spine bristled, and she crouched defensively on the branch. The woolly rhinoceros she had mistaken for a rock stood blinking in the sunlight. It snorted.

The man who had awakened it looked small beside it, his head not even coming as high as the animal's shoulder. He dropped his spear and walked backward, slowly.

The next man barked, and the others turned their heads toward him. So did the mammoths. Billie was getting impatient with the mammoths. Why didn't they run?

Another man backed away slowly, and another, and the remaining men grouped more tightly, growling and shaking their spears.

The mammoths moved warily, putting more distance between themselves and the other group.

The rhinoceros turned its head from side to side, looking at the men. Its massive horn glinted in the sunlight. A man darted forward, and the rhinoceros stamped its foot. The man threw his spear in a clean line straight for the animal's side.

The spear hit, and bounced off. The rhinoceros shook its woolly coat and brayed.

Two of the men advanced, spears in hand, and let fly. The first spear bounced off; the second stuck, but drooped in a manner that suggested it was only caught in the hairy coat. The rhinoceros lowered its head. It charged.

All the men ran. Billie could feel the vibrations in her tree branch, as the rhinoceros' hooves pounded the ground, faster and faster.

The men who hadn't retreated earlier to the safety of the woods were screaming. The rhinoceros was gaining on them, and they scattered, but it had already cut part of the group off, and now it smashed into a man from behind, hooking him on its horn and tossing him in the air. Blood jetted from the man's back, and his screaming intensified.

The other men out in the open stopped running and watched.

The rhinoceros wheeled, ran back toward the fallen man, and trampled him. The screaming stopped.

The rhinoceros turned its attention to the men it could see. They stood unmoving, and it swiveled its head from side to side, looking from one to the other.

The first man to have spotted the rhinoceros reemerged from the woods, but now he was carrying a stick that flamed at one end. He shouted and waved the fire at the rhinoceros, distracting it from the other men.

It charged him instead.

He dropped the torch, picked it up again hastily, but a patch of dry grass was already on fire. The man backed off and the fire spread.

The rhinoceros ran into the fire, but immediately retreated. The men got out of its way as it fled, bellowing, across the open tundra. Billie caught a whiff of singed hair. She was pleased to see that, finally, the mammoths had taken their cue from something and were thundering off as well.

As the fire spread through the dry sections of the meadow, birds took flight and small furry things fled their cover. The men gathered at the fire's edges, stomping and clubbing anything that moved in a frenzy from which rose terrified squeals.

There were cats among them.

Billie smelled the grass fire and, when the breeze shifted, the cooking fires redolent of meat. But not even roast peccary could tempt her down among those cat killers this afternoon. She clung to her perch, silent and longing for a chance to go home.

*

Emma left Cathy's with the rolled-up painting under her arm. When she reached her car, she noticed the United Parcel truck had gone, but two pickups had taken its place. In fact, all the parking spaces in front of Walter's store were full, and while Emma was putting the painting in the backseat, one of the pickups pulled away from the curb. Its place was immediately taken by a battered, light blue car, whose trunk was held shut with duct tape. There seemed to Emma to be a lot of activity for the Village of Lake Harrison on a weekday morning.

The driver's side door of the blue car opened and Petey got out. His hair was tied back in a ponytail, and there was a spring in his step. Emma immediately grabbed the painting from her backseat and called out to him, but he disappeared inside the store before she could get his attention. She followed, passing the plate glass window with its gold-lettered sign, "TYMESON'S SPORTING GOODS AND HUNTING SUPPLIES," and almost bumped into a man who came out carrying a new rifle.

A bell tinkled when Emma opened the door, but no one inside paid any attention. The cashier was busy ringing up a sale, and a line of grim-faced men, most of them carrying boxes of ammunition, waited their turns. From behind the counter, Walter was explaining the features of a variety of firearms to other men, who listened with concentrated attention. Walter seemed purposeful and serious, and his big hands on the firing assemblies looked competent. The wall behind him, where rifles were displayed, had several empty places.

Emma looked around and saw Petey examining a display of hunting knives.

"Petey," she said. "How have you been?"

"Oh, hi, Mrs. Vernon," he said, dipping his head in greeting.

"Petey, I have something I want to ask you. You remember that animal you saw the other day?"

Petey's smile vanished. "I don't want to talk about that. I'm sick of people ragging me. I mean, I saw a strange animal, some animal killed Jake, and nobody will even think maybe it's the same animal. Wasn't no beaver killed Jake, is all I get from them." He returned his attention to the knives. Beneath his snub nose and short upper lip, his mouth was sullen.

Emma unrolled Cathy's painting on the glass display case, interfering with Petey's view of its contents. "I want you to look at this," she said. "Does this animal look anything like the one you saw?"

Petey glanced over his shoulder, then looked at the picture. "This by one of your students?" he said. "This kid doesn't draw too good. This animal looks like a haystack, but the teeth are the same. Who drew it?"

"Cathy Witte."

Petey looked at Emma with an expression of impressed surprise. "Does she say this is what killed her father?"

"She didn't see what killed her father. She drew this for my class last year. I told her at the time that the scale was wrong, but she insisted that's how big it was."

"What's it supposed to be?"

"Something she saw on the lakeshore last summer. I remembered it because it seemed similar to what you saw just before the fire."

"The size is right, and the teeth are right," Petey said. "But what I saw was lot fiercer. I bet it's what killed her father."

"It's possible," Emma said. "How many large animals can there be wandering around out there?"

"So, you drew the art teacher a picture of your beaver?" Walter said suddenly.

Emma jumped and let go of the painting, which immediately rolled up. Walter moved lightly for a big man; she hadn't noticed him come to the other side of the display case. As he spoke, he opened a cabinet behind the counter.

"No," said Petey. "I come in to buy a knife. But maybe I'll buy it in Ticonderoga or Lake George, someplace where the shopkeepers are polite."

"It wasn't a beaver killed Jake. Not even a giant beaver," Walter said. "It's not their nature."

"Maybe you don't know everything," Petey said. He turned and stalked out.

"You're very busy today," Emma said to Walter.

Walter nodded, took out a rag, a can of oil. "This town isn't going to let that thing get anybody else. Not if we can help it." He shoved the drawer shut.

"So you don't think it was Petey's beaver?"

"We know it was a bear, a rogue bear," he said, as much to the men waiting for him by the guns as to her. Then he added quickly, as though the thought had just come to him, "Do you folks have a firearm?"

"No."

"Does anybody out your way have a firearm?"

"I don't know. Rutledge. Maybe Charles."

Walter nodded. "Rutledge. Rutledge is a good man. But you ought to think about getting yourselves a firearm. And I'm not saying that because I want to sell you one. I'm saying it as a neighbor. I saw what that animal did to Jake.

You tell your husband he ought to get himself some protection."

"We wouldn't know what to do with a gun, Walter," Emma said.

"Then lock your doors at night, and your windows, and don't go outside. Because that thing's not afraid to come close to buildings, and it's not afraid of people. And it's out there. It's out there."

chapter 12

Emma decided she needed to go to a library,
but for her purposes the one next door at Bootsy's
was probably the best one to visit. She dropped her
car off at home and went inside to touch base with Max. She
also wanted to reassure herself that Billie was all right. If the
town was going to be swarming with trigger-happy animal
hunters, maybe she should try to keep Billie in for a few days.

She went into the kitchen and to the top of the stairs
leading to Max's studio. She listened to him humming a
Simon and Garfunkel medley, drifting from phrase to phrase
and song to song, slightly flat. That meant he was semi-
involved in his work. She closed the stairway door.

Billie's basket was empty. "Billie," she called, and
opened the refrigerator door. When this brought no response, she went upstairs. She wanted to change, anyway, get
out of the skirt and panty hose she'd thought appropriate for
her visit to Cathy's.

"Billie? Are you here?"

Emma hung the skirt in her closet and peeled off the
panty hose. It was much too hot for panty hose. She sat on

the edge of her bed while she freed her feet from their clinging touch, then turned to drop them beside her on the bed.

Something furry and bloodstained lay on her pillow, and she jumped, stifling a cry. She stood up and looked at it more closely.

A present from Billie, but whatever was it? A rodent of some kind, she guessed, but while the head was squirrellike, the tail was long and skinny. The color was unusual, too: a soft, golden brown.

"Probably some brand-new mutation, and my cat killed the only one," Emma muttered. She put on shorts and sandals, then picked the animal up by the tip of its tail. With her free hand, she dropped the pillow onto the floor, so she'd be sure to remember to change the case before she went to bed tonight.

Dangling the stiff little body at arm's length in front of her, Emma went down to Max's studio. "Max," she said.

He looked up, did a double take. "What's that?"

"It's dead," Emma said unnecessarily. "I found it on my pillow."

"I'm glad your cat likes you better than she does me," Max said.

"Do you have any idea what it is?" Emma asked.

Max shook his head, squinted, grabbed a sketchpad. "Hold it up a little higher," he said, his pencil already scratching on the paper. "And twist the tail so the head turns this way just a little."

"Don't be long," Emma said. "Why do I have to stand here holding it for you, anyway?"

"Don't move."

"Poor little thing. She didn't even eat it. I have no idea what it is, do you?"

"Probably some rare Andean chinchilla, the beloved pet of one of the neighbors, who witnessed your cat rip it from its cage and run across our lawn with it. If I were you, I'd deny everything. Done. You can trash it now."

Emma dropped the little rodent into Max's wastepaper basket.

"Hey!" he said.

"A present," she said.

He held up the drawing for her inspection. "What do you think?"

"Pretty good, except for the x's where the eyes should be."

"I can't help it. I'm a cartoonist: the vocabulary's in my blood."

"I'm going over to Bootsy's for a while," Emma said. She stopped at the foot of the stairs. "I went into Walter's store. Everybody in town seems to be buying guns or ammunition."

Max nodded. "I know. How are Cathy and her mom?"

"Cathy was upset, but dealing with it. Her mom was out making funeral arrangements. She does have relatives to help."

"That's good. So Cathy didn't slam the door in your face."

"No, Cathy didn't slam the door in my face. How do you know everybody's buying guns?"

"Oh, Nelson stopped by. He told me," Max said. "He's called a meeting for tonight, and he wants us to come."

"Walter says we should buy a gun, for protection against whatever's out there."

"I understand his point, but I've never fired a gun, and

I have no confidence in my ability to hit what I'm pointing at. I suppose it's something to consider."

"Is that what the meeting's about?" Emma asked.

"Yes," Max said. "I think we should go. We voted for Nelson for mayor, and now that he's in office, it's only fair to give him some support when he asks for it."

Emma nodded. "Okay," she said. "I'll be back in a little while."

She went upstairs, grabbed Cathy's painting, and headed out the front door, intending to take her usual shortcut through the strip of woods separating her yard from Bootsy's. Halfway across the lawn, she stopped.

The trees were dense enough so she couldn't see through to Bootsy's house. That was the point. Emma liked the walk through the leafy space, past the poplar whose leaves shimmered silver in the mildest breeze, the fallen maple trunk with its display of fungi, the wild columbines whose red and yellow were a surprise in the prevailing green and brown. Because of this, the shortcut wasn't all that short: instead, it meandered from the front of Emma's property to the back of Bootsy's, taking a turn around a huge old maple whose roots provided a home for a raccoon family. Prolonging a walk through the woods was the real point of the shortcut.

But besides the raccoon, and the birds, and the chipmunks, what else might there be in the wood, napping lightly and waiting for the night, but ready to spring if disturbed? She remembered the flash of teeth she had seen at the edge of Bootsy's party.

Maybe she should drive.

Drive next door? That was silly. Bootsy would never let her forget it. Maybe she should walk in the road.

Emma walked in the sunshine, keeping to the center of the road. Her lawn ended, and treeshade closed over her; slender branches, reaching for the sun, trailed toward her. A twig snapped.

Emma ran. She kept running until she reached Bootsy's kitchen door.

"Bootsy?" Emma called, going into the kitchen.

Bootsy sat at the table, a scattering of open cookbooks in front of her. Her hair hung loose in a mass of red-gold fluff that brushed the shoulders of her black cotton dress. "Why are you out of breath?" she asked.

"I've taken up jogging. I jogged over," Emma said. "Do you have a map of Lake Harrison?"

"Probably. Dana has maps of just about everything. Why?"

"I want to look at it."

Bootsy's gaze shifted from Emma's face to the rolled-up paper in her hand.

"Is Dana around?" Emma said.

"He's in the library."

Emma walked toward that room.

"Do you want some tea?" Bootsy asked.

Emma paused. "Normal tea?"

"Earl Grey."

"All right."

"I'll bring some in," Bootsy said.

The library door was open, and Dana sat staring intently at something outside the window. His beard was shorter and more square today, which Emma thought was a good change. He showed no reaction to her entrance.

"Dana?" Emma said, tensing.

"Don't move. Look."

Something was moving in the trumpet vine that hugged the library windows. A hummingbird. Emma resumed breathing. It finished with one flower, flitted to another, hovered, was gone.

Dana relaxed. "They like the trumpet vine," he said.

"Yes," said Emma, and refrained from telling him what he'd just done to her nervous system. "Do you have a map of the Lake Harrison area?"

"Oh, I think so," Dana said, going over to the stand where he kept his maps. It was full of shelves that were broad and deep, but set close together, so a large number of maps could be stored alphabetically without being creased. He ran his finger down the listings and pulled a map out.

"Here you are," he said, setting it down on the library table.

Emma leaned over it. Lake Harrison was at the center. The outcropping or small peninsula where she and Bootsy and Rutledge lived was at its southern end. The village was northeast of her property, stretched out between the lake and the main road, long but not wide. She was surprised at just how much wooded area there was. The few roads twisted around the rocks, and so seemed long while you were driving them, but on the map, she could see they didn't really go very far. They just took the long way to do it.

"Is this map up-to-date? Is there really so much undeveloped land?" Emma asked.

"Published last year," Dana said.

"And the north. There's nothing up there," said Emma. "That's the 'Forever Wild' section, isn't it?"

"The beginning of it."

"How big is it?"

"Two million, a hundred some odd thousand acres," Dana said. "Why?"

Emma sighed. She unrolled Cathy's picture beside the map. "Do you remember that beaver Petey saw? And you said there were beavers like that in this area ten thousand years ago. Could they have looked like this?"

Dana raised one eyebrow. She hated when he did that. It was like his face was made of taffy, and somebody was pulling one side. "Hardly a precise rendering." He went to his shelf of oversize books, bent down, and pulled one out. He blew dust off its top and brought it to the table. Emma watched as he paged slowly through illustrations of ice age fauna. A line of mastodons spread across two pages. A bison made a furry lump against a snow filled landscape.

Bootsy came in with a tray of tea things. She set the tray down and looked at the materials spread out on the table.

"I'm not finding any," Dana said. "I know they're mentioned in the text briefly, but they're not one of the more spectacular animals, so they may not be illustrated."

"Wait," Emma said, "Turn back a page."

He did. The skeleton of a giant deer with outspread antlers dominated two pages. "That's a giant deer," he said. "Also called an Irish elk."

"How big were they?" Emma asked. Her voice came out in a whisper, and she cleared her throat.

"Big. Their antlers had a span of three yards."

"Sounds about right," Emma said.

"They never made it to this continent, though," said Dana.

They're here now, Emma thought.

"Is that what killed Jake Witte, do you think?" Bootsy asked, pointing to Cathy's painting.

"Hardly," Dana said. "If it's a giant beaver. They were vegetarians."

"It just looks like a bad drawing of a bear to me," said Bootsy, pouring tea.

But Emma was looking at the empty part of the map, the part labeled simply "Forest Preserve."

"I saw something swimming across the lake yesterday morning, something that could have been that animal," Emma said, accepting a cup and setting it down. Steam rose from the tea, wavering across the map's surface. "I thought it was coming from the island, but . . ." She pointed toward the map's uncharted region. "It could have been coming from the north. From there."

"You think a giant beaver could be living in the forest preserve without anybody knowing? What do you think, Dana?" Bootsy said.

Dana stirred his tea, frowned. "It's what I suggested the other day," he said at last. "Stranger things have happened. A shy animal, in an area without roads, a huge area that hasn't been fully explored. It's not impossible. After all"— he waved a hand toward the northern section of the map— "that's the unknown. In olden days, an uncharted area like that would be marked 'Here there be Tygers.' "

Emma sipped her tea. She wondered what the tygers in question would do when they discovered civilization encroaching on them. Would it look like dinner?

chapter 13

Billie waited high in the tree as the fire spread across the meadow. The flames fed on the dry brown grasses until they hit boggy ground and turned to smoke. On one side, the fire burned itself out against a rock face, but in the near meadow, where the men were at their killing, it continued to spread in long lines that first smoldered, then burst into flame.

The men coughed in the haze of low smoke that spread across the ground. Their clubbings slowed, became less accurate. Furry things made successful dashes into the woods. One by one, the men lowered their clubs and spears and looked around. They cried to each other.

A man standing in a smoky patch coughed and rubbed his eyes. The grass around him suddenly flamed, surrounding him in fire. He screamed and ran, trailing smoke from his hair and his fur skin covering.

The smoke rose toward Billie. She blinked.

The sounds of the men quickened. The one who had brought the fire in the first place made the loudest noises, waving his arms. Suddenly the group split, some running into the woods while the others took off their fur skins and beat at the edges of the flame.

Soon many more came running, women and children, too, and they were all beating at the fire, or pouring water from skins, or hacking bare places in the meadow between the fire and the camp.

Billie didn't like this smell, or the way the smoke stung her eyes. She squinted, and closed her third eyelid partway for protection.

At last the smoke thinned out. The people stood looking at the charred ground. One barked, and the others followed his example, their bodies shaking. After that, picking their way carefully around the meadow, they gathered the singed bodies of the animals the men had clubbed. Slowly they returned to the camp. One watcher stayed behind, looking at the burnt ground and occasionally poking at a smoldering tuft with his spear.

Billie stretched herself along the branch, forepaws tucked against her chest, tail curved neatly beside her. The sun made its way through the branches, laying its sleepy warmth on her fur.

A small group of people came to the meadow carrying two sticks held together by a patch of leather. They shifted the body of the man killed by the rhinoceros onto the leather, took the sticks by the ends, and carried him away. The wood and leather creaked under his weight.

The watcher remained by the meadow's burnt edge, sitting cross-legged in the fading sunlight.

At dusk, a pack of dire wolves came loping across the tundra. They sniffed the burnt ground. The largest gazed across the meadow, scanned the forest trees, and Billie could see his eyes flash yellow in the fading light. He sat, pointed his nose to the sky, and howled, a long, long cry that held all the vastness of the tundra. His jaws snapped around the sound, tearing its heart out and throwing it to the stars.

The sound made the fur along Billie's spine and tail stand up in a ruff of fright. She dug her claws into the tree branch.

The wolves moved cautiously, snatching up dead and dying animals the fire and the men had missed.

The watcher had gone.

The pack leader sniffed the air, shook himself. He bared his teeth, yipped softly, and moved off. The others followed, disappearing into the growing darkness with an easy, space-devouring stride.

The meadow was empty. Billie hooked her claws around the tree trunk and began her descent.

After supper, Emma cleared the table while Max loaded the dishes into the dishwasher. She put the meat scraps into Billie's bowl and set it on the floor, but no cat appeared.

"I'm getting worried," Emma said. "I haven't seen Billie since this morning."

"I'm sure she's fine," Max said. He looked down at his ink-stained T-shirt. "I'm going to change. Maybe she got shut in the guest room again. I'll check while I'm up there." He switched on the dishwasher and went upstairs.

Emma went onto the deck. The trees across the lake and on the island were black against a purple sky, and the dimpled surface of the lake was purple, too, as though the sky had spilled across it. Emma leaned over the railing.

"Billie!" she called into the still twilight.

There was no response.

Emma went down the deck stairs and into the garden.

The woods on either side presented blank faces, impenetrable in the growing darkness. "Billie!" she called again, and walked to the lakeshore.

Small waves slapped against the tethered rowboat, and a fish splashed. She looked at the island, then along the shore. At the end of the peninsula, on Rutledge's dock, she could see the silhouette of a man with a pipe between his teeth. A shadow of smoke rose from the pipe. Rutledge was taking his after dinner smoke. She couldn't imagine the lake without Rutledge. He seemed as old and fissured and strong as the oak trees growing on his property.

Emma climbed into the rowboat and pushed away from shore. She rowed toward Rutledge with long, steady strokes, pausing between to scan the wooded shore. She could see the lights in her house, and in Bootsy's, blinking through the trees. "Billie!" she called.

When she was level with Rutledge, she stopped the boat's motion. "Hi! Have you seen Billie?"

"Evening," Rutledge said. "Can't say that I have."

"I haven't seen her since this morn . . ." Emma was interrupted by caterwauling from the woods, followed by hissing and a frenzied rustle. She stood up in the boat. "Billie!"

A cat rushed out of the woods and ran toward the dock. Its tail looked like a bottle brush.

"You'd better sit down," Rutledge said.

Emma had to admit the boat was rocking unsteadily. She sat. "Billie?" She couldn't tell the cat's color in the darkness, but it seemed larger than Billie. It ran up to Rutledge.

"Eeuw, it's Pudding," Rutledge said. "And I believe he has had an encounter with a skunk." Rutledge moved farther down the dock. Pudding sat and growled at the woods.

"Don't you have to go to the meeting tonight?" Emma asked.

"I do at that. Just collecting my thoughts." He puffed at his pipe and the bowl glowed red.

"I think it's going to be a lively one."

Rutledge emitted a dry chuckle. "You might say that. You'd be surprised how many forms this animal is taking. Lillian even thinks it's a snake. And of course, since I'm the animal control officer, I'm supposed to have gotten rid of the thing before anybody saw it at all."

Emma looked at the rippled surface of the lake, darker now and pierced by a few still points of stars. "Do you ever see anything?" she asked.

Rutledge took a long draw on his pipe, let the smoke out slowly. "Like what now?" he asked.

"What's the largest deer you ever saw, oh, say, swimming in the lake?"

"Seen some pretty big ones. Seen some elk."

"Big even for elk?"

"Maybe."

"Me too," Emma said. "What do you think Petey saw? Do you think a beaver could be as big as a bear?"

Rutledge pondered the lake. "I haven't seen one that big," he said.

Emma followed his gaze, across to the dark shore of the forest preserve, where all electrical lines stopped. "The 'Forever Wild' part's pretty big," she said.

"Big enough to hold a beaver the size of a bear, is that what you're saying?" Rutledge's tone held amusement.

"I haven't seen one," Emma said. "Not clearly enough to be sure that's what it was. But I did see an animal swimming in the lake . . ." She broke off. Rutledge wouldn't believe her anyway. She looked up. The North Star shone now over the forest preserve, and a red star, or maybe a planet, was in line with it.

"I've lived here all my life," Rutledge said. "Animals swimming look different, mostly because they're wet. Pudding here's going to look different when I get tomato juice all over him. Also because they're mostly underwater. But still . . ."

Emma looked at him. He was drawing on his pipe again, and the red glow lit his weatherworn face, highlighting the creases. He blew the smoke out.

"It's a big preserve. Sometimes early in the morning, when the mist is on the lake, I'll see giant deer swimming, or maybe they're just tree branches. Sometimes, late at night, I'll hear big things moving. And once, in broad daylight, I thought I saw the biggest damn cat. But only for an instant, and it was probably sunlight reflected off some camper's backpack. And if you mention any of this at the meeting tonight, I'm going to deny it."

"All right, Rutledge, I won't say anything. Especially considering all the men are going to be armed."

"And the women and children, too." He shook his head. "Snakes," he said disgustedly.

Emma pulled on one oar, turning the boat around. "Keep an eye out for Billie, won't you?"

"Will do. Come on, Pudding."

Emma rowed home. Just as she reached her dock, and was fumbling with the rope, the moon rose. The night became softly luminous, the water liquidly metallic. Now that she could see, Emma tied a knot easily and ran through the garden to her house.

chapter 14

Billie made her way cautiously, searching for a suitable doorway. A bitter smell of smoke lingered near the ground, and also a smell of fear, but both were dissipating. The farther she got from the meadow, the stronger became the scents of pine needles, of decomposing leaves, of the territorial markings other cats had left on rocks and tree trunks. And a smell of roasting meat came from the people's camp.

Hunger drew her to the edge of the firelight. She crouched beneath a low-hanging branch near the cave entrance.

The fire at the center of the open space had meat on sticks suspended over it. The meat was golden brown, and clear juices dripped into the fire, making brief, crackling bursts of flame. While Billie watched, a woman prodded a roast with the tip of her stone knife, then turned the stick so another side was to the fire.

People sat near the fire, quietly eating roast peccary. A bare-chested man with singed, uneven hair, grimaced while a woman rubbed something on his head and back. All their skins were smudged, and they moved slowly, grunting occasionally. Even the children were subdued, watching the scene with solemn faces.

A pointy-nosed brown dog was sniffing round, and Billie gave it wary attention. It crouched submissively, begging for food, and a man threw it a meaty bone. The dog caught the bone and trotted off with it to the far edge of the firelight, where it lay down and gnawed its prize.

The dead man lay on the ground, and a woman sat silently rocking back and forth beside him. The woman tending the meat offered her a piece but, receiving no response, set it down near her and went back to the fire. Billie looked at the meat. So did the dog, although it was still chewing on what it had.

Suddenly a kitten toddled out of the cave. The kitten was a little ball of frizzy baby fur on unsteady legs, its tail held stiff for balance. This was probably the first time it had ventured from the nest. It looked around, opened its mouth, and mewed loudly.

A child saw it, smiled, tried to pull a piece of meat from the grasp of the man he sat near. The man frowned. The child's smile faded.

Billie tensed with anxiety for the kitten walking toward these cat killers.

The mother cat came running to the sound, picked the kitten up by the scruff of its neck, and carried it, her head held high, back into the cave.

The child pulled at the man's arm. Still frowning, the man gave him some scraps of meat, which he took into the cave.

Billie inched closer to the cave entrance, where the child sat feeding scraps of meat to the mother cat. Evidently these people were only dangerous sometimes, but Billie couldn't puzzle out the rule of it. She was concerned that the mother cat might be unwise in choosing to live among them.

The kittens were in their nest, mewing, and Billie saw the cat from the oak tree approach them. The cat's nipples looked swollen with milk. She glanced anxiously from the kittens to their mother, and back again.

The mother jumped in with the kittens and disappeared, then sat up again so her head was visible. She gave an encouraging trill to the other cat. The mother who had lost her kittens gave an answering cry, and jumped into the nest. Both cats settled down. There followed a sound of purring cats and kittens.

A light woof nearby startled Billie. She turned, arching her back. The dog had come up near her and was poking its nose inquisitively in her direction.

She hissed.

The dog whined. It opened its mouth, showing a lolling tongue and cruel, sharp teeth. Its eyes were bright and black and shiny.

Billie arched her back higher, bristled her fur, and growled.

The dog barked. It pushed its grinning jaws closer.

Billie howled. She lashed out, raking her claws on its beady nose.

The dog yelped. It ran toward the men, its tail between its legs, blood dripping from its nose.

They looked in her direction. A man got up and came toward her. He was a black figure with the fire behind him, a black shadow that grew and grew as it came closer. Behind him, another man poked a stick into the fire, then held it aloft and he, too, came toward her, carrying fire.

Billie ran. Leaves crackled, twigs snapped, as she ran as hard and as fast as she could, barely knowing where she went, just anywhere to get away.

Nelson banged his gavel again and again, trying to silence the roomful of people. A trickle of sweat ran down from beneath his captain's hat. Emma thought she'd never known the town hall to be so hot, but then she'd never been here with so many people present, so much body heat, and in August.

"Order! Could I please have order!" Nelson bellowed in a voice used to command a crew, but the buzz of excited conversation remained undiminished until Walter stood up. People quieted down then, not wanting to miss the confrontation.

"What's the village government doing about the situation, then, if you think it's so bad for people to arm themselves?" Walter said. An approving murmur came from around the room. Walter smiled and nodded, growing more confident with the crowd's support.

Nelson was red-faced and uncharacteristically flustered. Seated at the table beside him, Rutledge leaned back in his chair, relaxed but alert.

"I didn't say it's bad for people to arm themselves," Nelson said. He took off his cap and set it on the table, then mopped his forehead with a handkerchief. "I said it's getting out of hand, is what I said. You're selling guns to people who don't know anything about using them safely, panicked people. It's asking for trouble."

"There's a bear out there killing people. If you don't think we should defend ourselves, then tell us what the village government is doing to protect us," Walter repeated. He looked around the room, playing to the people, and they applauded.

Nelson struck his gavel again, and glared at Walter in a way that made it clear he wasn't going to put up with much more of this challenge to his authority. "That's what this meeting is about," he said.

"Did you invite the bear?" Emma recognized the voice of Rick Shannon, the gas station owner. He was a waspish little man, and his voice held a light sting, quickly withdrawn and prepared to strike again.

"We're here to plan a strategy," Nelson went on.

"What about the state police?" Lillian asked anxiously. She was seated at Nelson's elbow, and again she wore mix-and-match separates. It occurred to Emma that Lillian could throw her wardrobe into a suitcase and be ready to move on at any time, and that this was probably left over from Nelson's naval career. "What are the state police doing?" Lillian said.

Nelson shrugged. "No crime's been committed."

"A man's dead," said Walter.

"But no crime's been committed. He was killed by a bear. That means it's up to our animal control officer, with help from the Department of Environmental Conservation if he needs it."

"He needs Encon all right," said Lillian. "Rutledge, did anybody tell you about the snake that attacked me?"

"It's been mentioned," said Rutledge.

"Biggest snake I've ever seen. Came in the window down at Nelson's, went back out when I screamed."

"Jake wasn't killed by a snake," Walter said. "I think we should stick to the subject under discussion."

"I was plenty scared," Lillian said.

"Rutledge, have you called in Encon?" Rick asked.

"I called them," said Rutledge.

"Something killed two of my sheep," Howard Connely said. Howard had come to the country to escape the anxiety of the city, but he had brought it along with him. He had pouches under his eyes and his mouth was always pursed to contain his indigestion. He popped Tums constantly and was chewing one now.

"Why you want to have sheep right next to the woods . . ." Rick began.

"They're my lawnmowers, keep the motel grass just as neat as a golf course," said Howard. "And something slashed their throats and did some heavy feeding."

There was a gasp and a moan from the side of the room: Mary Witte, Jake's widow. Mary looked like an older version of her daughter Cathy, but with the hair under control and with thinner cheeks. Howard broke off in obvious embarrassment.

"I'm not sure that was done by the same animal as attacked Jake," Rutledge said.

"I'd still like to know what Encon had to say," said Rick.

"They were real sympathetic," Rutledge said drily. "But they're understaffed. What it comes down to is, if we can find it, they'll come and kill it."

"If we can find it, we can kill it ourselves," Walter said amid a general murmur of approval.

"But not with everybody running around and maybe shooting each other," Nelson said.

"I think we know more than that in this town about hunting," Rick said. "We need somebody to organize." He turned to Walter with what Emma thought was a preset cue, but Nelson interrupted.

116

"That's Rutledge's job as an elected official," Nelson said.

Walter's jaw took a firmer set. "Is that what you're going to do, Rutledge? Organize a posse?"

"A bear-hunting posse," Rick said, and sniggered.

"If it comes to that," said Rutledge.

"But first, you're going to want to handle it on your own, aren't you?" Walter said. "You always want to handle things on your own. But this is too big for that."

"What are you going to wait for, before you ask for help? Wait for it to kill somebody else? No offense, Mary," Rick said.

Mary stood. "I have something I'd like to say," she said, and everyone gave her respectful silence. "I want this thing caught and killed before it can kill anyone else. And I'm prepared to offer a reward of five thousand dollars to whoever kills this bear that killed my husband."

"That's fine of you, Mary," said Nelson. "But it's not necessary. Everybody's going to do all they can to get this animal without your offering a reward."

"I think its a fine and generous offer," said Walter.

"Good for you, Mary," Rick said.

"I'm going to publish it in the *Post Star*, so everybody will know the offer's for real," Mary said.

The sound of the gavel drew Emma's and everyone else's attention back to the table, but she was surprised to see it was Rutledge, not Nelson, wielding it.

Rutledge stood. "Don't you know what'll happen if you advertise a reward for that bear? You'll have people from all over coming here bear hunting."

"The more people after it, the sooner it'll be found," Mary said.

Murmurs of assent and resistance beat against each other. Rutledge banged the gavel again.

"Haven't you people seen that movie, *Jaws*?" he said. "What happened in that when they offered a reward? They got people from all over, out of state even, swarming all over the town with all kinds of weaponry. Only this isn't some fish that's going to stay put in the lake. This is a bear, and they'll be after it in your backyards. Do you really want some clown from Long Island shooting off a rifle at anything furry he sees? Could be your wife in her fuzzy robe, going out to pick up the morning paper."

"Rutledge has a good point there," Nelson said. "I hope you won't publish that ad, Mary."

"The quieter we keep this, the better," Rutledge said.

"How are you going to keep it quiet?" said Walter. "It's already been on television."

"No, I was wrong. I wasn't thinking it through," Mary said. "I wouldn't want anybody getting shot because of something I did."

"We don't know for sure it was a bear at all," Petey said, but the room filled with groans of dismissal and people turned away from him. He flushed, looked at Emma.

Emma stood. "Petey's right: we don't know it's a bear."

"It's close enough to a bear for me," said Rick.

"But if it's some other kind of animal, it might have different habits. Wouldn't it help to know more about what you're tracking?" said Emma.

"You've learned a lot about hunting in the last ten hours. Bought a gun yet?" Walter said, and the room filled with laughter.

Emma sat back down. Petey gave her a sympathetic look, shrugged his shoulders, and slumped in his seat.

"I want everybody to take precautions," Rutledge said. "Lock your doors and windows, and don't go into the woods at night. Don't let the kids camp out in the backyard. And don't be firing off weapons in the village. I'll be hunting it with a tranquilizer gun. If you see it, call me. Nelson, could I borrow your beeper so they can reach me wherever I am?"

"Sure thing." Nelson handed it over, with relief clearly written on his face.

Walter, who had been tipping back in his chair, brought the legs back down to the floor with a thump. "This isn't a job for one man," Walter said.

"That's why I'm asking for help, asking people to let me know what they see. But I don't need an army walking through the woods, spooking every bear in the county."

"If I see that thing around my trash cans, I'm shooting it whether you like it or not," Rick said.

"There's a law against discharging a firearm within the village limits," said Nelson.

Walter stood up. "Nelson, I don't care about that law. If that bear is threatening me or my family, I'm going to kill it. And I don't believe any judge or jury would tell me I was wrong to do it. You've got twenty-four hours, Rutledge, to find it on your own. After that, we form a hunting party." He looked around the room for support, then turned and walked out.

More than three-quarters of the people present walked out with him.

chapter 15

"I just hope we get through this without anybody else getting killed," Rutledge said, his voice raspy with stress, his lined face looking tired. He was sitting on the railing of Nelson's porch, a mug of coffee in his hands, the starlit lake black behind him. Emma thought the lake seemed bigger from Nelson's, probably because the island was on the other side of the peninsula and didn't interrupt the view.

Nelson was seated in a wicker chair with his legs stretched out and a beer in his hand. His wide mouth drooped at the corners. "I don't think I like being mayor. People don't do what you tell them," he said gloomily.

Lillian, seated in the chair beside his, leaned over and patted his hand. "Nelson misses the navy."

He smiled at her touch, his smile as tender as his frown had been morose. "No," he said.

Max, leaning against a post, stared across the lake. Emma couldn't see his face. A bug light made disconcerting sizzling noises at the end of the porch.

Nelson turned toward Rutledge. "Where are you going to start?" Nelson asked.

"Behind Jake's restaurant," Rutledge said. "See if it comes back for more."

"But weren't Howard's sheep the last things it went after? Wasn't that its last feeding place?" said Nelson.

"I don't think the same animal did both," Rutledge said. "I didn't want to go into details in front of Mary Witte, but the sheep had their throats slashed, then they were partly eaten. It happened fast, right where they fell, because all the blood was in one place. But Jake . . . Jake took longer. Jake put up a struggle, and his throat was chewed out, not slashed."

"So there are two bears out there?" said Lillian.

"Two animals," said Rutledge. "Maybe not two bears."

Lillian looked out into the dark nervously. "I don't know why these wild animals can't just stay where they belong. Why do they have to come hanging out around people?"

"If people are going to put out garbage cans full of food, I don't know how you explain to a bear this isn't free lunch," Nelson said. "Not to mention fat sheep near the woods."

"Do you have to kill it?" Emma said, and they all looked at her in silence for a moment.

"This bear did more than freeload out of a few garbage cans," Max said.

"But it's not a murderer," Emma said. "It was hungry, so it ate something. You can't really blame it for that."

"You can't blame people for wanting to shoot something to keep from being eaten by it," Nelson said.

"I know, but . . ."

"Emma, you of all people, defending the animal? After what happened to your father?" Lillian said.

"I know. But that made me think about this sort of thing. A lot," Emma said. "And my father wasn't murdered. He was just . . . caught up in nature some way. The way Billie catches mice."

"We're not mice," said Lillian.

"We are to the bear. I mean, if the only way to stop it is to kill it, fine. But do you have to kill it, Rutledge?"

"Probably I do. You want me to repatriate it to the middle of the forest preserve?"

"Something like that."

Rutledge shook his head. "These bears that hang around people aren't altogether wild. They're like Bootsy's mouse."

Emma smiled.

"Your sister has a mouse?" said Max.

"She doesn't want a mouse," Emma said. "But she had one in her kitchen. Bootsy came in one night, turned on the light, and there it was, sitting on the counter and eating its way into a loaf of bread, right through the wrapper. So they both screamed and ran, and then Bootsy bought a trap."

"A Havahart trap," Rutledge put in. "Caught the mouse, too."

"That's where Rutledge and I come into the story," said Emma. "Because we saw her coming out of the house with the trap. Saw her on the lawn. And she gave us a lecture about what a fine thing she was doing, returning this mouse to the wild and letting it run free with all its little mouse brothers and sisters. Returning it to the fields where it belonged, where it could be happy. Then she opened the trap and the mouse ran straight back toward the house."

"She didn't take it far enough away," said Lillian.

"No, Lillian, that's not the point," said Rutledge. "The point is that mouse belongs in a house. It's a house mouse, like its father and its grandfather and its great-great-great-grandfather before it. It'll starve in a field, or get caught by Billie or Pudding." Rutledge finished his coffee. "I'd better get going. I've got a long night ahead of me."

"Want me to come along?" Nelson said.

Rutledge shook his head. "Thanks for the offer, but you're a fisherman, Nelson, not a hunter. Walter's the one I'd like to have along, but I couldn't get him without getting half the town, and I don't want that big a chance of getting shot." The beeper on Rutledge's belt sounded.

"It'll show the number they want you to call on the side," Nelson said. "You can use my phone."

Rutledge nodded and went indoors.

"We ought to be going, too," Emma said. "I want to try to get my cat in."

"Just what do you expect people to do about mice?" Lillian said. "I know they're cute, but they're dirty things, they foul people's food supplies, chew on electrical wiring, and spread diseases."

"I don't know, Lillian," Emma said. She stood up and went over to Max, who put his arm around her. "I don't have an answer. I just don't think you can divide things up neatly according to how you think they should be."

"I'd like to know a better way to do it. If you're going to live in the country, you can't be sentimental."

Rutledge came out hurriedly, picked up his jacket on his way toward the porch stairs. "Nelson, I have to get over to the motel. Somebody's shot something, a bear maybe, or maybe a dog, I'm not sure. Different people kept grabbing the phone." He paused on his way down the steps. "You'd better call the state police, just in case nobody else has."

"Got your firearm in the truck?" Nelson asked.

"I'm all set, I . . ."

A howl came from the distant woods, a long and piercing wail that brought all the people together to the edge of the porch, peering into the darkness.

"What was that?" Emma asked in the silence that followed.

"Coyote, maybe," Nelson said.

Rutledge was already running to his truck. He climbed in and drove away, tires squealing, in the direction of Howard's motel.

Out of breath and tired, Billie hid in the shadows beneath a pine tree. She crouched, listening for the sounds of pursuing men: trampling feet, a panting dog, twigs snapping. She heard leaves rustle, a rodent squeal suddenly cut short, the cry of a night bird. In the distance, frogs sang.

Gradually, the tension in her muscles relaxed, her fur lay down sleek and smooth again. She crept out from under the tree and looked around.

The night revealed structures in a subtly detailed way the multicolored light of day only obscured: the black, unreflective mousehole in the speckled ground could no longer fool the eye into taking it for a sun-cast shadow; the thing that moved was a thing separate, and its color couldn't tie it to the plants it lived among. Everything that wasn't shadow glowed with the simple red that was also the color of the doorways.

The ground rose to her right, and the sounds of frogs, lake sounds, came from beyond the ridge, where the old man's machine and the large door should be. Going through the big door would put her on the island, and that wasn't the best thing she could do, but anywhere home seemed good.

She looked up at the night sky, checking for the moving shadow of a bird of prey, but nothing came between her and the stars. It must be busy eating the rat she'd heard it catch. She crossed the clearing and climbed to the top of the ridge.

The big door glowed red, but it looked weak, its energy fading. She hurried down, knowing there wasn't much time before it closed. As she neared the door, she was assaulted by the scents of otherside animals: cats and wolves, mammoths and peccaries. She turned sharply and hissed, but they weren't around. The smells came from the ground, from the multitude of overlapping footprints leading to the door. Billie realized this too late. She prepared to leap through, but the door had closed before she could spring.

She was in otherside, on a muddy, dense mat of hoofprints and pawprints. Its edge was sharply defined: a line in the grass with animal signs thickly layered on one side, and on the other, untouched grass. She could see the lake, and above it, the wide moon with its two accompanying bright stars.

Billie sat and cried.

No one came to help her. The door didn't open.

She got up and walked with weary purposefulness along the lakeshore, stepping around pebbles and tufts of grass, climbing over fallen logs, her moon-cast shadow by her side. She leaped onto larger rocks and back to the ground beyond, moving her head from side to side to gauge the distance. She crossed the meadow that would be lake bed on the home side, and sat down to wait where the ground rose again.

After a while, the light on the island throbbed, then rippled until it formed the big doorway and, farther from the old man's machine, the smaller openings that were the little doorways. She leaped through onto neatly mowed lawn.

And there was her house, where she knew it would be. She ran up the stairs to the food room door, put her paws against it, and mewed.

No one came. She could see into the kitchen plainly, could see her food dish, with food in it. She cried again.

There were no sounds within the house. She should be able to hear the television, and she wanted to go in and lie on the box's warm top. But still no one came.

She walked around to the other door and cried there, but it did no good. The sky here, too, was bright with moon and stars, and owls might be hunting.

She retreated to the shadows by the door, and waited.

chapter 16

Emma and Max left immediatly after Rut-
ledge. Emma waved from the passenger seat to
the two remaining figures on Nelson's lit porch
while Max drove the car onto the road.

"You're going right home?" she said, seeing the direction he was taking.

"No?" said Max, surprised.

"Don't you want to follow Rutledge?"

"No. It sounds like there are too many people involved
in this already. I don't think we'd help by showing up," Max
said.

"Who said anything about helping? I want to see what
they shot. If you don't want to go, I'll drop you off at home
and go by myself," Emma said.

"If you really want to go, I'll go with you," said Max,
making a U-turn. "But why do you want to see a dead bear?
I thought you felt sorry for the animal."

"I don't think it's a bear. There wouldn't be all this
'maybe it's a dog' business . . . whoa!"

A siren sounded behind them. A police car, lights flashing, streaked round the bend. Max pulled over to give it room to pass. "Making for Howard's," he said. "So if you don't think it's a bear, what do you think it is? Petey's beaver?"

"Maybe."

"You still think there's something strange going on, don't you?" Max said.

"Maybe. But it's not something I'd talk about to somebody who'd only laugh at me."

"I didn't laugh at you. I just think you've got emotional baggage and you're projecting it into this situation. It's understandable, given the circumstances."

"But it doesn't make for a real giant beaver."

"No, it doesn't."

"I'm not the one who saw the beaver, Max. There! On the lawn."

Max pulled up onto the edge of the motel's lawn beside the police car, which stood empty, driver's side door open, light flashing on top.

Farther out on the lawn Emma saw a tangle of moving figures surging around something. They blocked her view of whatever it was, but she heard snarls and growls. Someone screamed, and the people ran back, revealing an animal and a man struggling on the ground. The man screamed again, a shot sounded, and the animal yelped. Another shot, and another, and it fell.

The people moved closer.

Max got out of the car. Emma, noting that it was dark on the lawn, took a flashlight from the glove compartment and followed him.

A state trooper sat on the ground, a gun in one hand, the other arm dangling by his side. His jacket looked wet.

"Call the Emergency Squad, Howard. Now!" Rutledge said, giving Howard a push when he didn't move immediately. Howard seemed dazed, but walked, then ran, toward the motel.

"I think it broke my arm," the trooper said, his voice tense with pain.

A group of strangers, probably motel guests, stood around awkwardly. "You," Rutledge said to one of them, "go get blankets. Fast. We don't want him going into shock while we're waiting for the Emergency Squad." The man ran in the same direction as Howard, and two others went with him. Rutledge bent to examine the wound. "Can't see worth a damn," he muttered.

Emma switched on her flashlight and shone it on the trooper. He was a young man, his mouth grim with pain. The wet patch on his jacket was suddenly bright red. Rutledge glanced at her, nodded, looked inside the jacket. "Needs a compress," he said.

"Here," Max said, taking off his cotton cardigan. "Will this do?" He folded up the sleeve and Rutledge held it firmly in place beneath the jacket.

"Damnedest thing I've ever seen," the trooper said, his breath shallow. "What is that, anyway? That dog belong to one of you?" He directed the last question to the remaining hotel guests.

A chubby, fair-haired man holding a dog leash cleared his throat. "No. The other one is mine. The one it killed," he said unhappily, pointing at a mound lying on the dark lawn. There were others, too, Emma could see, but she couldn't tell what they were until she could point the flashlight in their direction.

The sound of an approaching siren cut in.

Emma looked at the trooper. "He's shivering," she said to Rutledge.

"What's taking them so long with those blankets?" Rutledge said. "Hang in there, Bruce."

"They're coming," said the man with the leash. And they were. Emma could see two people coming from the motel. But before they reached the trooper, the Emergency Squad sped onto the lawn and abruptly stopped, cutting off its sirens but leaving its headlights shining on the scene. Squad members quickly surrounded the trooper.

Emma got out of their way and went to explore, shining her flashlight on the furry things that lay dead in the darkness. Two of them were sheep, and the third, the one the man with the leash had pointed to, was a German shepherd. All had had their throats torn out.

The last one, the one the trooper had had his struggle with, was by far the largest. It was doglike, with black-and-silver fur, shaggy, a cold climate animal. She paced it off at six feet in length. She'd never seen a dog so big. Was it a wolf? The wolves she'd seen in the zoo were nowhere near so large. And its jaws, snarling in death, the rows of white teeth still frightening, were jaws that could break a man's arm. And that's what they had just done.

"What is that?" Max said, walking toward her with Rutledge beside him. The ambulance turned, drove away.

"I don't know," Emma said.

"Wolf, maybe," said Rutledge.

Max ran toward the car.

"I didn't know wolves came that big," Emma said.

"Neither did I," said Rutledge.

"Well, it's not Petey's beaver."

"It's not a bear, either. But I think it's what killed Jake."

132

Max came back, a sketchpad and pencil in hand. "Hold the light on it," he said to Emma. "Steady."

"It's the same style of killing as Jake: a worrying kind of attack, until the victim's weakened and it can go for the throat. I put two tranquilizer darts into it and they didn't do a thing. Unless I maybe slowed it down enough so Bruce could shoot it."

"Is that what we heard howling earlier?" Emma asked.

"Yes," said Rutledge. He looked across the lawn, into the darkness of the surrounding trees. "And it wasn't howling to us. It was howling to others of its own kind. Wolves just like this one."

Emma shivered. Max, absorbed in his work, went right on drawing.

chapter 17

Emma was relieved to find Billie waiting when she got home. At the sound of car doors slamming, Billie came running from the shrubbery, mewing excitedly, and ran straight for Emma.

"There you are! I was worried about you," Emma said, picking the cat up. Billie rubbed the top of her head against the bottom of Emma's chin and purred raucously.

"You'd think we'd abandoned her for weeks," Max said, unlocking the door.

Emma went inside. Billie had both paws round Emma's neck and, still purring, was rubbing her head against Emma's ear, but as soon as they reached the kitchen, Billie leaped down and went straight to her food dish. She ate hungrily, purring and growling alternately.

"Misses one meal and she behaves like an animal," Max said.

"So do you," said Emma. She went to the kitchen's sliding glass door, but could only see her own reflection, so she opened the door and stepped out onto the deck. She looked across the lake, to the place where the glimmering water gave way to the duller black that was the island.

Max followed her. "What?" he said, putting his arms around her.

"Do you think something like that wolf or whatever it was killed my father?"

"Could be," Max said. "But how would it get out on the island?"

"Swim."

"Why would it swim out there?"

"I don't know. A stopping off place? Maybe it was swimming from the forest preserve and it stopped to rest."

"Could be. But it can't do any more harm," Max said. "And you're tired, I'm tired. Let it go. The cat's home, the big bad wolf is dead, let's just put it behind us."

"One of them's dead," Emma said. She leaned against him, letting herself notice how tired she really was. She closed her eyes, and saw dead sheep, dead furry things. "I'm exhausted," Emma said, "But I'm not going to bed until we lock every door and window, and you do something about the window Billie goes out."

"All right," Max said, "But I don't think wolves can turn doorknobs."

When she had checked every door and window twice, Emma sagged onto the bed.

"I stapled the screen, so Billie's in for the night, but I left the bathroom window open. We need the cross-ventilation," Max said, coming into the room. "You closed the bedroom window? It's too high up for anything to get in." He opened the sash, and a summer breeze billowed the curtain.

Emma leaned back, expecting to rest against the soft cushion of her pillow, but her head hit only the mattress. No pillow. Of course: it was on the floor. She got up, changed the case that had had Billie's animal on it, and sank wearily into bed just before Max turned out the light.

Billie jumped onto the bed and settled down, kneading Emma's pillow and purring. Emma fell asleep, lulled by the sound.

· When she woke, it was because Billie was standing on her hair and growling. The room was grey with predawn light. Emma moved her hand to push Billie off her hair, but the cat jumped across the bed and ran to the window. She climbed onto the sill and stood looking out, growling, her back arched and fur bristling.

Emma went over to see what the problem was.

There was a cat in the garden. No, a lion. With no mane. And no tail. All sleek and silvery in the early light, with well-defined muscles moving under its coat as it walked toward the house.

"Max," Emma whispered, not wanting to attract the big cat's attention. "There's a lion in our backyard." She pulled her jeans on, slid her bare feet into tennis shoes. She poked Max. "Wake up."

He mumbled something unintelligible and rolled over.

Emma grabbed a sweatshirt, which she put on while going downstairs. She pushed her hair back out of her face and went into the kitchen.

The lion sat on the deck, on the other side of the glass door. It was looking around, apparently enjoying the view. Was there a circus in town? Emma wondered.

Billie came up beside her, still growling, staring at the lion. Emma put a reassuring hand on Billie's back and Billie jumped, spit, an explosive little sound that must have caught the lion's attention, because it turned toward them and looked into the kitchen.

Billie went completely still and silent.

Emma decided to follow her example and crouched motionless, staring at the animal on her deck.

It wasn't a lion after all, at least not a lion like any Emma had ever seen. It was bigger and its teeth were different. *If this is a lion, it has one problem of an overbite,* Emma thought. Its top fangs gleamed long and white, extending well below the bottom jaw. *This is a sabertooth cat. There are no sabertooth cats,* Emma told herself as she looked at the one that sat on her deck.

The great cat came suddenly alert, peering into the kitchen. It stood up and hissed, opening the largest, most tooth-filled mouth Emma had ever looked into. Then it pawed at the glass door.

Billie crouched so low to the floor she looked like she had melted. Emma hoped the latch on the door would hold.

The sabertooth moved its head from side to side, apparently trying to get a clearer look at something, although it seemed to be looking directly at Emma and Billie. Then Emma realized that, in the early light and with the dark kitchen behind it, the glass door must be acting as a mirror. The cat was seeing itself; it was certainly behaving the way Billie did in front of a mirror. It even had the same puzzled expression.

The sun rose, and the big cat squinted in the door's reflected glare. It turned its head away, opened its mouth, and stood breathing. Emma found this profile almost as intimidating as the frontal view: its mouth was open a full ninety-five degrees, wide enough to let the tips of its fangs clear the teeth in its lower jaw. *The better to eat you with, my dear,*

Emma thought. Although it didn't seem particularly aggressive at the moment. It was just breathing.

The cat closed its mouth, stretched, and sharpened its claws on the deck. It moved slowly out of sight, toward the stairs leading to the garden.

Emma went very slowly toward the glass doors and looked out. The world was sunny, cheerful, normal, the deck empty except for its usual furniture. She hadn't seen what she thought she had just seen. Except there were large, clawed-up splinters sticking out of the floor of the deck.

Emma slid the door partly open and slipped outside. The stairs were empty. She looked over the railing onto the dew-covered lawn and garden.

The sabertooth was walking across the lawn, leaving dark green pawprints on the silvery surface. Its coat was tawny in the sunlight, its movements graceful and self-possessed. It walked to the lake's edge and drank. Emma could hear the lapping sounds its tongue made.

She went back into the kitchen and slid the door shut. With shaking hands, she picked up the receiver and punched Rutledge's number into the phone.

Come on, come on, she thought, listening to it ring.

On the tenth ring, Rutledge picked up and muttered a groggy hello.

"Rutledge, this is Emma. Are you awake?"

"Guess I am now."

"Listen: there's a sabertooth cat in my backyard. I think it's heading toward the woods between your place and mine."

"A what?"

"A very large cat. Bigger than a lion and with teeth the

size of butchers' knives. It was sitting on my deck, and now it's walking toward your place."

"Emma, this is?"

"Yes, Emma."

"This isn't a joke, is it, Emma?"

"Rutledge. No."

"I was hoping it was. Okay, I'll take care of it."

"Rutledge, you're not going to kill it, are you?"

"I'm going to stun it."

"That's why I called you: there's no reason to kill it. Rutledge, it's beautiful."

"It's following the lakeshore?"

"Yes. I'll meet you."

"Stay where you are," Rutledge said.

"It's by the water. I'll come along the road and across Bootsy's yard. We can head it off," Emma said, and hung up. *I must be crazy,* she thought, but she had to know what was happening.

"Billie?" she said.

Billie sat on the kitchen table and stared out at the deck, a serious expression on her face. Emma scratched Billie behind the ears.

"Stop worrying," Emma said, and went into the entrance hall. She hesitated at the foot of the stairs. Should she try again to wake Max? He'd probably want to stop her, and besides, by the time she got him awake enough to understand what was happening, the cat would be gone. She left through the front door.

Emma jogged along the road and cut across Bootsy's lawn. Rutledge was walking along the lakeshore, and he waved to her to slow down. She followed cautiously, looking for the cat.

It wasn't hard to find. The sabertooth was by the water's edge, sunning itself on a rock. It was stretched out with its head on its paws, and it was snoring.

Rutledge raised his rifle to his shoulder, and Emma wondered how you could tell whether you'd adequately stunned a sleeping cat. Rutledge fired a tranquilizer dart, and Emma's question was answered: as soon as the dart hit, the cat rose snarling and turned to face them. Rutledge fired another dart, and the cat sprang toward them, fury in its eyes and its bristling fur.

"Fall back!" Rutledge yelled, and Emma ran toward Bootsy's while looking over her shoulder at Rutledge and the cat.

The cat hesitated, deciding which prey to hunt, and Rutledge fired again. It hissed at Rutledge and raised a threatening paw as it wobbled on its other three legs. It tried to leap, but collapsed instead. Rutledge lowered the rifle.

Emma went over to them. "You've got it!" she said.

"Yeah, I've got it. Now what do I do with it?" Rutledge said, running his hand over the grey bristles on his chin.

Emma looked down at the cat. There was quite a lot of it. "When it wakes up, you mean?"

"We've got a tiger by the tail here, in a manner of speaking, although this cat doesn't seem to have one," Rutledge said, retrieving the tranquilizer darts from the cat. He ran his finger down the length of one white fang. "This is some cat. I guess I ought to call Encon."

"Couldn't we just take it into the 'Forever Wild' section and let it go? That's got to be where it came from. Encon's going to want to shoot it, or put it in a cage."

"Not necessarily. Mostly they ignore me when I ask for help." Rutledge looked across the lake. "If I found a bobcat in these parts, that's probably what I'd do with it. We could have just found a bobcat here," he said, looking at her significantly.

Emma nodded. "How about a mountain lion?" she said.

"Mountain lions are extinct in the Adirondacks."

"But not everywhere. And if somebody should happen to see us, don't you think mountain lion is more plausible than bobcat? Given what we've got here."

"Point taken," said Rutledge.

"We could put it in a boat and just row it over," Emma said.

"I gave it enough to stun a grizzly, but there aren't exactly any recommended doses for sabertooth cats. I don't exactly know when this drug is going to wear off, or how long it would take to load the cat into a boat and row it across." Rutledge said. "Do you want to be out in a boat in the middle of the lake with it when it wakes up? We've got to get it into the animal control truck, the back's caged in. Then we can drive it around the lake to the protected area."

"Okay," said Emma.

"Only the truck's parked on the road, and this is a lot of cat to drag up there." He lifted a paw. "Heavy bones, and the rest is all muscle. I'd say it's got to be over six hundred pounds. Do you think your sister would mind if I drove over her lawn?"

"No, we just won't wake her up and tell her," Emma said. "Try to drive quietly."

Rutledge went for the truck and Emma sat by the cat and marveled that it was real. It was deeply asleep. She stroked the broad surface of its head, the round ears as big as saucers. It had whiskers, just like Billie, but its teeth were unlike any teeth she had ever seen. The enamel was shiny and white, smooth to her touch, and on the curved inside edge she felt little serrations. Big as it was, it seemed so helpless, sleeping here with its paws limp, the claws retracted. Even awake, it would be no match for a rifle with real bullets. "Don't worry, kitty. You'll be safe."

"What is that?" said Bootsy. "Is it dead?"

Emma jumped, turned. Bootsy stood there in a pink silk wrapper that emphasized the pink tinge in her hair. Her thin legs were bare, and on her feet were the bunny slippers Emma had given her last Christmas as a joke, never expecting her to wear them. Her hair was tousled, and her expression was suspicious.

"It's a cat," said Emma. "Rutledge caught him for me. He's just tranquilized."

"You're not going to keep it, are you?" said Bootsy.

"Of course not," Emma said. "It belongs in the wild."

"It's enough you kept Billie when she strayed in." She circled the sabertooth, peering at it critically. "What kind of cat is that?"

"Mountain lion," Emma said.

"It sure has big teeth." Her attention was distracted. "What is he doing?" she asked, pointing across the lawn.

Emma glanced in that direction. "That's Rutledge. He's driving across your lawn."

"I know it's Rutledge. You and Rutledge woke me up. Why is he driving across my lawn?"

"We have to pick up the cat, Bootsy," Emma said reasonably. "Before the tranquilizer wears off."

Bootsy looked at the cat's teeth, took a step backward.

Rutledge stopped the truck and came around to the back. "Morning, Bootsy," he said sheepishly, opening the grillwork back door.

"Bootsy came out to help," said Emma. "Bootsy, grab a hind leg."

"I will not. It probably has fleas."

"Suit yourself. But if we don't get it into the van, it's still going to be in your backyard when it wakes up," Emma said.

Bootsy sighed. Rutledge grabbed the cat's front quarters, and Emma and Bootsy grabbed the rear. They lifted him and tried to get him high enough to slide onto the truck.

"This thing weighs more than a refrigerator," Bootsy grunted. "Don't you have a dolly?"

"I'm not a moving man," Rutledge said. "We usually put big animals in a sling and get several people to help lift them. I don't think an old man and two skinny women are going to do the job."

"I could wake Dana," Bootsy said.

"No," Emma said.

"It's all right," said Bootsy. "I think he'd be interested. What you've got here looks an awful lot like a sabertooth cat."

Emma grabbed Bootsy's shoulders. "They're extinct. And there are a lot of jumpy people running around with guns. What we want to do is return this mountain lion to the wild before anybody knows it was here, and before anybody can shoot it."

"Oh. I see." Bootsy frowned at the cat. "In that case, why don't I get my clothesline, and we can attach the pulley up there in the truck, tie the rope around the cat's middle, and haul it in that way?"

"Yes!" said Emma.

Bootsy crossed the lawn to detach the pulley from beside her kitchen door.

"That's a remarkably practical idea for a woman wearing bunny slippers," Rutledge said.

"Bootsy's very practical. She just chooses to be practical about odd things," Emma said.

Emma climbed into the truck and grabbed the pulley from Bootsy.

"Put it on one of the hooks we use to secure cages. That should be strong enough," Rutledge said, tying the rope around the cat's middle. He took the free end of the rope and pulled. The cat rose, and Emma grabbed its neck while Bootsy pushed from below. They got the head and shoulders onto the truckbed. The cat opened its mouth and snored.

"We're getting there," Rutledge said, and dropped the rope.

Emma held on while the other two lifted the cat's hindquarters up and rolled it over.

"That's it!" Emma said. She grabbed the pulley and jumped down; Rutledge untied the rope and closed the grill. "Thank you, Bootsy," Emma said, returning the clothesline. "I promise not to tell anyone you wear those slippers in public." She got into the passenger seat.

"I'll be back later to take care of the ruts in the lawn, in case Dana gets upset," said Rutledge.

"You two do have interesting projects," Bootsy said. Then, after a pause, "Did that thing kill Jake?" she asked, sounding as though she'd just made the connection.

"No, a wolf killed Jake," Rutledge said, climbing into the van.

"Put on your television," Emma said as Rutledge drove away. "The police shot it last night. I'm sure they'll have a story about it."

chapter 18

Billie sat on the kitchen table and twitched her tail in annoyance. She couldn't believe her person had gone out the front door without opening a can. Oh, there was dry food, but it was morning and time for her can.

She jumped to the floor and stalked into the living room. Going past her scratching post, she walked to the chair her person usually sat in and unsheathed her claws. She reached up and scratched the upholstery vigorously, putting her back muscles into it. There was a satisfying sound of ripping fabric.

That done, she gave a flick of her tail and, holding it aloft, pranced upstairs. She cast a reproving look toward the front door as she passed it. At least her person had had sense enough to go out the front door, instead of out the kitchen door, where the sabertooth was.

She went into the bedroom and leaped onto the bed where the man slept. She walked along his body and, standing with her paws firmly placed on his chest, she purred in his ear. When this got no response, she licked his ear and the side of his face, avoiding the raspy places on his cheek.

He grunted and shifted his weight, but she held on and nuzzled his neck, grooming him.

He pushed her away and sat up, looked at the woman's side of the bed, groaned, and flopped back onto his pillow. He closed his eyes.

Purring, Billie licked his ear. He pushed her away and she rubbed against his hand, mewed. He looked at her. She stared at him. He sat up, swung his legs over the side of the bed. Billie jumped down and stood in the doorway, waiting. He got up, and she went before him into the hall.

He closed the bedroom door.

Billie sat and stared at it. Then she got up and, mewing, scratched with both paws at the bedroom door, her claws sheathed but banging hard enough so the door shook in its frame. He bellowed, but she kept banging at the door and crying until he opened it.

He went downstairs and into the kitchen, and Billie followed. He kept up a gurgling complaint as he rattled the can opener drawer and opened the can. He dumped the food into her dish and slammed the dish down on the floor, then went back upstairs.

Billie ate. Then she cleaned her paws and whiskers, and behind her ears. It was time to go outside.

She ran upstairs. The bedroom door was shut.

No matter. She went into the bathroom and jumped to the window.

The screen was fastened shut again. How many times did she have to push it open before they caught on that that's how she wanted it? She clawed at the screen, and pushed against it, until finally it came loose in her preferred corner.

Billie slipped through onto the roof.

"I'm hungry," Emma said. The morning sun shone in the passenger side window of Rutledge's truck and Emma reached up to lower the visor against the glare. A couple of parking tickets fell out.

"There's a granola bar in the glove compartment," Rutledge said, shifting the old truck into a lower gear. Emma didn't think she could work the stiff gearshift, but Rutledge's arms were strong from a lifetime of paddling canoes and chopping wood.

Emma rummaged among the assorted maps and warranties, found half a granola bar that had seen better days, shoved it back in, added the tickets, and slammed the compartment door. "There's a McDonald's coming up."

"You want to stop at McDonald's with that cat in the back?"

Emma peered through the little window into the back of the truck. "He's still sleeping. And we could go through the drive through. Come on, Rutledge: we've got another half hour before we get there, then we have about forty-five minutes to get home, and I haven't even had coffee yet."

"What if somebody pulls up behind us and sees him?"

"His head's at this end. From the back, he just looks like a big, tawny animal. He's got no tail. We could even say he's a dog. A Great Dane."

"I don't relish the idea of somebody waiting behind us with nothing much to do but stare into the back of the truck," Rutledge said, driving into the McDonald's parking lot. "So I'll go in, and you can wait out here and keep people away from the cat. Do you want anything besides coffee?"

"Egg McMuffin," Emma said, climbing out of the parked truck.

Emma looked around the lot. There were a few cars, a camper, and a station wagon at the near end. Once Rutledge had gone inside the restaurant, Emma went to the back of the truck.

The cat was asleep, his hindquarters with his stubby little tail pressed against the grille. It could be a dog, Emma told herself.

He stretched, pushing his paws against the side of the truck and flexing his claws. The feet definitely gave him away.

"What's him?"

It was a child's voice. Emma looked around, then down, and as she turned almost knocked over a very small boy who was standing close to her. Where had he come from? She saw a big-hipped woman leaning into the station wagon's rear seat and buckling in an even smaller child. This one probably belonged to her, too.

"What's him? A cow?" the boy said again. He was a chubby blond with traces of a milk mustache, and he sounded perplexed.

Emma hated to lie to a child. "It's a cat," she said.

The boy frowned. "Him's not a cat. Cats are little. This little." He held out his hands, measuring an imaginary cat.

The sabertooth chose that moment to lift up its head and yawn.

The boy's eyes went round and huge and his mouth dropped open. Then he gasped, and snapped his jaw shut.

"Jason, don't bother the lady." The woman from the station wagon was walking toward them, her eyes warily on Emma.

"Mommy, Mommy!" Jason said.

"I hope he hasn't been any trouble. They do wander off," she said.

"No trouble at all," said Emma.

"Mommy, him has big teeth!"

"Does he, dear?"

"Him's a cat!"

His mother laughed and took his hand. "I don't think that's a cat, Jason."

"Him is! Him has teeth and whiskers and claws."

The woman looked at the animal in the truck.

"It's a Great Dane," Emma said.

"I saw him's teeth," Jason said. "They're big as me."

The mother looked into the truck with more curiosity.

"We're bringing him in to test him for rabies," Emma said.

"Come away, Jason," his mother said, snatching him up and carrying him to the station wagon. "What have I told you about staying away from strange animals?"

Emma was relieved to see Rutledge crossing the parking lot toward her, a cardboard tray and paper bag in his hands. "Let's get out of here," she said.

Emma snapped the little triangles out of the coffee's plastic lids while Rutledge started the truck. She was sipping hers when he bounced onto the street. Coffee splashed onto her lip, and she grabbed a napkin.

Rutledge stopped for a traffic light and unwrapped an Egg McMuffin. "I used to do this with your dad," he said.

The smell of bacon made Emma hungrier. She took her own sandwich out of the bag. "Do what?" she asked, and took a bite.

"Drive through McDonald's for breakfast," he said, the

words somewhat muffled by the food he was eating. "Mornings when we were going hunting."

He pulled onto the lake road, and Emma found it easier to drink coffee now that they were out of the village's stop-and-go traffic. "I don't remember you two going hunting."

"This was before you were born. Your mother didn't approve of hunting, so he stopped."

"You went to McDonald's before I was born? They're that old?"

Rutledge nodded. "They're that old."

Emma looked through the little window at the cat.

"How's he doing?" Rutledge asked.

"He's rolled over. I think he's enjoying the sun. I think . . ." She put her ear to the window. "I think he's purring."

"I'm glad he's happy," Rutledge said.

Emma looked across the lake. The reflected sunlight hurt her eyes, but she could make out her house on the other side, and Rutledge's, and she could see the island.

"Why do you think my father was killed?" she asked.

"Why? That's a big question."

"Do you think he did something wrong?"

Rutledge shrugged. "He wouldn't have done something stupid, he knew enough for that. But sometimes a person's just in the wrong place at the wrong time. Sometimes the unexpected happens."

"Like a bear showing up on an island where there shouldn't be any bears?"

"Like that," Rutledge said. "I was always sorry he stopped hunting. I missed his company. But your mom wanted to move back to the city, and he was trying to keep her happy."

"It didn't work," Emma said.

"No. It didn't work."

"You still got plenty of chances to hunt, though."

"Guidework? Guidework's not hunting, not for the guide. It's more like baby-sitting."

The road was pleasantly free of traffic, more so as they traveled north. Tree branches that should have been cut back trailed into the way of the truck's passage, and chicory hugged the shoulder, spilling its green leaves and blue flowers onto the asphalt. Emma glimpsed the waving stalks of purple lythrum in the ditch beyond.

The road veered away from the lake, and Rutledge stopped to open the gate to a service road. He drove into the forest preserve. The dirt road hadn't seen an application of gravel recently, and the truck bounced along, smashing through twiggy growth that sought the sun.

Emma looked at the cat. He seemed to be paying groggy attention to the shaking he was getting.

Rutledge stopped in a clearing and turned off the engine. In the silence, a bird called.

"Time to return him to the wild," Rutledge said. "Better roll up your window. I'm going to go back there, open the grille, and run back in here." He got out, leaving the driver's side door open.

Emma watched through the window and saw the grille go up. A moment later the truck bounced lightly as Rutledge climbed back in and slammed his door shut.

"What's he doing?" Rutledge asked.

"Sleeping. He did stretch out more, so I think his paws are poking off the back."

"He's not getting out?"

"He's not getting out."

"I got Danish, too." Rutledge rattled the McDonald's bag. "We could eat Danish while we wait."

Emma rolled her window back down and listened. "I think he's snoring."

"That tranquilizer should have worn off by now," Rutledge said. He looked through the window. "It's the sunlight. He's sleeping in the sunlight. Cat's just plain comfortable."

"What do we do now?" Emma asked. "Just wait for him to wake up?"

Rutledge was chewing on a Danish. He washed it down with a sip of coffee.

Emma tasted her coffee, found it cold. "What if he doesn't wake up 'til nightfall?"

"Damn cat," Rutledge said.

Emma looked through the window. The sabertooth yawned, displaying his jaws. "What if he wakes up hungry?" she said.

"We're not waiting 'til nightfall. And we're not waiting around to be canned cat food," he said, patting the metal wall of the truck. He honked the horn. "What's he doing?"

Emma looked through the window. "Flattening his ears. I think he's annoyed."

"Just what we need: six hundred pounds of mad cat. I told you to roll up your window."

Emma rolled up her window. Rutledge turned on the engine and rolled forward, put in into reverse and rocked back, repeated the procedure several times. "Now what's he doing?"

"I think you'd better stop. He looks like he's going to be sick."

"Oh, terrific."

"Wait, he's getting up. He's turning around. He's lying down again."

Rutledge honked the horn.

The cat hissed, giving Emma a frontal view of his weaponry. "He's getting really mad, Rutledge."

The sabertooth shook himself, turned, and jumped out of the back of the truck.

"He's out!" Emma said.

They watched the cat walk slowly across the clearing. He stopped, opened his mouth, and breathed, then closed it again and went to the edge of the forest. There he paused and sprayed on one of the trees.

"I'm glad he waited to do that til he was out of the truck," Rutledge said.

The cat came toward them, curiosity in his expression.

"Can he smell us?" Emma asked.

"I don't know, but I'm not turning off the engine in case we have to leave in a hurry."

The cat rose up on his hind legs, put his front paws on the truck, and looked at them through the windshield.

"Jeez!" Rutledge said, and jumped, accidentally turning on the windshield wipers.

The sabertooth watched the windshield wipers go back and forth, back and forth, turning his head in time to the metronome-like motion.

Emma laughed and laughed.

"Are you getting hysterical on me?" Rutledge said.

"No," Emma choked out, "But I just may die laughing."

He turned the wipers off. The cat paused, got down. He walked a few steps away from the truck, stopped, opened his mouth.

"What do you suppose he's doing?" Emma said.

"I think it helps them smell," said Rutledge.

The cat walked north, into the forest, and disappeared.

Emma felt relief wash through her body. "I hope he'll be all right," she said.

Rutledge got out of the truck. "I want to check something," he said. "Holler if he comes back."

Emma watched, but the dense shade was quiet, and she imagined the cat padding to safety in the unpopulated forest. She felt good about that.

Rutledge got back into the truck. "There's a lot of tracks out there," he said. "I thought I saw moose tracks when I went to let the cat out, but there's others, too. Moose, bear, wolves, stuff I don't even recognize. There's some big round ones, if I didn't know better, I'd swear were elephant."

"Why would all those animals be leaving the forest?" Emma asked.

"They're not," said Rutledge. "They're going into it. All the tracks I saw were coming from the direction of town, or from the lake, and heading north."

"But that doesn't make any sense," said Emma. "How could they be coming from . . ." She looked through the trees that lined the shore, caught a glimpse of water. "Could they be coming from the island?"

"Only if there's a zoo that we don't know about on that island."

"It doesn't make any sense," Emma said again. "I'm going out to the island. Do you want to come?"

"There's nothing out there. Do you have any idea how much I have to do today, to settle things down after what happened last night?"

Emma looked at the lake. It seemed to her that if you were swimming from the island, this would be the nearest point on the northern shore.

"Emma, I don't like the look on your face,". Rutledge said. "Don't go out there alone."

"All right," Emma said.

"I mean it."

"I said all right."

"I don't believe you. I'm going to tell Max to lock you up."

"I'll go with Charles. He wants to go out there, anyway."

"Make sure he brings a gun."

"A gun? I don't want to kill anything. You said there's nothing out there anyway."

"Emma . . ." Rutledge looked ready to explode. He lunged forward to the glove compartment, slammed it open. "You take this and you keep it with you," he said, pulling out a pistol and giving it to her.

"I don't want a gun. I don't know how to work one, and I . . ."

". . . Don't want to kill anything," Rutledge finished for her. "It's a tranquilizer gun. It's loaded. It might keep you alive."

The thing felt heavy and cold in her hand. She thought of the trooper last night, his arm dangling. "All right. I'll take it with me."

"Good girl," said Rutledge. He turned the truck around and headed home.

chapter 19

Billie jumped from the roof to a tree branch and climbed down to the garden. A doorway opened, but she sauntered past it. She didn't feel like going to otherside today. There was plenty of otherside on this side, too much, as far as she was concerned. It offended her sense of propriety that animals different from cats were coming through.

She walked to the water's edge. A sticklike insect with bright blue wings hovered above the surface, but it was too far out to catch without falling into the lake. She sat and watched little brown fish swimming in the shallows. If one came near enough, it might be worth risking a wet paw.

A sound of chewing made her turn her head. Pudding was crouching beneath a nearby bush. He was eating a mouse, and he growled when he saw her looking at him. He dug his claws more fiercely into the small mouse. She flicked her tail contemptuously. A smell of skunk came from Pudding, overlaid with something else, as though he'd been rolling in crushed tomatoes. He continued to glare at her and growl as though he'd caught a whole haunch of peccary.

Billie stalked away from Pudding and his territory. She was going in the general direction of the trap full of birds, and decided this would be a good time to check on them. She hadn't been there in a while. She cut across the lawn and through the narrow strip of trees to where the cage stood, a tall thing big enough for many birds.

The sun was on the other side, and silhouettes of birds sat in a row on a branch of the dead tree at the cage's center. A yellow bird hung from a feeder, pecking at seeds, and a tray of water was full of splashing, feathery things sending out sprays of water glittery with the light behind it. Billie crouched and moved cautiously forward.

A blue jay saw her and gave shrill alarm. Suddenly all the birds were screeching and fluttering, flying if they could, hopping if they couldn't, flapping a good wing and dragging an injured one. Billie sat and watched the spectacle, her nose close to the wire mesh. One bird came near her, and she pounced at the mesh, clinging to it and climbing the side of the cage.

There was an angry scream: the white-haired person who lived here ran toward her waving a broom. Billie tried to jump down, but one claw was caught in the mesh. Still screaming, the woman swung the broom and whacked Billie's side and head.

Billie fell, the claw breaking off in the mesh. Her side hurt, and her paw. The woman's face was red, and she shook the broom and screamed. Billie crouched, getting her breath back, and flattened her ears. The broom waved near her face, and she scrunched up her eyes to protect them.

The woman screamed again and gave Billie another whack. Billie ran, and the woman ran after her, swinging the broom and shouting and gasping.

Billie escaped into the woods and looked back. The woman stood leaning on the broom, one hand on her middle, breathing heavily. Behind her, the birds gave triumphant witness to Billie's flight. Billie remembered now why she hadn't been over here in a while.

She went home and walked up the stairs to the deck. Her side hurt when she breathed deeply, and her paw hurt. She licked it, cleaning blood away from the broken claw. There was no accounting for some people whatever side of the door you were on.

The sun was soothing and warm. She climbed onto a cushioned deck chair, curled up, and went to sleep.

Rutledge dropped Emma off in front of her house, and she noticed he waited until she was inside even though it was bright midmorning.

The house seemed quiet. "Max!" she called, but there was no answer. She went into the kitchen and put the stun pistol into the drawer with the dish towels. Max must have gotten up, because there was coffee keeping warm. She was pouring herself a cup when the she heard the front door open.

"Max?" she said.

"It's me. I went for milk," Max said, coming in with a grocery bag. He set the bag down and took out a newspaper, a bag of donuts, and the milk. "Lake Harrison made the tabloids," he said, pointing to the newspaper.

Emma read the headline. " 'Restaurateur Eaten.' That's disgusting. What kind of sick mind would think up something like that?"

"Everybody's talking about the wolf now. Have you listened to the news?" Max said.

"No, I just got in."

"They had Dana look at it, and he thinks it was a dire wolf. Supposed to be an extinct species. It'll be a big deal if he's right." He poured himself coffee. "So where were you?"

"There was a giant sabertooth cat on our deck this morning. Rutledge and I took it into the forest preserve and let it go."

"No, I mean really."

"All right then, there was a mountain lion on our deck this morning. Rutledge and I took it into the forest preserve and let it go."

"Emma," Max said, annoyance in his tone.

"Really," Emma said. "Look." She pushed open the kitchen's glass door, stepped outside, and pointed to the section of deck where slivered wood stood up at odd angles. "He was scratching there."

Max looked at the deck, then at Emma, a bemused expression on his face.

"If you don't believe me, ask Rutledge," she said.

"I believe you. I believe something was here," he said, throwing his hands up in surrender. "How did you know? Did you hear it tearing up the wood?"

"No. Billie woke me."

"She's good at that. I wish you'd fed her before you left."

"I was in a hurry."

Max bent to examine the jagged splinters. "It was probably a raccoon, Emma. How many strange animals can there be wandering around Lake Harrison?" He pulled out a sliver. "I'm going to have to replace this section of deck. And speaking of replacing: that cat of yours pushed the screen open again."

162

"It was a very large wild cat," Emma said, and sat on the lounge chair. Billie slept curled up on the cushion, and Emma stroked her head and back. Billie looked up sleepily, purred, and settled down again. "Rutledge shot it with a tranquilizer dart and we let it go in the woods. Rutledge can tell the difference between a cat and a raccoon, and so can I."

"Rutledge likes to join you in these imaginative games about the mystery of nature. Rutledge is a bad influence. He's never going to grow up. Why would it have come to this side of the lake?"

"We were wondering that, too," said Emma. "But with all the guns and ammunition ready to hand in this town just now, it's lucky for the cat that Rutledge and I saw it first."

"What, you wouldn't want a nice sabertooth tiger rug for the living room?"

"It wasn't a tiger," Emma said. "It was tawny, like a lion."

"Here comes Peggy," Max said.

Emma turned. Peggy was crossing their backyard with a purposeful stride.

"Emma, I have to talk to you about that cat of yours," Peggy said from the ground below the deck.

"Come on up and sit," Max said. "Can I get you some coffee?"

"No, thank you, dear," Peggy said, coming onto the deck.

Billie looked at her and drew farther back into the cushions.

"That cat of yours has been upsetting my birds again." Peggy's voice quavered with emotion, and she pointed her finger and shook it at Billie.

Billie hissed.

Emma wondered what Peggy had done to make Billie so fearful. "Don't do that, Peggy, you're upsetting the cat," she said.

"Well, really! You encourage her, Emma," Peggy said.

"Sit down, Peggy," Max said, placing a chair for her. "Would you rather have water or coffee?"

"Coffee would be lovely, dear."

Max waited. Peggy sat. Max went inside.

"What did Billie do this time?" Emma said.

"She's trying to get my birds! She was climbing the outside of the flight cage, trying to get in." The pitch of Peggy's voice rose as she talked about what she had seen.

Max came out and gave Peggy a mug of coffee. "But there's no way she can get into the cage, is there?" he said soothingly.

"No, but she upsets them. They were flying all around and screaming."

"Peggy, you can't expect a cat not to be attracted to a cage full of birds," Emma said, trying for a calm and reasonable tone. "And your birds are safe. I don't know what you expect us to do about this."

"Keep her in. She doesn't have to be out terrorizing the neighborhood."

"Yeah, well, that's easier said than done," Max said jokingly.

"I don't think it's funny. I don't think it's funny at all. And if you don't keep her home, I'm going to get a shotgun and make sure she doesn't bother my birds!"

"That's enough!" Emma shouted, jumping up. She threw her coffee mug at the deck, where it smashed into fragments. "Hasn't there been enough of guns, and shooting, and blood? Hasn't there been enough dying? When your birds are rehabilitated, you let them loose and they go flying into my garden, pecking at the corn and the peas, and I don't go threatening to shoot them, but I don't like it . . ." Emma noticed the other two were looking at her in stunned silence. "Sorry," she said, and sat down again. She put her hand out toward the table, reaching for her coffee mug, but of course it wasn't there.

"I didn't mean to upset you," Peggy said. "It's just that it bothers the birds so much when that cat comes over."

"There's a kind of double standard here," Emma said. "The cat has to be locked up for being a cat, but the birds should be free to be birds." She was trying to be calm, but she could hear the quaver in her own voice.

"Hey," Max said. "This is nothing to fight over. This is silly."

"Shut up, Max," Emma said.

"Dear, why don't you go inside and get Emma some more coffee?" Peggy said.

Max looked surprised, then threw up his hands and went inside.

Emma looked at Peggy, shrugged. "My baby would like to eat your babies," she acknowledged.

"I didn't mean that about the shotgun," Peggy said. "You know that, don't you?"

"I know."

Peggy came over and gave Emma a hug, sitting on the end of the lounge chair as far away from Billie as possible. Billie growled anyway.

"I shooed her away with a broom," Peggy said. "I didn't hurt her."

"Maybe you should try a water pistol," said Emma.

"That's supposed to work with cats. Scold her first, and if she doesn't leave, use the water pistol."

"I'll have to try that. It's just that she gets the birds so upset."

"Birds cry to warn each other. And they're smart. The ones that come to the window feeder know they're safe when Billie's on the other side of the glass. What I'm saying is, is it really the birds who get so upset?"

"Maybe it's me." Peggy patted Emma's hand. "You have to let your father go, dear. Don't make every death in the world into his death. You'll never get over it."

Max poked his head out the door. "Is it all right if I come out now?"

"Of course, dear," Peggy said. "Everything's fine. Well, I have to go home now and fix Charles his lunch." She stood up.

"Oh, Peggy," Emma said. "Has Charles gone out to the island yet?"

"No, I don't believe he has."

"Would you tell him I'd like to go with him?"

Peggy smiled. "Yes, of course. That's very sensible of you. I'm so pleased." She went down the stairs and across the yard.

"Maybe this afternoon," Emma called after her. "If he's free."

Peggy nodded.

chapter 20

"**Are you all right?**" Max asked, massaging Emma's shoulders. "You're all tense."

"I'm fine," Emma said. Peggy turned and waved before going into the woods between their properties, and Emma waved back, smiling.

"Maybe we should take time out, go away for a weekend or something. Would you like that?"

"No, I wouldn't Max," Emma said, pulling away from his hands. "There's too much going on here."

"That's why I think we should get away."

Emma looked at him, saw the worry in his eyes. "There's stuff I have to work through, that's all."

He nodded. "I can understand that."

"And there's stuff going on. You don't want to admit it, but there is."

"That's over now. They killed the wolf, and it's over."

Emma smiled. "Right. So there's no need to get away from it. I'm starved: let's have lunch." She scooped Billie up and carried her inside. "Come on, cat: there's a slice of ham in it for you if you stay out of trouble."

She noticed the worried expression didn't leave Max's face.

After lunch, Emma ran upstairs and kicked off the loafers she was wearing. They were too floppy. She wanted to be able to move fast on the island if she had to. And she was going this afternoon, with or without Charles.

The phone rang while she was tying the laces on her sneakers, but it stopped halfway through the second ring. Max must have picked it up.

She finished lacing the sneakers and wondered if there was anything she ought to bring besides the stun gun. They didn't have much that would be useful in the way of self-defense against a sabertooth cat or a dire wolf. A kitchen knife would be a joke, even if she got close enough to use it, and if she were that close, the animal would probably be doing a good job of tearing her apart. Her courage faltered at the images her imagination presented, and feeling weak-kneed, she sat on the edge of the bed.

She was only going out there to observe. Besides, the idea was to find a way through this without any more killing. That was the point, wasn't it? She was there to look, and run. And she was prepared, she knew what to expect. Her father hadn't.

"That was Charles on the phone," Max called up the stairs. "He's rowing by to pick you up in a few minutes."

"Great," Emma said. And it was great. It was remarkable how relieved she felt not to be going alone. She ran downstairs.

"Max," she said, surprised to see him still in the kitchen, "how come you're not working?"

"I was just waiting." He waved his arm in the direction of the lake.

"To see me off? Don't be silly. Go on downstairs." She kissed him lightly. "Go on. I'm only rowing out to the island with Charles."

"Do you want me to come?"

"No." He was watching her with that worried expression that was beginning to annoy her. "You know you don't want to come. This is just avoidance behavior. Go get something done, or you'll be miserable to live with the whole rest of the day," she said, pushing him toward the door.

He went.

Emma took the stun pistol out of the dish towel drawer and went out into the sunshine.

Charles' boat came gliding along the shoreline. He pulled his oars in, water dripping down the sides, and stopped beside her dock.

"Ready?" he said, smiling up at her. He wore a straw fedora. The sunlight coming through the brim made a pattern of golden checks across his forehead and cheeks, already patterned with wrinkles. He seemed fragile and soft, compared to Rutledge. She felt a twinge of guilt at bringing him into this, but he intended to go anyway.

"Yes," Emma said, climbing into the boat. It dipped with her weight, righted itself as she sat down in the center of the backseat.

"What's that for?" Charles pointed to the gun.

"Just in case," Emma said, setting it down on the seat. "It's a stun gun Rutledge wanted me to carry."

Charles snorted. "You won't need it for anything. They killed the wolf last night."

The sun lay heavily on the boat as Charles rowed toward

the island. Emma could smell the water, lake smells of vegetation, of organic processes taking place in unhurried water. The little fish that hung around the dock darted away from the boat's shadow. Emma held tight to the edge of her seat. The oarlocks creaked, stopped. Emma looked up.

"Did you say something?" she asked.

"It was just small talk," Charles said. His wire framed glasses glimmered under the hat brim. "This upsets you, doesn't it? Would you rather go back?"

Emma looked at the island, dark with cedar, its interior hidden. "Everybody's worrying too much about upsetting me," she said. "Let's just get it done."

"Good girl," Charles said.

He skirted a patch of water lilies and made for the old dock that belonged to the lodge. The building itself, partially overgrown, swung into view.

"It needs paint," Emma said.

"If that's all it needs, I'll consider myself lucky," Charles said. He hooked a rope over the dock and pulled the boat close. "Careful where you step."

Emma stuck the gun into the waistband of her jeans. She accepted Charles' hand getting out, not because she needed help, but because she didn't want to hurt his feelings. The dock was in poor shape, and she tested the strength of each board before putting her full weight on it.

They walked through a tangle of vines and saplings that had once been a lawn. The Victorian lodge, under its growth of ivy and creeper, still jutted out turrets and bits of gingerbread trim. White paint flaked away from clapboards that had weathered a grey almost as dark as the slate roof.

"The roof should be good," Emma said. "Don't slate roofs last forever?"

"If they're kept in repair," Charles said. "Do you see any missing slates?" He walked across a porch whose boards creaked under his step and pulled creeping vines away from the door.

While Charles searched his pocket for the key, Emma looked round. She could see across the lake to Charles' house, but her own was not in sight. Cedar grew to the water's edge on either side, cutting off the view of much of the lakeshore, and their dark seedlings dotted the low growth that ran from the porch to the water. "We ought to come out and mow this, just to keep the trees from taking over," she said. She listened for animal cries, but heard only birds and the jingle of Charles' key ring.

"There!" he said.

Emma turned just as the door swung open.

They went into a large, shadowy room, apparently a combination lobby and gathering place. A counter with a wall of pigeonhole boxes stood by the stairs leading to the second floor, but the remaining space was taken up by a billiard table and by chairs grouped for conversation. A fieldstone fireplace dominated the far wall, the ashes of its last fire still on the hearth. All round the room, the stuffed and mounted heads of deer, of bear, even a mountain lion, looked down with blank stares.

On the billiard table lay her father's cameras, unexposed rolls of film, some tools, and a pair of night goggles he'd borrowed from the air force base in Plattsburgh. They were elaborate things with a complicated arrangement of lenses. They should be returned, too. She picked up the goggles and saw they were set for infrared.

She put them on, and the dim room was filled with

green light. Why green? Must have something to do with the construction of the goggles.

Charles unbolted and opened a window shutter, and Emma's eyes were filled with blinding white light.

"Jeez! Charles!" Emma said, hastily taking off the goggles. Spots swam before her eyes, and she waited for them to fade.

"What's wrong?" Charles asked.

"The light," said Emma. "It's a really bad idea to shine light into somebody's eyes when they're wearing those goggles."

"I'm sorry. Are you all right?"

Emma could see again. "Yes."

Charles opened the rest of the shutters, spotlighting the room's features, one by one, with sunlight. A chandelier made of antlers hung from the rafters, its half-burnt candles drooping from the heat of many summers. Spiderwebs trailed from it in profusion, attaching it tenuously to the edges of the billiard table, to the immobile balls. A layer of dust covered everything, and Emma saw mouse tracks on the leather chair seats, and chewed holes from which sufficient stuffing had been removed to make room for nests. An elaborate sideboard stood against the interior wall, its shelf supports and drawer pulls carved to look like the heads of bears and wolves, its legs like animal feet, so that the whole seemed to be some conglomerate animal, a hunter's dream or nightmare. Kerosene lamps stood in a row on its top shelf.

"No electricity?" Emma asked.

"No. That's one of the reasons it was closed: too costly to bring it out here, but the competition on the mainland all had it."

"Then what was Dad going to use to power the maser?"

"Where is the maser?" Charles asked.

"I don't know. It's not on the table."

"What does it look like, anyway?"

"Kind of like a vacuum bottle with tubes coming out of it. And there will have to be electromagnets with it." She looked around the dusty room. "If the rest of the place is as full of antiques as this room is, you might get back a fair amount of the purchase price by selling the furniture off," Emma said.

"You think this junk is worth something?" said Charles.

"I would say so. Getting it off the island might be a problem. That sideboard would sink a rowboat."

"We had thought the furniture might come in handy if we wanted to reopen," Charles said, dusting his hands on the legs of his jeans.

"Does this lead to the kitchen?" Emma asked, pointing to a swinging door.

"Yes. I'm going upstairs to check for leaks."

Emma listened to his slow footsteps on the stair treads, on the floor above. Otherwise, the house was silent. She pushed open the kitchen door and went through.

This room, too, was dull with dust and shaded by boarded windows. Faint light came through cracks in the boards. Shards of glass lay on the floor, their dull gleam barely visible beneath a coating of dust. Emma stepped over them and undid the various latches and bolts that held the back door closed, including a two-by-four that served to bar it, and swung the door open.

She expected an overgrown yard, or trees crowding up to the house. She expected decrepit outbuildings. She expected neglect. She didn't expect what she saw: an open area where the plants were trampled, the trees and bushes broken back to their largest stems, all within a height of maybe eight to ten feet. Above that, the leaves were untouched. It looked . . . grazed. Like something had come through and eaten whatever leaves and twigs it could reach. The grasses and Queen Anne's lace and buttercups had been flattened by something large.

The deer she had seen? Maybe a herd of them.

She went to the edge of the porch. The damage had been done recently. The flattened plants hadn't wilted, the broken twigs were sharply white. Deer wouldn't have fed so leisurely if there were a large predator on the island. Taking courage from that, Emma stepped off the porch and looked for tracks.

The unyielding ground was rocky. She walked across the grazed area, up an incline, until she stood on a ridge of rock and looked down into a shallow ravine. The rock face opposite was covered with photoelectric cells. So that's what her dad had planned to use for power. And there was the maser, sitting on a rock and wired to the photo cells.

She climbed down. The ground at the bottom was springy, but not saturated. The grass was smooth, flattened by its own limp habit of growth. To her left, the ravine widened and was filled with trees. To her right, she saw the lake. Emma walked toward the lake, the ridges of rock on each side becoming both narrower and lower. Abruptly, the untouched grass gave way to thickly trampled ground, as though a great number and variety of animals had been summarily dumped there: hooves, padded feet in several patterns, the round depressions with toe marks that Rutledge had commented on. They were all oversize. Emma set her sneakered foot inside a hoofprint and had room to spare.

Some of the prints went up the low sides of the ravine

and disappeared on the rocky ground. Others followed the shore for a while. Most went either immediately or eventually into the lake. Somehow the animals were coming from this little island.

It would not be easy to convince anybody, even Rutledge, of that.

She should have brought a camera and considered going back for one of her father's.

An icy prickling went down her spine as she remembered that's what he had been doing when he died: taking pictures.

She didn't want to be here anymore.

She had turned and started climbing toward the lodge when the first cry sounded.

chapter 21

Emma, pulling herself up the rocky slope with the help of a branch, lost her grip, and stumbled backward. The gun fell out of her waistband. The cry came again from across the lake. A wheezing, large animal noise sounded like somebody killing bagpipes. She shaded her eyes with her hand and looked across the water, scanning the shore for the source of the sound.

An elephantine creature, its fur sleekly black from the water it had just swum through, stood on the shore below Nelson's. While she watched, it lifted its trunk and brayed again, its huge, curving tusks flashing white in the sunshine.

A mammoth.

Of course: its trunk was Lillian's snake. Or the snake was a mammoth that had come earlier, and this one was calling to it. Lillian was as trigger-happy as the rest of this town.

Emma grabbed the stun gun from the ground and scrambled up the rock, scraping a hole in the knee of her jeans getting over the top. She ran across the flattened grass and stumbled up the porch steps, into the lodge.

"Charles! Charles!" she shouted.

Charles came downstairs in a leisurely fashion. "Sounds like one of the neighborhood kids has taken up trumpet lessons. He has no talent. I hope he doesn't practice diligently."

"Come on!" Emma said. "We have to get over to Nelson's." She ran out the front door and down to the dock.

"Why, what's happening? I think it's damp in one of the bedrooms. I have to go into the attic and check it out," Charles said from the front porch.

"You have to come with me now." Emma dropped the gun into the bottom of the rowboat and untied the rope. "There's a mammoth outside Nelson's. We have to get over there," she said, pulling the boat closer to land. Why had he tied it out on that rickety dock in the first place? The boat bumped against the shore, and she held out her hand to him, but he hadn't moved from the porch.

"A mammoth what?" Charles asked.

"A woolly mammoth," Emma said.

Charles stared at her. Downy seeds, disturbed by her passage, floated in the air between them. Charles batted one aside as though the gesture would clear his thoughts.

"The sound you heard was a woolly mammoth crying over by Nelson's. Come on," said Emma.

Charles pushed his glasses up to set them more firmly on his nose. He looked past her shoulder. "You're losing the rowboat."

Emma had let the rope slip from her hand. Unsecured, the boat was drifting away. She splashed into the water, grabbed the boat. She was tempted to leave him and come back for him later, since it was so hard to get him to move, but a vision of him lying dead and bleeding, torn apart by some unknown animal, sprang into her imagination.

"You have to come," she said. She looked up at him. "Please."

Charles nodded. While he fussed with the padlock on the door, she climbed into the boat. She decided to tell him later that she'd left the kitchen door wide-open.

Sun-dappled water swirled past her vision as she turned the boat around. She stopped the circular movement and pushed the stern against the shore. She was prepared to take off as soon as he was seated.

Charles got in, but instead of sitting in the stern, he moved toward the rower's seat.

"I can row," Emma said.

"We can both row," said Charles, sitting beside her. "We'll move faster."

They skimmed toward Nelson's with long strokes.

"Did you say you saw a woolly mammoth?" Charles asked.

"Yes. Row," Emma said.

They rounded the end of the island, shot past Rutledge's and into the cove where Nelson kept his boats. Emma glanced over her shoulder at the activity around the boatwright's shop. "Something's going on," she said.

"Where did you see whatever you saw?" Charles asked. They approached the dock, looked for a place to tie up the boat.

"On the shore," Emma said, "But it's not there now. Wait, there it is!" she said, standing up and rocking the boat.

"Whoa!" said Charles, grabbing the dock.

Emma scrambled ashore and ran toward the mammoth, which stood in Nelson's vegetable patch. The mammoth brushed its curved tusks along the ground, loosening the plants. It twisted its trunk around a bell pepper bush, pulled the plant up, and ate it.

Lillian shouted excitedly, men ran in and out of the shop. Walter came out with a rifle.

"No!" Emma screamed, running toward Walter.

Nelson came onto the porch. "Put the rifle down, Walter," he said. The others watched in confusion, ready to jump off the porch or go back inside, depending on events.

Loading tranquilizer darts into his rifle, Rutledge walked toward them. "I'll take care of it, Walter!" he called out. Emma remembered the gun she'd left in the boat.

Walter took aim.

"No!" Emma shouted again. She was nearest to him. There wasn't time to get the gun, although she'd like to use it on Walter, so just as he squeezed the trigger, she hit the barrel of the gun, deflecting it enough to ruin his aim.

The mammoth screamed.

Everybody on the porch ducked.

"Don't ever do that!" Walter shouted, red-faced. He shoved Emma away. She lost her balance and fell.

The mammoth's hairy shoulder was wet with blood. It backed up, lowering its head.

"It's going to charge!" Walter said. He raised his rifle.

"Put that thing away," Rutledge said, stepping between Walter and the mammoth. "You can't stop an elephant with that. You'll only get it mad."

"And I suppose you're going to get those little old darts through its hide?" Walter said. He moved to get a clear shot.

Emma got up off the ground and grabbed the rifle barrel. She pulled the rifle out of Walter's surprised grip and threw it in a long, slow arc toward the lake. It fell into the water with a splash and disappeared.

"Hey!" Walter grabbed Emma and spun her around. "That was a thousand-dollar Weatherby!" he shouted.

"Let her alone!" Rutledge said.

The mammoth was back near the tree line, whimpering and rubbing at its shoulder with its trunk.

"Damn you, Walter!" Emma shouted, pounding his arm with her fists. "You hurt it!"

"Hey!" Walter protested, putting a hand up to shield himself. "It was going to attack!"

"No, it wasn't. It's a herbivore, Walter. How ferocious can it be?"

"The bullet hit the clapboard here," Nelson said. "He must have just grazed it."

"I'm going to have you brought up on assault charges," Walter said to Emma.

"Walter, you're six-three and 250 pounds. She's maybe five-foot-two and a hundred pounds, soaking wet. You're going to look a fool," Rutledge said, stepping between Walter and Emma.

"Well, she owes me a thousand for the rifle," said Walter.

"Somebody should call a vet," Emma said.

"I will," Lillian said, and went inside.

Charles came up to the group by the porch. "Is there a circus in town?" he said. "What is that thing?"

"It's a woolly mammoth," said Emma.

"They're extinct," Charles said. "It must be some kind of gimmick. Some circus owner glued hair on an elephant."

"It does look pretty tame," Nelson said. "Walter, you're lucky Emma stopped you from shooting somebody's valuable animal."

Lillian came out. "Vet's on his way."

Rutledge drew Emma away from Walter.

"It's a mammoth," Emma said so everyone could hear. "Not an elephant. Look at the tusks: elephants' tusks don't curve like that. And its shoulders: elephants don't have such high shoulders."

"You're an expert?" Walter sneared.

"Ask Dana if you don't believe me. He's got pictures of them in textbooks."

"But they're extinct," Charles said again.

"Like that wolf that got killed?" Rutledge said.

The mammoth cried softly, directing its attention to the woods. The brush parted, and a baby mammoth toddled out clumsily. It went over to the big mammoth and they twined their trunks around each other in a caressing gesture.

"Ah!" said Lillian. "Isn't that sweet?"

"That don't look like extinction to me," Nelson said. "That looks to me like something that could put this town on the map."

chapter 22

"I think they're coming from the island," Emma said to Rutledge.

"How could they be coming from the island? It's too small," said Rutledge.

"I don't know how, but there are tracks out there . . ."

"Here's the vet. I'd better go help him."

Rutledge went over to a grey-haired man getting out of a car, and soon they were deep in consultation. Emma watched the mammoths. The mother pulled leaves and twigs off a maple and stuffed them into her mouth; the baby went beneath her to nurse. The two shaggy coats blended together, a brown so dark it was almost black, and slightly curly now that they were drying.

Arms at their sides, Rutledge and the vet approached the mammoths slowly. The vet carried a leather bag, and Rutledge had his stun gun in a lowered position. The mother watched with a mild eye; the baby came out from under her and toddled round the men, its expression bright with curiosity under its tousled fur.

The vet spoke soothingly and set his bag down. Concentrating on the mother, he opened a bottle, poured brown liquid on a gauze pad. The baby inspected the open bag with its trunk, stepped backward, and sneezed. The vet cleaned the graze on the mammoth's shoulder. She whimpered and pulled back, but he patted her head and she let him finish.

"They're magnificent."

It was Dana's voice. Emma turned and saw him standing beside her, his gaze on the mammoths, his expression rapt.

"They're woolly mammoths, aren't they?" Emma said. "Aren't they supposed to be extinct?"

"Supposed to be."

"They seem so gentle."

"Absolutely magnificent," Dana repeated. "There must have been a small population in the forest preserve all this time."

"There's no way things could become extinct and then just come back again," Emma said to herself, thinking of the tracks going into the preserve and the ones that suddenly appeared on the island. "What happened to them before? Why did they die out . . . or almost die out?"

"Changing habitat: they were tundra animals, and the ice age ended. Also man appeared on the scene. There's an unfortunate correlation between the appearance of man and the extinction of other species."

"Could cavemen have eaten enough mammoths to make them go extinct?"

"Probably not. But there's evidence of man herding large numbers of animals together and stampeding them over cliffs, or driving them with fire and killing them in huge numbers. A kind of annual hunt. I'm so pleased these escaped." Still wearing an awed expression, Dana walked toward the mammoths.

Nelson strode onto the porch. Emma hadn't noticed he'd gone inside. "The *Post Star* is coming, and the *Times Union*. And Channel 6," he exulted. "And when this hits the local papers, I'll bet we'll have CNN and the Associated Press here, too."

"Don't forget, I saw it first," Walter said.

"It's on my property," said Nelson.

Emma looked at the mammoth placidly letting Dana stroke its tusk and wondered how safe it was in this enlightened age of man. She went over to Rutledge.

"Rutledge, will you come out to the island with me? There's something I want to show you."

"Can't right now. I'm the animal control officer, and I'd better hang around here for a while in case I have to control some animals," Rutledge said, looking at the people on the porch.

"Okay. I'll just go out there with a camera. Charles . . ."

"I'm going in to call Peggy. She's got to see this."

"So she'll give you a ride home. Is it all right if I take the rowboat back then?"

"What? Sure. Sure, I'd appreciate it."

"Emma, take the gun," Rutledge said.

"It's in the boat."

As Emma pulled away from the shore, she saw a pickup truck arrive and disgorge what appeared to be several families of children. Rutledge and the vet were trying to keep them back, and Nelson brought out a rope which he strung from tree to tree. Before she turned at the peninsula, the police had arrived to help with crowd control, which was good, because the crowd had already increased considerably.

Emma rowed to her own dock and went into Max's studio. He was bent over his drafting table, absorbed in his work.

"There are woolly mammoths down at Nelson's," Emma said, searching the cupboard for their camera.

Max grunted.

"A mother and baby." Emma found the camera behind a box of Tootsie Rolls. "Does this have film in it?"

"I believe so." Max paused to sharpen a pencil. "Taking pictures of these mammoths?"

"No. There'll be plenty of those in the newspaper."

"Right, right," Max said in a disbelieving tone.

Some people won't accept what's in front of them until it bites them, Emma thought. Then, upset by the literal possibility of that happening, she locked the door that led from the studio to outdoors. "I'm going out to the island," she said, slinging the camera over her shoulder. A pang of dismay at the idea of going out there alone caused her to add, "Want to come?"

"I thought Charles was going with you."

"He did, we went together, but he's at Nelson's now, with the mammoths."

Max joined her in saying the last three words, then shook his head. "So if you've been out there, then you know it's safe. I really ought to finish this. If you can wait . . ."

Emma grabbed a couple of rolls of film from the drawer where they were kept and dropped them into her pocket. "That's okay. Catch you later." She started up the stairs, paused. "How come you believe in the wolves but not in the mammoths?"

"What? I saw the wolves, wolves are plausible . . . You're kidding about mammoths, aren't you?"

"Watch the news tonight," Emma said, and ran upstairs. She went through the kitchen, where Billie was sleeping. In passing, Emma scratched behind the cat's ears, and left the house.

Billie woke up when her person passed through the kitchen. She jumped out of her basket, giving a quick, staccato cry, but the woman was out the door, closing it behind her, before Billie could make it known she wanted attention.

In the quiet house, Billie heard a chair squeak. She ran downstairs.

The man was there, seated at a table with a stick in his hand. She jumped onto the table and, purring, rubbed her chin against the stick.

He yelped, picked her up, and plunked her down on the floor.

He was always slow to understand. She rubbed against his ankles, purring loudly, then jumped onto the table and sat watching while he rubbed a lump back and forth on the paper-covered table. He picked up the stick again and she reached for it, curling her claws around it and pulling.

He yelped again, threw down the stick, and picked her up roughly by her belly. He went to the door, turned the knob, grumbled, fussed with the lock, turned the knob again, opened the door, and dropped her onto the ground outside. He closed the door.

Billie sat and washed his touch off her fur, taking care to look over her shoulder at him to make sure he got the point.

She would find the woman. Billie sauntered around the corner of the house in time to see her rowing toward the island.

No matter; a shimmer above the trees told her the big door was open. She could take a roundabout way and avoid the water. She found a small door, and jumped through to otherside. If she hurried, she could catch up with her person.

Emma left Charles' rowboat tied to her dock and took her own, remembering to transfer the gun. She rowed not toward the lodge, but toward the rocky outcropping where she had seen the deer. Once there, she tied the boat to one of the metal rings attached to the rock and sat looking up at the island.

She was at eye level with the ground at the narrow end of the ravine, and its grassy center gave her a view into the island's heart. Trees rose thick and tall on either side, but sunlight reached the clearing and scattered daisies turned their flowers skyward. A field mouse of ordinary size ran from one tuft of grass to another, and disappeared into the meadow. The boat thumped softly against its rocky mooring.

It all seemed harmless enough. Emma slung the camera over her shoulder, stuck the gun in her waistband, and climbed ashore. She'd keep an eye on the woods, and not get too far from the boat.

The footprints were nearby, where the rock gave way to soil. Emma found a circular depression she now knew to be a mammoth's footprint and photographed it. She should have brought something to set beside the animal tracks, for scale. A ruler would have been ideal.

She found a pawprint, clicked the camera, then, on impulse, bent down and set her hand inside the depression left by the pawpads of whatever beast had passed this way.

Her hand fit inside the pawprint easily. If its foot was this big, how large would its mouth be? The gun could show scale. She slid it next to the pawprint and photographed them both.

Emma stood and looked uneasily into the woods. Thinking that whatever had made this track had gone into the lake, she turned her attention to the water.

A touch of fur against her leg made her heart jump. She looked down, and in her relief took a deep breath.

"Billie! How did you get out here?" Emma picked up her cat. Billie purred and put her paws around Emma's neck. "Did you follow me to the rowboat, and I just didn't notice you?"

Billie rubbed her cheek against Emma's, and Emma stroked the cat's back several times, then shook the loose cat fur off her hand. It drifted slowly through the air.

Emma set Billie down and moved inland, taking pictures as she went, wondering if they'd develop. *I should have brought plaster,* Emma thought, annoyed with herself for not thinking of it sooner.

Billie ran between her legs, twisting around her ankles. Emma tripped, but managed not to fall. Billie walked in the direction of the boat and meowed.

"I know, you want to go home. I'll take you soon. Just be patient." Emma focused on a hoofprint, clicked the shutter, moved farther inland. The tracks were thicker there.

Again, Billie ran between her legs, tripping her.

"Billie! What's the matter with you?"

Moving from paw to paw, Billie looked at her anxiously and cried.

"Please, Billie, I won't be long. Can't you just sit still for a few minutes?"

Emma followed the tracks of paws and hooves until the trail suddenly stopped. Untouched, smooth meadow lay beyond. It was as though the animals had suddenly appeared out of nowhere. And this was where the maser sat. Could the maser have something to do with the animals' presence? That was silly: it was just an amplification device. She photographed it and continued toward the interior.

She took a few steps forward and the air seemed suddenly colder. She looked around. The trees seemed different somehow. Yes, of course: she'd thought the island was covered with cedar, but this was a mixed forest of evergreens and oak and birch. It must be just the shoreline that was all cedar. And the area at the wide end of the ravine seemed much bigger than she'd thought.

She glanced back past the maser to see if Billie were waiting, but there was no sign of the cat, who had to be around somewhere.

Odd: she could smell meat cooking. Somebody on the mainland must be having a barbecue.

Billie suddenly appeared at her side, meowing frantically. "All right, sweets," Emma said, picking her up, but Billie remained tense in her hands and jumped down as soon as she could.

Maybe Billie was aware of something, of some animal, Emma thought, looking into the shady forest apprehensively. She put her hand on the stun gun for reassurance. "All right, we'll go," she said, but Billie had disappeared again.

Emma walked toward the lake. The cat would be waiting there, that's where she wanted Emma to go. And it would probably be a good idea to listen to Billie's senses and get off the island. She hurried along the rock to the lake's edge.

The rowboat was gone. In fact, half of the lake was gone. The center of it remained, but the space between the island and her house was dry land covered with grass and scattered rocks. She didn't need the boat: she could walk home, except it wouldn't do much good because her house was gone. She ran to the edge of the rock, where the deer had stood, and looked across the plain, across the water. Rutledge's house was gone, and Bootsy's, and beyond the trees, where Nelson's roof should have been visible, there were only more trees.

Emma felt her heart beating faster. She told herself she must have gotten turned around somehow, come out of the ravine some other way. But how could anyone get lost on an island the size of this one? And even if she had become disoriented, this was still an island. There should still be water all around it. What had happened to the lake?

"Billie!" she called.

There was no answer.

There had to be a reasonable explanation. Maybe she hadn't come back out the way she'd gone in. She could swear she had, but maybe she hadn't. Retracing her steps was the way to find out.

Emma walked onto smooth grass, unmarked by animal tracks. Her hopes rose. Maybe she had taken a wrong turn somehow. She looked at the ground more closely and saw that there were animal tracks, but just a few. While one pawprint and a hoofprint were fresh, the others were worn by rain.

She walked inland, came to an invisible line of demarcation, the ground thick with tracks on one side, the grass smooth on the other, but reversed. The tracks were inland, the smooth grass led to the water. The maser was where it should be. The photoelectric cells, however, were gone.

Thoroughly confused, Emma continued walking between the rocky ledges, which grew wider apart as she walked toward the island's interior. The right-hand ledge curved, blocking her view, and she couldn't find where she had made the wrong turn. On the left, the ledge grew lower and gave way to meadow.

Emma saw a man dressed in fur and leather walking in the meadow. His hair was long and he carried a long, pointed stick. She couldn't be sure from this distance, but she thought there was a spearhead at the end of the stick. He went into the woods at the far side of the meadow.

She could still smell meat cooking. Some back-to-nature group must be playing at being Indians, camping out on the island. She was annoyed. Why didn't they use the public campgrounds? There were plenty of them.

She'd come back out with Max and Charles and deal with him later. It was best not to try to confront crazies alone. But she felt reassured, knowing she wasn't the only person on the island. Things couldn't be as strange as they seemed.

The reassurance vanished when, continuing beside the right-hand ledge, she at last stepped from behind it and saw a vast plain dotted with occasional stunted trees. In the distance was a shrunken version of the lake, and beyond that, a horizon covered with ice.

A herd of mammoths grazed, stretching out their trunks to pull up shrubby plants. To the left of the mammoths was another grouping of animals, half a dozen or so deer. Two of them had wide antlers similar to those of the deer she'd seen. They seemed to be traveling north.

A woolly rhinoceros stood up nearby and yawned. The

beast was covered in black hair, like the mammoths, but was built lower to the ground. It had a horn prominent on its nose. It shook its head, small ears flapping, and walked toward the lake. Emma held still as it passed by her, either not seeing her or not caring that she was there. Its brown eyes had a mild, vague look. Perhaps it was nearsighted. When it reached the water, it waded in and drank.

She wasn't home anymore. She was wherever the mammoths and the giant deer and the sabertooth had come from. But where was that?

The Pleistocene? How could she be back in the Pleistocene? Ten thousand years back? If she wasn't there, she was some place very like it. Never mind how, it was a good working hypothesis. It was the only one she had between herself and mental chaos, so it would have to do.

She looked at the rhinoceros, lapping water and snorting. She looked at the distant mammoths, at the open, grassy plain that stretched to a horizon white with ice. Emma felt small. And alone. And bereft of home.

How was she going to get back? That line where the tracks appeared and disappeared had to be the answer. That must be where she crossed over, back by the maser.

The maser. What had her father done? Not photographs at all, not recordings of space-time, but a passage of some kind from one part of space-time to another. She had taken a wrong turn after all, but it was a very different kind of wrong turn from any she'd ever taken before. And when her father had taken it, it had killed him.

She ran into the ravine and back to the lake, her heart beating fast with exertion and fear. At the end of the tracks, she stepped over.

Nothing changed. The lake was still missing, her home

was still missing. And where was Billie? Billie had been there. Billie had been on both sides, she was sure of it, so there must be a way.

Again, she stepped over the line. Again, nothing happened.

But the maser was there. She went to it and examined the fiberglass outer casing and the wires that fed into it. But from what? The power cells were gone, at least in this time. But they had been there. She looked at the indicator on the side. The maser was charging up. There was no power supply, but it was charging up. The maser must be in both times.

She tried to remove the lid, but it was screwed on and she didn't have a screwdriver, and she certainly couldn't borrow one from the man with the spear.

And who was he? She remembered him with foreboding. It was probable he was from this time and place and that there were more like him. What had Dana's book called them? Paleo-Indians. They had as much in common with today's Native Americans as she had with some Cro-Magnon living in a cave. Would the Paleo-Indians help her or kill her? And what if they found the maser?

Emma's legs felt wobbily and she slid to the ground, her back against the rock wall. What did she know about these people? Nomadic hunters, tribal, Stone Age technology. Nothing would make her trust her life to them.

Stay calm. Stay calm and think. What did she know about the maser? She wished she'd paid more attention when her father was explaining it. About an inch and a half of man-made ruby rod inside a vacuum with a nitrogen coolant. Electromagnets powered by an outside source, in this case way outside. Electrons in the ruby charging up, gathering energy through the waveguide. And when it was charged, did it emit its signal automatically, or did somebody have to trigger it? And how would she know when it went off? She hadn't noticed a thing coming in.

And what modifications had her father made to it, to get it to make an opening through space-time? *Daddy, what have you gotten me into?*

chapter 23

When Billie turned and looked behind her, she saw the doorway had closed. Her person hadn't followed. Feeling bereft, she sat and looked at the blank air. Then she cried outside the door, but it didn't open.

Billie thought of the other doorways. Her whiskers twitched as she remembered the feel of their sides going through. They were all too small. Her person would have to come back out through this one.

It would open again. She settled down to wait.

The rock was warm, and after a while she dozed in the sunlight, her ears remaining alert for signals of change. Birds sang out of reach, and the lake water lapped against the rock and the rowboat. Eventually the light dwindled and the air grew cooler. Billie ruffled her fur and looked for signals the door might be opening. There were none. Perhaps when the little lights came out in the sky, there would be an opening.

She heard splashing and turned toward the lake. A boat was coming toward her. The man was rowing toward the island. She stood at the end of the rock and cried to him.

He called to her, then tied his boat next to the other one and climbed onto the island. Billie held her tail aloft in welcome, and he ran his hand along her back. He stood, held his hands on either side of his mouth, and shouted.

He walked toward the center of the island, shouting as he went, and Billie followed him, keeping to the edge of the rock ledge where it was easiest for her to walk. At the end of the clearing, he stopped, looked around, and peered through the thin border of trees at the water beyond.

He came to where Billie stood on the ledge, at face level with him. He seemed to need reassurance. Billie leaned forward and licked his forehead.

He stepped back and wiped his hand across his forehead, then climbed up the rocks and walked toward the island's house. Billie followed.

He went up the steps and opened the door. Billie slipped inside with him, and he paused to cry out before going through a second door. Keeping closer to his feet, Billie again went with him.

He walked across the large room, crying as he had outdoors. Billie was sure it was because he missed the woman, but for all his cleverness with doors, he was looking behind the wrong ones. She watched him run his hands through the fur on his head, making it stand up untidily.

She sneezed. The room was full of dust, especially down here on the floor. She looked up for a better place to jump to, and saw animals staring at her from all around the tops of the walls. Their eyes were bright, their mouths snarling or their antlers ready to attack.

Billie uttered an explosive hiss and took refuge under a heavy piece of furniture. There was dust below, and mouse smell, and she hid all the way in the back.

The man knelt and looked into her hiding place. He crooned to her, but he didn't sound sincere. He sounded like he was going to give her a pill. He reached his hand in and she swatted it.

He pulled it out quickly, shook it, grumbled.

Billie growled.

He pushed on the furniture, but it didn't move. He poked a broomstick under, pushing against her, and she hissed, fighting it, then felt his grip on the scruff of her neck.

She howled and clung to the carpet. He pulled her, getting hold of her back with his other hand, dragging her toward him. Her claws ripped through the carpeting, but he got her out.

Billie flailed in the air, but he held on to her, making angry noises all the while, and went back outside with her, where he dropped her. He stood alternately sucking at the scratches on his hand and muttering.

Gradually, Billie's fluffed-up fur subsided to its usual smoothness. She noticed with distaste that she had dust and spiderwebs in her coat.

He shook his head and complained, then reached for her. She pulled back. He threw up his hands then and walked back the way they had come, toward the boats. The darkness was growing and he stumbled as he went.

Surefooted in the red light of evening, Billie followed him as far as the rock, where she sat again to wait for the large door to open. It should happen soon.

The man fussed with the rowboat, rocking it about and rattling the oarlocks. Then, just when she expected him to leave her in peace, he suddenly scooped her up, plunked her down in the boat, and pushed away from shore.

Just as the door opened. Billie stood and meowed, but

he ignored her. She bent this way and that, judging the distance to shore, but he was rowing away from it all the while. She couldn't make the jump. She gave a series of urgent cries, because the door was fully open. Although he was facing that direction, he didn't even slow down until he reached the dock by their house. Then he tied up the boat, grabbed Billie, and dropped her ungently onto the shore.

She followed him to the house. There was little else she could do. Once inside, he picked up the shrill thing on the wall even though it was quiet at the moment, and made noises into it.

Billie went to the refrigerator and meowed.

Scowling and still making noises, holding the thing on its cord to his ear, he opened the refrigerator, pulled out a piece of meat, and threw it to her.

In spite of his rudeness, Billie grabbed the meat and ate it. She was still hungry when she finished, and she tried asking him for more, but he was so absorbed in his lament, leaning against the wall there, that he didn't notice her plea from beside the refrigerator door.

To get his attention, she reached her paws up the side of his legs and scratched at the fabric covering.

He yelled and kicked her away.

She made do with some dry food, then went upstairs.

In the room where they slept, moonlight defined all the shapes in distinct shades of grey. Billie jumped onto the bed and walked across the taut surface. A light scraping noise caught her attention, and she looked back across the indentations her paws had made in her passage across the bed. The sound came from the window curtain, moving in a light breeze and rubbing against the sill. The curtain drifted into the room and she considered pouncing on it, but she was too dispirited to want to play.

Billie climbed onto the pillow and kneaded it, taking comfort in its softness and in the smell of her person that lingered in the fabric. She rubbed her cheek against the smell, wanting her person back. The other one was a poor substitute.

She left the bedroom. Going toward the hole in the screen that opened onto the roof, she heard several voices downstairs, but not the voice she wanted to hear. Maybe they had brought the woman back. Hope rose, and Billie ran downstairs to the kitchen.

The room was bright with light and color. The man who lived with Billie's brother stood playing with one of those sticks they carried at night, the kind that lit up. He kept switching it on and off. The grey-haired man who lived in the house by the birdcage stood beside the table, chattering and moving his hands, and Billie's man leaned against the refrigerator.

Billie jumped onto the table. Pudding's man stroked her back, but she could tell he wasn't paying attention to her. Then all three nodded, almost at the same time, and went out the kitchen door.

Billie followed and watched from the deck. They walked across the lawn, their cries interlacing and interrupting each other. They stood at the lake's edge, waving their arms and looking at the island. When the grey-haired man climbed into the rowboat, followed by the others, Billie ran after them and reached the boat just as her man was untying the rope.

She jumped in.

Her man picked her up and threw her out again.

The door was still open. She could see the shimmer. She called up her courage and stretched her muscles. The boat had moved away from the dock, but Billie jumped, and reached the boat.

The men barked. Hers picked her up and threw her back onto the shore. She felt herself sail through the darkness and come down onto the grass. When she turned, they were too far away for another attempt.

She watched them row toward the island, but not toward the door. Instead, they went ashore at the island's old house. She didn't see how that would be of much use.

Billie looked for a doorway, found one above the catnip, and jumped through.

chapter 24

Emma waited for the maser to recharge. She looked at it carefully for a triggering device, but could find only an on/off switch. Was there something she had to do to get it to breach space-time?

Of course she didn't. It had been here for a year, operating on its own. It had to be self-triggering. Probably when it built up enough power it would discharge.

Where should she be when that happened? Would she get hurt if she was standing close to the maser when the power discharged?

She stood and looked around her. The forest came to the edge of the ravine on each side, and branches drooped into it, their leaves motionless. She heard birdsong and the cry of a mammoth. The sun was behind the trees, and the rock face opposite her cast a long shadow. Night was coming.

The more she looked at the rock walls narrowing to a point with the lake beyond, the more the place looked like a potential trap. She had the stun gun, but she wouldn't want to face a dire wolf or sabertooth cat with it. And didn't wolves hunt in packs? She probably shouldn't spend the night on the ground.

What if the passage home opened? She could climb a nearby tree and watch, but how would she know? She hadn't seen anything special when she'd come to this time: she'd just suddenly found herself here.

A wolf howled. It sounded far away, but it prickled the hairs along the back of her neck in spite of the distance. She should climb to the safety of a tree while she had enough light to find a good one.

She started to climb the left-hand side of the ravine because it was lower, but she hesitated. The man had gone into the forest on this side, and the cooking smells had come from this side.

Emma went back to the maser and stepped over the line one more time. Nothing happened, and the machine was still recharging.

She scrambled up the right-hand rock wall and climbed into a decent-sized oak. She could see into the ravine, and out across the shrunken lake. The air was cold now that the sun was going down, and she shivered inside her cotton sweater. How cold did it have to be before you had to worry about hypothermia?

Billie made her way through the otherside night toward the red light of the big doorway. She hoped her person would be waiting there and would come home and open a can.

She was almost to the ravine when she heard dry leaves rustle. She stopped. Eyes shone: a pair behind her and a pair farther over. Billie growled. She didn't like the smell drifting through the forest, a smell of ungroomed fur. She could make out doglike shapes standing beneath the trees.

From the darkness beyond the eyes, something snarled, something yelped. The eyes disappeared into darkness as the smelly things looked behind them. One raised its snout, and howled a long, piercing cry that made Billie's fur stand on end.

Wolf. A smell of wolf.

Snarls and hisses came from the ravine. The wolves hurried toward the sound of a big cat, cornered.

Billie ran in terror toward the trees, overshooting the oak in her panic, continuing to the pine beyond. She climbed, all the while aware of the battle taking place just beyond the rocky ridge.

Billie clung to the tree and looked down. Between the ridges of rock a sabertooth stood, its back to the open doorway. Its escape to the tundra was blocked by the wolves, their eyes yellow, their jaws grinning in the moonlight. A chorus of growls rose ominously from the group. The sabertooth hissed, displaying its own white fangs. It was a match for any of the wolves, but not all of them at once.

Curious about the fight, Billie crept out onto a branch to see better. Her weight made it dip, and she clung to the bark, looking at the scene below. More yellow eyes joined the group ready to attack. Billie felt a wave of revulsion for pack hunters. She hissed, too, but no one noticed her.

A wolf nipped at the great cat's hindquarters, and when it turned to defend itself, another tore at its shoulder. The cat yowled in fury and slashed the nearest wolf. It retreated, yelping, but another took its place.

Through the open doorway, Billie saw the three men at home walk into view, Pudding's man going first with the light. They stood on the rock beside the big lake at home.

In the ravine below Billie, a wolf sprang for the great

cat's throat, but the sabertooth slashed the wolf's side open, and it lay yelping in pain. Other wolves attacked it where it lay; the remainder of the pack sprang at the cat, whose fangs were now dark with blood. In the frenzy, a wolf grabbed the tip of the branch where Billie sat and shook it determinedly, apparently thinking he'd got hold of an enemy.

Billie dug her claws in, used her tail for leverage, but the shaking was too much. She lost her grip and fell into the melee.

Suddenly the air above her was full of snapping jaws. Springing for the sabertooth, a wolf kicked Billie. She recovered her balance and, keeping her belly as close to the ground as possible, ran for the doorway. Behind her, another wolf howled in pain. Ahead, the men calmly chirruped to each other.

Billie burst through the doorway into the beam of light. Her fur bristled, her heart beat fast. Her man looked at her in surprise, then looked behind her in amazement. Billie swerved, sure from his expressions that something was following her.

The sabertooth leaped through heavily, blood flowing from its shoulder and side, blood suddenly red on its fangs in the cone of light. It hissed at the men, and hers jumped to the side, as did Pudding's, dropping his lightstick as he went. The stick rolled, sending the sabertooth's shadow moving along the rocks behind it. When it stopped, it shone on the cat and the grey-haired man, who stood unmoving, staring, between the cat and the lake.

The other men called out in warning. The sabertooth hissed again, raised its paw, and struck the man out of its path, then ran into the lake. Billie could see the ripples it left on the moonlit water as it swam toward the far shore.

The injured man sat on the ground. Blood welled from his shoulder. The others went to his aid, clucking and fussing. Behind them the doorway loomed, firmly open.

Billie rubbed against her man, trying to get his attention. He pushed her away. The wolves could come through any minute. She jumped into his lap where he knelt, put her face close to his, and meowed.

He pushed her down, stood up. He and the other helped the injured man to his feet. They took a few steps, making noises to each other all the while, but then the injured man stopped, shook his head, sank to the ground.

At least they were out of the direct path from the doorway to the lake. Billie sat uneasily, looking at the doorway, afraid to go near. There would be no getting her person through tonight.

The uninjured men untied the rowboat the woman had left attached to the rock, and together helped the injured man in. Hers got back out and lifted Billie into his arms. He held her with unaccustomed gentleness and took her into the boat with him. When they were out on the water, the doorway closed.

They rowed home. In the kitchen light, the bleeding man sat on a chair. Red drops fell to the floor. Billie's man opened the top part of the refrigerator and made rattling noises, taking things out and dropping them onto a cloth. He bundled the ends of the cloth together and held it against the hurt shoulder.

The other man just made noises into the box on the wall.

The man on the chair looked pale. His head drooped. The others chirruped encouragingly, walked back and forth for no reason Billie could see.

A siren wailed outside, grew louder, stopped abruptly at its loudest. Her man ran to the door and let in booted men with a wheeled machine. Their steps shook the floorboards.

Billie hid under the kitchen cabinet and watched the feet go back and forth. After a time the men and machine left, taking the injured man with them, but a stranger stayed. Hers gave a long series of cries, angry and upset, but the other just sat making tracks on paper with a stick. He stood up, put on his hat, and left.

Her brother's person, who had been leaning against a wall, came forward making comforting noises. He patted her man's shoulder, then left.

Alone, her man turned off the light and sat staring across the lake.

Billie came out from under the cabinet. She rubbed against his leg, jumped onto his lap, and sat looking into his face.

He glanced at her. The sadness in his expression didn't change, but he stroked her back, then returned his gaze to the water and the night sky.

They sat together until the moon set. Then he put her gently down and went upstairs.

Billie slipped through the opening in the kitchen door, out onto the patio, where she jumped onto the railing and stretched along its narrow width. The sky at one end of the lake was purple. She closed her eyes and dozed, but kept her head high, her mouth open, to taste the air for dangers.

chapter 25

Dozing in the tree, Emma was shocked awake by the sounds of a tremendous animal fight. In the moonlit ravine below her, a sabertooth cat fought with a pack of wolves. The cat was bleeding from several tears in its flesh. One wolf lay dead, its throat severed, and the others were worrying the cat, who had been forced into the narrow end and hadn't much room to maneuver. In spite of the one dead wolf, their size and number made it likely things would go badly for the cat. Emma clung to the tree.

Suddenly she saw Billie running away from the fight. She ran past the maser and disappeared. The sabertooth, as if taking its cue from Billie, leaped after her, and it, too, disappeared. The maser had made its breach in space-time and, with the snarling pack of wolves at the base of her tree, Emma couldn't get to it.

Emma saw fire across the ravine: men had come with torches. The men attacked the wolves, throwing spears into the snarling pack. There were yelps of pain, and much confusion, much sniffing and searching for the cat. It was clear to Emma that they couldn't smell where it had gone.

One of the men tossed a torch into the pack, the flame arcing high over the milling bodies before falling among them. The wolves bolted then, running for the tundra. The largest paused and howled back at the people standing on the rocks. The sound made Emma's stomach turn to ice. Then the wolf ran straight for the North Star, stopping once to howl again. Emma could see dark shapes following it, the pack regrouping, moving on.

A man grunted, looked into the shallow ravine. Emma followed his gaze. The torch still burned, sizzling on the damp ground. Blood was smeared everywhere and the dead wolf stared at them. The man grunted again, and, moving as one, the group of hunters went away.

Emma waited. When she was sure the men were gone, she climbed shakily down from her tree and into the ravine. She picked up the guttering torch. Once off the damp ground, it burned more brightly, and she held it high, examining the place where both cats had disappeared.

She saw rocks, grass, and beyond them the foreign landscape and diminished lake. But she was sure both cats had gone through here to her world. She took a deep breath and, holding the torch, stepped forward, walked to the end of the rock that overlooked the lake.

Nothing happened. Nothing changed. She was still here, in this world of fierce animals and brutal people.

The cats had been running. Maybe that was it. She went back into the funnel, stuck the torch into the ground, and ran, ran to the edge of the rock. Still, nothing changed. No house lights appeared. When she looked behind her, the torch still burned beside the dead wolf.

Emma slumped onto the rock. She looked at the night

sky, but tears blurred her vision, and the moon wavered. "Billie," she called. "Billie!"

A frog croaked, jumped, splashed. Insects hummed. The lake lapped the rock. There were no other sounds.

Emma went back to the torch. As she passed by the dead wolf, she noticed movement in its fur and looked closer to see what was causing it. Fleas. The fleas were leaving the cooling body, crawling to the ends of the fur and jumping. Emma pulled back hastily, brushing at her jeans with her free hand. She climbed onto the rocky ridge and back to her perch in the tree.

Emma waited for morning. The moon set, and the darkness around her became impenetrable. Small animals rustled in the fallen leaves, and once an owl shrieked. She didn't even try to sleep. Her arms around the tree branch ached, and she felt stiff and cold all over. And very hungry. At the first grey light of dawn, she unhooked her camera from a neighboring branch and climbed sorely down.

The ravine was bloodstained. The body of the wolf lay too near the maser for comfort. What if the people came back by daylight for its fur? They were sure to see the machine. Emma couldn't move the wolf and daren't move the maser for fear of disrupting its connection to her own world.

This was where the cats, big and little, had disappeared, this narrow place between the rocks. The grass was flattened from the fight last night, and caked with dried blood.

Could she get through now? With a feeling of nervous excitement, Emma stepped forward. And onto the rock with the shrunken lake on one side, dry land on the other, leading to where her house should be, but wasn't.

What did the cats know that she didn't? She looked at

the maser. It was charging. There were broken branches in the ravine from last night's fight. She dragged an evergreen bough over to the maser and positioned the foliage so that it hid the machine. If the people weren't looking for it, she didn't think they'd find it.

Discouraged, Emma walked toward the lake. She sat on the rock and looked across the water. It was clearer than the lake she knew. Not so much algae, probably because of the glacier sitting like winter on the opposite shore and making the water too cold for algae. She dipped her hand in. The water was the temperature of snowmelt, and although she felt dirty, she abandoned any idea of plunging in. Maybe she'd try that in the afternoon, when the sun was stronger, and she could at least dry herself on a warm rock.

Emma knelt and looked into the water. The granite bottom sloped toward depths where plants had established a green, underwater bed. Winged insects landed and skimmed along, their feet making dimpled impressions on the surface tension. Suddenly the plants moved, parting as a fish rose through them to snap at the flies, its mouth opening a hole in the surface of the water, its scales flashing iridescent in the sunlight.

Ripples spread from the encounter toward Emma, and lapped the rock where she knelt. They moved through a floating image: herself, backed by the sky. When the water stilled, she considered her reflection. Pale face streaked with dirt, a puffed-out tangle of hair with bits of leaves and twigs in it, rumpled shirt, also dirty and twiggy.

She'd feel better if she were clean. She'd feel more in control. Emma searched through her pockets for a comb, but all she could find was half a roll of LifeSavers and film. She ate one of the LifeSavers. It was lint-covered from her pocket, but she'd never had a LifeSaver that tasted so good. Bootsy would have a comb. Probably a mirror, too, but Emma didn't even have a handkerchief.

She took the stun gun out of her belt and set it beside her on the rock. She took off her shirt and shook it out, then leaned forward and washed her face and upper body in the lake. The cold raised goose bumps on her arms and chest, and a cloud of dust and leaf fragments floated in the water when she'd done. She hurriedly put her shirt back on, glad for the warmth. She felt a little better.

Was there anything to eat around here? At least she had water. She moved away from the leaf litter she'd dropped into the lake and drank, cupping the water in her hands and bringing it to her mouth. It had a cold, clean taste, like water from a well.

Should she wait by the maser? Her stomach cramped with hunger. She couldn't eat pine cones, and while she had to get back home, she also had to survive long enough to cross over. The maser was charging now, anyway.

She picked up the gun and went into the woods. Surely the wolves would be sleeping now, but she kept the gun in her hand just in case. Maybe there would be berries or fruit growing in the sunlight at the edge of the forest.

chapter 26

Billie heard the refrigerator door open. She jumped down from the deck railing and found the man standing in front of the open refrigerator, moving things around inside. He was chirping in a complaining sort of way until he grunted and grabbed the milk container, which was in front, and set it on the table.

Billie liked milk. She jumped up beside the container and rubbed her chin against it.

He picked her up and dropped her onto the floor. So much for his friendliness last night.

She sat down to wait. He was making that repulsive hot brown liquid they liked to drink in the mornings, and he poured himself a mug of it. She watched the milk container as he carried it to the mug, poured milk in, set it down. He drank, tilting his head back the way it seemed they had to. She'd never seen a person drink properly from a bowl, and suspected they had a defect of the tongue.

He set more mugs on the table and poured milk into a pitcher. When he turned his back to return the container to the refrigerator, she jumped onto the table. She was familiar with this pitcher. Its neck was too small for her to get her nose in, but its top was open. Billie stuck her paw in, took it out wet with milk and licked it. She was getting a second pawful when he turned, saw her, and barked. She calculated the time it would take him to reach her, finished cleaning the milk off her paw, and jumped down just before his hand could strike her.

He picked up the milk pitcher and went toward the sink. Billie mewed.

He stopped, slammed the pitcher down, and got her bowl out of the cabinet, making grumbling noises all the while, the way some dogs do when they've got a bone. He put the bowl on the floor, poured the milk from the pitcher into it, stepped back, and gave a short bark.

Billie lapped the smooth, cool milk, then sat and cleaned her paws and whiskers. Before she was done, the man let in other men with clomping boots, and they all came into the kitchen and gathered round the table. The man filled mugs for them, and they drank. They were a poor substitute for her person, and that brown stuff was a waste of good water. Billie walked out, tail held high, her gait stiff with disapproval, but none of them seemed to notice.

The morning was still new, the grass nastily wet. She stepped on it, shook her paw, stepped again, shook another paw, but there was no getting away from the wetness. She was thinking about trying to get back inside through the downstairs door when a machine's roar startled her and she bolted for the bushes. From their safety, she looked toward the sound.

A boat was coming across the lake, a fast, noisy boat that splashed water behind it. It pulled up at the dock and became quieter.

The men came out on their big feet and walked down the deck stairs. Billie saw the stair treads sag beneath them, saw them cross the lawn and get into the boat. Her man was with them. The boat roared again and took off, leaving the lake rocking behind it. Billie watched it pass the island and go toward the far shore.

What was that all about? Sometimes they made no sense.

It was clearly up to her to do something about getting her person home. She walked toward the shore, flattening her ears in annoyance at the wet grass, and looked for a small door close to the lakeshore. Finding one, she leaped through to otherside.

Billie plodded across the otherside lowland that was the bottom of the lake at home, reaching the location of the big door just about the time the sun rose high enough above the trees to shine on the ravine floor.

The place stank of wolf and blood. She had hoped to find her person waiting, but no one could hang around this smell for long, and the ravine was empty. The door had closed, anyway.

Thirsty from her walk, she went along the rocks to the lake's edge and crouched to drink. The water here tasted better than the lake water at home, cooler and without the musty, vegetative smells and the underlying trace of boat engines. She sat for a while and watched a bird make swooping flights, catching insects from the lake's surface. It flew near her once, and she chattered excitedly, but it veered off and kept its distance after that.

When Billie felt rested, she went to the otherside camp and checked on it from a hiding place beneath the oak tree. Maybe her person had come here. She was nowhere in sight, and Billie felt discouraged.

The otherside people weren't crowded 'round. An old woman sat by the fire with some little ones. Two cats from the cave approached the fire. They were the solid grey who had lost her kittens and the grey tabby who had hers hidden in the cave. The tabby found a fish head on the ground and ran with it into the cave; the grey cat continued to search.

None of the people seemed to pay any attention. Enticed by the smell of fish, Billie stepped into the clearing. She jumped onto a rock and stretched her neck, sniffing the air.

A child came toward her, holding out a piece of fishtail. Its expression seemed friendly enough, but the grey cat backed out of its path and Billie, remembering the killing after the grass fire, sat and hissed. Just a warning, to see what it would do.

The child spoke soothingly, holding out the fish. Billie waited for it to put the offering down. The child stepped closer, and Billie stood up, growled, prepared to run. At this, the child set the food on the ground. When she had seen it take two steps backward, Billie jumped down.

The grey cat got there first, pounced, and ran off with the fish.

Billie sat and cleaned her paws, soothing her pride by pretending that was what she had intended to have happen all along.

The child grinned and barked and held its finger out to Billie. She sniffed, but smelled no food. The child barked some more, and the old woman barked as well. Then, watching Billie, the old woman's grin faded and she chirped something to the child, who looked at Billie more carefully. Offended, Billie jumped back onto the rock.

The tabby came back from the cave and approached the

cooking fire. She hesitated, looking first at the child, then at Billie.

The child sat and crooned to the tabby. It took a chunk of something smoky and oily-smelling from its pouch and held it toward the tabby, glancing sidelong at Billie as it did so. A cat treat, Billie thought. The tabby took the morsel and ate, allowing the child to stroke her back lightly as she did so.

The child took out another treat and held it toward Billie.

Billie was tempted. She was certain from the smell that there was a concentration of flavor in the treat.

The tabby was interested, and approached the child's hand, but it pushed her away. Billie found this rude, since she assumed this was the tabby's own person, and rudeness made her wary. She stood on three paws, considering whether to reach with her fourth paw for the treat.

The tabby hissed suddenly, not at Billie, but at the woman who had approached silently. Distracted by the offered food, Billie hadn't noticed the woman either, and was startled. The woman took another step and the tabby ran.

Billie ran, too. It was axiomatic not to trust a person whom another cat didn't trust. She scrambled up the oak tree, digging in her claws, feeling her muscles stretch and grip in an invigorating way.

Billie sat on a branch overlooking the ravine. Sunlight reached the branch, making it pleasantly warm, and it swayed gently in a breeze that carried a smell of mammoth. She stretched along the branch, let the breeze ruffle her fur, and waited for her person to return.

Emma walked through the woods. Leaves crunched underfoot, but the forest was remarkably free of dead wood. Most of the trees seemed young. Even the mature ones had recently grown to their full height; nowhere did she pass an ancient giant, fissured by time and broken by forgotten storms from which it had recovered. It was a new forest, a forest encroaching on the tundra. She came to its edge, but took care to remain hidden from the view of anyone who might be looking her way.

A treeless expanse of grassland rolled into the distance where it struck against peaks of stone and ice. The horizon itself was a line of white against a blue sky. Emma knew she was looking at a retreating glacier. She put the gun back into her belt and took a photograph.

Clouds patterned the fields and hills with shadow. A small storm seemed to be breaking against one of the hillsides. She could see haze near the ground, but when she looked up, she was puzzled not to see rain coming from the quickly moving cloud. A herd of woolly mammoths turned their backs to it. Then she realized the haze must not be water, but dust blowing from the newly exposed earth in the north. She focused on the mammoths and took another photo.

A human shout made her heart jump into her throat. She looked toward the sound, saw men coming onto the tundra from the forest. Three of them lifted tools and hacked at the grass; two others piled wood in a heap. She didn't think they had seen her.

There were already several piles of wood along the strip of cut grass. What were they doing?

To avoid the men, she retreated into the forest. The ground rose, but it was an easy climb. There was sunlight ahead, and a noise of birds. She hoped the birds were eating something.

Emma came out into a field of brambles at the edge of a cliff. The birds were feasting on berries that grew on the brambles. Emma went closer and the birds flew away. The berries looked very much like blackberries. She tasted one, and it tasted like the sweetest blackberry she'd ever had on her tongue. When it didn't make her sick, she ate a lot more of them.

A mammoth cried. The sound seemed to be coming from the base of the cliff, but Emma couldn't see past the bushes, which were a tangle of thorns on top. Underneath they thinned out, and she crawled through to the edge of the cliff. She wanted a picture from up here, especially if there were animals around. She'd been so upset yesterday that she'd wasted a lot of opportunities to prove she'd been here.

When she reached the edge, she was glad she had approached it under cover, because a group of men was walking toward the cliff. They carried spears. Dogs ran beside them.

On the tundra below Emma, a woolly mammoth was trapped inside a pit, and trying to get out, had worn the sides to mud. It looked exhausted.

Emma didn't understand how this had happened. It was too large a pit for these men to have dug as a trap. Then she saw traces of ice mixed with the mud, and thought she understood: a pocket of ice that had been part of the permafrost had melted, leaving a layer of grassy dirt on top that had collapsed when the mammoth stepped onto it. She remembered illustrations of the process in Dana's books, but those had been line drawings. This was a tired, trapped animal looking up at her with fear. It raised its trunk and whimpered.

The men jumped into the pit. For a brief, wildly hopeful moment Emma thought they had come to rescue the mammoth. The idea was quickly dispelled as they plunged in their spears, their knives. Blood was everywhere and the trapped animal screamed. It seemed to Emma it was looking directly at her when it died. She hoped they killed it before they started butchering it, but was never entirely sure afterward. She retreated into the brambles, was overcome with nausea, and vomited.

Emma felt drained of all emotions but one: she wanted more than anything to get back home. She'd go back to the ravine and wait. She didn't care if she starved.

When she arrived in the ravine, she found that the dead wolf had been carried off. Her heart beat faster as she approached the branch she had put over the maser. She moved it aside, and found to her relief the machine was still there. But it was charging. Damn. The breach had probably opened while she was gone. She shouldn't have gone off for so long. Judging by the sun, it was midday already.

She sat down to wait. The machine had discharged its energy sometime late at night, and probably again before noon. It must be less than twelve hours between opportunities. She had the stun gun, in case any men came along. She would sit here and wait, and get home before midnight. If she didn't miss the opening.

A cat's cry came from the woods. Emma turned toward it, and saw Billie climbing down from a tree. Billie ran toward her, mewing excitedly. Emma picked her up. Billie purred raucously and rubbed her head against Emma's chin.

"Billie, I don't think I've ever been happier to see anybody," Emma said.

Billie pinched Emma's chin in a love bite.

"Do you know the way home, Billie?" Emma asked. "You do, don't you?"

The maser was still charging. With Billie in her arms, Emma stepped over the line anyway, just to try it, but she wasn't surprised when nothing happened. She went back and sat down. Billie curled up in her lap and went to sleep.

Emma stroked her cat and watched the machine. Time wore on. Billie stretched and turned her belly to the sun.

Billie had come back earlier in the morning, because Emma had seen her leave last night. And she had left on purpose. So had the other cat: they had run toward the opening. They had known it was there.

How had they known? Had they heard it, smelled it, seen it? They were better at all three than people were.

How had her father known? Or maybe he hadn't. Maybe death had surprised him, and he'd never known how he'd succeeded. No, he'd had a plan, a design. So what had he used to carry it out? The maser. Cameras. Film. Goggles.

Goggles. Night goggles. Cats could see better at night than people. And the maser amplified microwave and infrared radiation. That was it.

"Billie, do you see things I can't?"

Billie yawned and stretched, then pulled her paws tight over her face. Apparently she didn't see anything special right now. It was just nap time.

No wonder. The sun was warm. It was making Emma drowsy, too. She had to stay awake, but after a sleepless night and with nothing to do but wait, that was difficult. She slid back against the rock, where she'd be somewhat hidden, and took the gun into her hand. She slumped against the sun warmed rock and closed her eyes for a few moments.

When she awoke, the sun had set. Billie was gone from her lap.

Emma sat up in sudden panic. "Billie?"

Billie sat a few yards off, grooming her toes. She looked at Emma and blinked in the moonlight. Then she looked toward the narrow end of the ravine. Billie stood up, her face and body suddenly alert.

Emma went toward her. Billie ran, and Emma ran after her, stumbled, and came down on her hands and knees on the rock. She came down almost in the water, which shouldn't have been there.

Emma looked up. All of the lake was back. And across the lake, she could see house lights and streetlights and even a car moving along the road.

"Billie, we're home!" Emma said.

Billie rubbed against Emma and purred. Emma sat and held her cat close. "We're home," Emma said again.

chapter 27

But where was the rowboat? Emma had left
it tied to the rock, and it was gone. She supposed
she could swim. Looking across the lake, she estimated the distance. Something bobbed on the moonlit water
beside her dock: the rowboat. Somebody had thoughtfully
rowed it home.

Billie rubbed against her ankles. Emma could swim
home, but she didn't want to try it while holding a cat. And
she didn't want to leave the cat on the island as she went for
the rowboat.

Emma turned and looked apprehensively into the
ravine. The photoelectric cells on the rock wall were dully
metallic, and the maser sat in its accustomed place. She saw
nothing to justify her fear. Grass and rocks and shadowy
cedars crowned both sides. The dark cedars, comforting in
their familiarity, stood thick against the sky. They were from
the island she knew in her world, her island, and their smell
of freshly sharpened pencils went back to her childhood.

She thought about the island's configuration. They
were at the end farthest out in the lake, but the lodge was

closer to shore, and very close to Charles' house. Shouting distance, she hoped.

"Come on, Billie," Emma said, picking the cat up. "Let's see if we can rouse up some help."

Emma walked toward the lodge. As she got closer to the end of the ravine, Billie stopped purring and tensed, her claws digging into Emma's shoulder. "You don't want to go in there, do you?" Emma said. "It's all right, we're just cutting through the forest." When she made the turn, Billie relaxed again.

It was darker among the trees, and Emma walked with one hand on Billie and the other stretched in front to ward off branches. But as long as she kept going straight ahead, she knew she had to come out in the clearing behind the lodge, and when at last she stepped free of the trees, there it stood, its weathered siding silvered by moonlight.

Emma felt great affection for the building for being where it was supposed to be. She went round to the front and looked across the water at the lit windows of Charles' house.

"Charles! Peggy!"

A lamp burned in the living room window, and the kitchen light was on, but there was no movement, no flicker of television light, nothing to tell her whether they were at home or had just left a couple of lights on.

The aviary was silent.

Maybe if she threw some rocks across, she might be able to hit the side of the house and get their attention. Failing that, she could strike one into the flight cage and rouse the birds. That would get Peggy out. She might be too mad to come across and get them, but it would definitely bring her outside.

Emma went to the edge of the lake to look for rocks, and saw Charles' rowboat tied to the dock.

"Well, look at that, Billie: transportation. I don't know why they traded rowboats, but something has finally happened to make our lives easier."

She got in with Billie and rowed home, and together they climbed the stairs to the kitchen door.

It was locked. Billie put her paws on the glass and mewed. Emma pushed, but nothing happened. She could see into the lit room, where dishes were piled in the sink, Max's jacket slung across the back of a chair, and a map spread on the table. The coffee machine's light was on. He must be near.

"Max!" she called. There was no answer.

Emma moved farther over, so she could see down the hall, and there he was, standing in the open front doorway, talking to someone. The light beyond the doorframe seemed unusually bright, and she wondered if he'd installed a floodlight.

"Max!" she called again, and rapped on the glass, but he obviously didn't hear her. "I've got to go 'round front, Billie. Then I'll come back and let you in," Emma said, but Billie followed her, crisscrossing between her legs so she tripped on the stairs. "Come on then." Emma picked up the cat and went to the front of the house.

A harsh glare came from tripod-mounted spotlights evidently belonging to Channel 6, since its news van was parked in the driveway. People clustered round the front door, most of them neighbors trying to get a look at the TV crew, but there were also several strangers in T-shirts bearing the station's logo. A man pointed a video camera at Max, and a perky blond woman wearing heavy makeup held a microphone in Max's face. Poor baby, he didn't look at all happy.

Emma stepped over a coil of heavy black electrical cable and tried to get round a skinny, T-shirted figure wearing a baseball cap with the peak turned to the back. He grabbed her arm, whispered, "You can't go up there, they're taping."

Emma felt her temper flare. She'd been struggling to get away from savage beasts and people for two days now, and she wasn't about to be kept out of her own house by some geek with his hat on backwards. "Let me go!" she said, jerking her arm free and stumbling backward into the cameraman.

"Hey!" he protested, his camera swerving.

"Emma?" Max shouldered his way past the reporter and the cameraman. "Emma!" He hugged her tight. Billie, caught in the middle, squirmed. Max released his hold. "Are you all right? Where have you been?" he asked, relief and happiness in his voice.

"Is this your wife, Mr. Vernon?" the reporter asked, in their faces with the microphone.

"Yes, it is," Max said, putting his arm protectively round Emma's shoulder.

"I'm sure you must be very happy to have her back. Where have you been, Mrs. Vernon? Did you know about the search and rescue effort that's been under way on your behalf?"

"No," said Emma. "I've been . . ."

The cameraman came up close, his lens a black and shiny eye pointing at them. Billie hissed.

"You're upsetting my cat," Emma said.

"Could you tell us where you've been?" the reporter asked again.

"On the island," Emma said. "I was . . ." A headline flashed into Emma's mind: madwoman lost among savages, claims she witnessed mammoth hunt, saw wolves attack sabertooth cat. "I was trapped in the cellar of the lodge. The door shut on me accidentally." Emma hoped the lodge had a cellar, but they accepted the lie readily. Emma thought she probably looked like a woman who'd been buried in a cellar for two days.

"But we looked on the island," Max said. "Didn't you hear us calling you?"

Emma shook her head. "The walls are thick," she elaborated.

"Do you know anything about the wild cat that attacked your neighbor?" the reporter asked.

Emma looked at Max. "Somebody got hurt?"

"My wife's already told you she was locked in a cellar. I'm sure she knows nothing about what happened on the island, and I can tell she's very tired," Max said, drawing her toward the front door. "That will have to do for now."

He pulled Emma inside and closed the door. She dropped Billie, and Max put his arms around Emma and kissed her.

"I must smell terrible," Emma said, coming up for air.

"I'm so glad you're home," Max said. "Where have you been? We've all been frantic."

There was a knock on the door.

Emma slumped with fatigue.

"I'll get rid of them," Max said, and stepped outside.

Emma went into the kitchen and set her camera down on the hutch, pushing it toward the back, where it would be safe. She poured herself a mug of coffee from the pot that Max was keeping warm. She put cream in her coffee and in

Billie's bowl, then sipped from the hot mug, holding it with both hands. It was the best coffee she'd ever tasted, thanks to two days' caffeine deprivation.

Billie lapped noisily and messily, splashing flecks of cream on the floor around her.

Emma sat at the table, which was covered by a map of the region. Somebody had drawn lines, dividing up the lake area. There was a coffee stain on the village. Toast crumbs were sprinkled across the lake.

Billie finished quickly, cleaned her face, and sat by the empty bowl, looking at Emma expectantly.

"Still hungry?" Emma asked, and set down her half-empty mug. She got a can from the cabinet and was opening it when Max came into the room.

"I got rid of the reporters. The neighbors said they're happy you're back, and Peggy said she'll call after you've had a chance to settle in," Max said. "Are you making a sandwich? Do you want me to make you a sandwich?"

"Who got hurt?" Emma asked.

"Charles. But he's all right, it was just a scratch. Literally. That is, it tore open his shoulder but there won't be any permanent damage."

"The sabertooth did it?" Emma spooned the contents of the can, liquid and all, into Billie's bowl.

"That's people tuna," Max said. "Fancy white albacore."

"She deserves it."

Billie ate from her bowl, purring loudly.

"Were you really in the cellar?"

"No. I was where the sabertooth came from. What's been going on here? Why are you using a map for a table-cloth?"

"We've been searching for you all day. Divided up the area, sent out different parties. Emma." He put his arms around her again and held her tight. "I was afraid you'd been killed."

Emma felt safe and wanted to stay in his arms forever. She leaned against him and the stun gun pressed uncomfortably into her hip, reminding her there was still a lot to do. She stepped back. "What happened to the sabertooth?" she asked, putting the gun on the table.

"The cat? I don't know. Last I saw, it was swimming across the lake."

"Heading north?"

"Yes. Why? Where have you been, Emma?"

"Have things been quiet otherwise? Any more animal attacks?"

"Depends on what you mean by quiet. Nelson's had tourists blocking the road, waiting to see those mammoths. Offers are coming in from zoos all over, and there's a movement to have them put on the endangered species list. We've got news teams in town from all the networks, and the wire services. I think the population has doubled, with all the extra people we have around. Petey's beaver story has made national headlines, and somebody's started a scholarship fund for Cathy Witte. Walter winged a reporter poking around Jake's garbage cans early this morning. Emma, where the hell have you been?"

"It's a long story, Max. And I'm starving. Could you make me an omelet or something? I'm going upstairs and get in the shower and use up all the hot water. Then I'll tell you." She walked toward the stairs, stopped and looked back. "Is Rutledge around? And Nelson? Do you think you could get them to come over?"

"I can try."

"Tell them it's important, Max. But Max? Just you and Rutledge and Nelson. Nobody else. Okay? There are some things we have to figure out," Emma said. "I want to do the right thing."

chapter 28

"And I took pictures," Emma said, putting the camera down on the middle of the map on the kitchen table. She waited for their reactions to the story she'd just told, and in the pause her fatigue began to catch up with her. Her legs ached from the morning's hike, her face and arms were sore with sunburn from a ten thousand years' younger sun.

Max pulled the camera thoughtfully toward him. The strap trailed across the irregular blue patch that represented the lake.

"Could you find your way back?" Rutledge said.

Emma shook her head and tendrils of wet hair brushed her cheek. "I don't want to go back. I want to set a watch around the island so that we can take care of any animals that come through."

"I wonder if we could use that machine of your father's to go to other places in the past," Nelson said, a faraway look in his eyes. "There are battles back in the days of sailing ships that I would dearly love to see." Emma felt she should have guessed that a mermaid tattoo was a mark of a dreamer.

Max's eyes were the slate blue color they became when he was serious. "I'd like to go back and photograph more of the Pleistocene," Max said, playing with the camera. "Sketch it, maybe."

"We have to be careful we don't change the past," Emma said. The thought he might actually go back there gave her a sinking feeling in her stomach. What if he got trapped? "And I think we need to get somebody who knows about quantum physics out here to look at that maser, somebody who can figure out how it works."

"It explains a lot," Rutledge said. "Do many things go through to the past, or wherever it was?"

"I don't think so," said Emma. "They wouldn't be likely to, would they? Because in this world, the entry is from an island. It's much more accessible from the other world. Anyway, I didn't see any animals that looked like they were from here. Except Billie."

"Except Billie," Max said. "Do you think she knows what she's doing?"

"She showed me the way home. And when she wanted to get away from the wolf fight, she ran straight for the opening to the present. So did the sabertooth. I think cats can see the breaches in space-time that the maser makes. Was she home at all while I was gone?"

"Yes."

"Maybe it's just another kind of door to her. The lake's smaller over there, and she can walk to the island."

"Where is Billie?" Rutledge asked.

"Sleeping in her . . ." Emma looked at the cat basket, saw with anxiety that it was empty. "I don't know. She was here a little while ago."

"She can take care of herself," Max said, putting his hand over Emma's.

"It's a good thing you and Charles still own that island," Nelson said. "Maybe we should put up some no tresspassing signs."

"What if we fenced off that area, just the part where animals come through," Max suggested.

"It might stop some of the smaller things, but there aren't many small things over there," Emma said, her memory oppressed by the sheer bulk of the animals she had seen. "I can't think of any fence we could put up that the rhinoceros would do more than glance at as it crashed through."

"Let's hope that one doesn't find its way over here," Rutledge said.

"Do you hope that?" said Emma. "I'm not sure I do. These are fabulous animals, animals that are extinct in our world." She gestured with her right hand, noticed it was shaking. "I feel like we're being given a second chance."

"And you think we won't blow it?" Rutledge's tone was grim. "Walter and his buddies are more like your mammoth-killers than you know."

"But we're not all like that. We could try."

"Why do you think these animals are coming here? Is it accidental?" Nelson said.

"I don't know," Emma said. "Partly, I suppose. But they are on the move."

Rutledge looked down at the map "Where to?"

"North," said Emma. "Both over there and here. North." She slid aside her coffee mug and the plate that had held her scrambled eggs, and cleared their view of the northern section of the map. "They'd have a couple million acres of forest preserve to move around in. It is supposed to be forever wild."

"I don't think the legislature meant it to be that wild," Max said.

"There are other dangerous animals in there," said Emma. "Aren't there, Rutledge? Couldn't we get them all put on the endangered species list or something?"

"Dana's in Albany working on that," said Nelson. "We have to keep it quiet where the animals are coming from until then, or the hunters will be here looking to bag what they can while its legal."

"I suppose we'll have proof when the film gets developed," said Max. "Enough to get the media on our side. Speaking of which . . ." He got the remote out of the drawer and turned on the television. "Let's see if we made the eleven o'clock news."

Emma was dismayed. "Media? Do we have to get them involved?" She turned her attention to the news anchors with their determined smiles. "I'm especially not going to tell those people. They blow everything out of proportion. They make a major event out of the weather. Every day."

Rutledge tipped back in his chair. "Thing is, we've got a lot of visitors in town, and we have to warn them. It won't be good for the community's image if they get eaten."

"It won't be good if they go swarming all over the island, either," said Emma. "They're going to start off thinking I'm a crackpot, then they're going to disappear or get mauled or killed. And what if they disturb the maser? We don't know what might come of that."

Max patted her shoulder, probably to calm her down, but it only hurt her sunburn. Then he ran his finger along the line on the map that marked the inhabited shore of the lake.

"Maybe we could protect the town more quietly. If we could discourage the animals from landing in populated areas . . ."

"We could set up a shore patrol," Nelson said. "But I can't promise nothing would get shot. Whoa, there you are, Emma." He thumped the chair legs back down on the floor.

Emma looked at televised pictures of an angry, disheveled woman holding a malignant cat. "Oh, we'd pick up a lot of sympathy, wouldn't we? Hecate and her familiar." The cat hissed at the viewer. "That does it. We're the bad guys."

"They didn't show much of me," Max said.

"You weren't as colorful as Billie and me. Rutledge, couldn't we tell people we're trying to stop these animals from coming out of the preserve?"

"People already think that," Rutledge said. "The shore was lined with them all day, watching the forest preserve with binoculars."

Emma leaned her head in her hands, covering her eyes.

"The shore patrol's the way to go," Nelson said. "I can get the town council to authorize it. We want to keep the animals alive. That's the only way they'll bring in tourists. We could get a few men out there on the lake with stun guns, to head off anything dangerous that insisted on coming this way."

Emma took her hands away from her eyes. "What about Walter? He wants to be a hero and kill big game."

"I haven't talked to Walter lately, but we'd have to buy the extra stunners from him."

"And he sells cameras, too," Max said.

"But he likes glory," said Emma.

Nelson stood up. "You get some sleep, Emma. You look worn-out. I'll call on a couple of people, see what we can do. The animals don't seem to come through more than one at a time, and the town should be able to handle that, once we're prepared."

"But quietly," Rutledge said.

"We want to preserve the mystique," said Max.

"Maybe we just have to worry about loose cannons until we can get fines or a prison sentence attached to killing these animals," Rutledge said as they walked to the front door. "I'll just walk up with Nelson now and help him set it up."

But Emma grabbed the doorknob. "No, you won't! Max will drive you both."

"I'm armed," Rutledge said, picking up his stun rifle from beside the door and holding it so it pointed downward.

"She's right," Max said. "I'll drive you."

Emma watched them leave, then closed the door. She dimmed the hall lights and the shadows grew. The mantel clock ticked, the television mumbled.

"Billie!" Emma called.

There was no answer.

Emma went into the kitchen and turned the TV off. Billie's basket was still empty except for some cat hairs and the impression of a small body on the cushion.

She couldn't have gotten out. But then again, maybe she could. She had ways of getting farther out than they'd imagined. It would certainly explain her habit of disappearing and then turning up unexpectedly in places they would think she couldn't have gotten to.

Like the island.

Emma slid open the glass door and carefully looked out at the section of lawn and garden revealed by the kitchen light spill. When she was sure there were no animals around, she stepped onto the deck.

The island lay out there in the darkness. She could just make out the tops of some of its trees against the newly risen moon. A breeze rustled the leaves near the house, and Emma jumped at the sound.

"Billie!" she called again.

There was no reply.

Emma sighed, went back inside and upstairs to the luxury of clean sheets and a soft, familiar bed. She fell asleep without any awareness of the transition.

chapter 29

Billie pushed her way through the screen and onto the roof. It was quieter here, just the sounds of wind in the trees and of insects chirping. Logy from all the tuna she'd eaten, she stretched out on the pleasantly warm surface and rested.

Bats flittered in the darkness. She could see them clearly, but they kept out of reach, circling the house in that irritating, teasing way they had. She liked bats: crunchy things, but hard to catch.

In time, the car left and came back. The squares of light on the lawn winked out, as did the lights in the neighboring houses. Traffic on the road dwindled, stopped. A raccoon came by, and Billie crept to the edge of the roof to watch it. It stared at her with yellow eyes, then moved into the woods.

Billie stretched, sharpened her claws on the shingles. She crossed the roof toward the tree, then moved her head from side to side, gauging the distance. She leaped, grabbed a branch, and climbed down.

Pudding was in his usual spot in the catnip. He purred when she came near, and she chewed a few leaves, then wrestled with him for a while. A crackle in the woods interrupted them, and they both jumped up, backs arched, but it was just the raccoon passing by, a tomato in its mouth.

When the sky lightened, the red glow of a small door near the lake tempted Billie to cross to otherside. She stepped through.

And was immediately assailed by smoke, sharp and thick and hanging low to the ground. Billie gasped, turned, but the door had closed. The smoke came toward her, and fire crackled across the grass. Through rifts in the smoky cloud, she could see men of otherside, clubs in hand.

Billie panicked, running blindly first from one arm of the fire, then from another, terrified of the men, the smoke, the flames. Her heart raced, she panted from exertion. Where was there a door?

Billie ran, knowing she was going in a circle, looking for a way to break out, but in her haste it seemed as if the fire was coming at her from all sides. When she passed that stupid brown dog that hung around the otherside men, it barked, then coughed on smoke. Stupid thing, standing in the smoke.

A man's legs appeared, solid in the haze. Billie backtracked to the dog, turned and hissed. The dog wagged its tail. Smoke was clearing behind it, flowing somewhere. The breeze from the tail? Billie caught a breath of fresher air. A doorway. There was a doorway behind the dog.

The dog tilted its head and looked at Billie.

Billie unsheathed her claws and gave it a sharp whack on the nose. It yipped and got out of her way. She burst through the doorway.

And found herself at home, on the grass behind her house. The air smelled clean, but a stench of smoke clung

242

inside her nose and mouth, and she could taste it unpleasantly. Her brother was there and, mewing an invitation to play, he came toward her, but slowed down as he sniffed her. The fur round his neck rose and he growled.

Billie was in no mood for any of this. She'd had enough, she was tired, she didn't feel good. She looked him in the eyes and set her paw firmly on his forehead.

Pudding sat.

Billie chewed grass, turning her head to use her side teeth most efficiently. When she had swallowed enough, she was seized by a hacking cough and she crouched, holding her head low and forward, backing up, until finally she sicked up the grass and a lot of the smoke-poison she had swallowed.

Feeling better, she climbed the tree to the roof and went inside to share her person's soft bed.

Emma was wakened by the chewing noises Billie made grooming herself. Why did she have to do this on Emma's pillow? Plus her fur smelled of . . .

Of smoke.

Emma sat up. Billie blinked at her in the predawn light, and purred. Emma stroked Billie's head and back, then put her nose close to the cat's fur. Definitely smoke.

"What's burning?" Emma asked.

Billie swiveled her head to lick her back.

Emma got out of bed. The bedroom door was closed, probably by Max reaching over after Billie came in, or maybe the wind. Emma put her hand on it. The wood felt cool, so she opened the door and stepped into the hallway.

The hall was dark, its window a pale, floating oblong shape admitting barely enough light to keep her from bumping into things. But the space smelled of summer coming through the windows: the lake, the lilies in Peggy's garden, and a slight mustiness that seemed to go with living among trees. It didn't smell of smoke.

Emma returned to her bedroom and hurriedly pulled on jeans, sneakers, a cotton shirt. She looked at Max, sleeping deeply, and thought she'd like a chance to sleep past dawn one of these mornings. Billie waking her up was getting to be a habit.

She went downstairs and stepped cautiously onto the deck. Mist rose form the lake in a way that made it seem like this could be the beginning of time as easily as the beginning of a new day, but there was no smell of burning.

So Billie had probably gone adventuring. Maybe she'd picked up the smell of the Paleo-Indians' campfire. They had to have fire. She had smelled meat cooking.

Emma felt incapable of going back to sleep. She went inside and flipped on the coffeemaker, put a filter in place, enjoying the ordinary ritual more than usual because she'd been deprived of it for a couple of days. She ground beans, releasing their fragrance in a sudden burst.

Billie had never come in smelling of their campfire before. But if there was food available, Emma suspected she'd been near it pretty often.

Emma poured water into the machine and watched coffee drip out.

Could the campfire have spread?

She took a mug of coffee out onto the deck and looked across the lawn, checking for dangerous animals. The day was in that lull between first light and dawn, when birds barely stirred, and Emma saw no suspicious movements. Only a lone fish broke the surface of the lake.

So what could have happened? Where had she seen fire back there? The torches. And they must have a cooking fire. That was all. What else would they use fire for? Emma sat suddenly straight, tipping her mug and spilling coffee on her hand in the sudden movement. She hurriedly transferred the coffee to her other hand and blew on her scalded fingers.

Scorch marks. She pictured in her mind the field where they were hacking at the turf and stacking wood. There had been scorch marks on the field where they were digging. Had they gotten tired of the slow progress and set fire to the field instead, to clear it? It was possible.

How did they use fire? To cook on. For light: the torches. She remembered them throwing a torch at the wolves. Did they sometimes chase animals with torches? Could they have had an accident, the fire gotten out of hand?

She wished she'd read Dana's books more carefully, but if she'd known she was going to need them as a travel guide, she would have. And although she didn't plan any more trips to the Pleistocene, maybe she'd better look them over just in case.

She thought of the smoky smell of Billie's fur.

Maybe she'd better go read through those books now. She wouldn't have to disturb anybody; she knew where Bootsy kept a key.

She ran lightly up the stairs to the bedroom. Billie was grooming her tail, and Max snored lightly.

"Max," Emma said.

The snore hesitated, then continued.

"I'm going over to Bootsy's," Emma said.

Max rolled onto his side and stopped snoring, but showed no signs of consciousness.

It was hopeless. She'd be back before he woke up, anyway. She kissed his ear and ran downstairs.

Should she drive and wake everybody up with the sound
of the engine, or walk, and risk an encounter with some
oversize predator? It seemed foolish to drive next door, and
foolish not to. Emma wondered what the chances were that
she'd meet some animal, and decided they were far less than
they'd been in days. After all, she was just back from their
world, and she'd survived. She'd walk.

It was quiet at dawn. Emma kept to the center of the
road, her sneakers soundless on the hard-packed dirt. The
sky had brightened to mauve, and there was enough light to
see by, although it was diffuse and dim and she cast no
shadow. Leaves on either side of her drooped, pulled down
by the weight of dew. She moved through a glistening cor-
ridor, until Bootsy's house came into view past the end of
the woods.

A frenzied rustling erupted in the underbrush, and something that looked like a pig darted across the road and disappeared with equal brouhaha on the other side. Emma
moved forward steadily, not wanting to be in the way of
whatever was chasing it, and not wanting to distract any pur-
suer by making sudden movements. She hoped she didn't
smell of fear, because she certainly felt it.

But nothing else came out of the woods. Maybe nothing had been chasing the piglike thing; maybe they just ran
around like that in the early morning. Or maybe it was
Emma's passage that had startled it from its cover.

Emma paused at the edge of Bootsy's lawn and looked
back at the road, the woods. Just then the sun rose, and
muted colors became brilliant, birds exulted. The woods lay
still and impenetrable. Emma crossed the cleared space care-

fully, alert to the blank face of the woods and what might be moving behind it like a dangerous thought.

She went to the kitchen door and parted a sweet-smelling tangle of phlox that grew beside it. Beneath the phlox she found the white-painted rock that hid Bootsy's spare key, and picked the rock up. The key was there, along with a couple of slugs and a misguided earthworm.

Emma let herself in. The kitchen was silent, semitidy: last night's dishes had been cleared, but left to air-dry in the rack. Bootsy's coffeemaker was set up, waiting for the first person into the kitchen to turn it on.

That was Emma. She flipped the switch: if they heard her moving around downstairs, and they also smelled coffee, at least they'd know she wasn't a burglar. Burglars don't make coffee for the people whose houses they rob.

Emma went into the library and pulled out the oversize book Dana had earlier shown her. She set it down on the library table and paged through it, going over the pictures once again.

They looked different now that she'd seen the real things. More approximate, less convincing. Not right, some-how, in the way they summed up the personality of each an-imal. But how could the artist have known just how sweet the mammoths were, or what determined machines the at-tacking wolves could be?

Bootsy poked her head through the doorway, grunted, withdrew. Emma knew better than to speak to her before she'd had coffee.

Emma turned to the section on Paleolithic man. There were lots of cave drawings, mostly of wonderful animals: huge bison oddly light on their feet, deer swimming, horses reaching their heads forward, running. Stick figures of men beside fully realized animal drawings.

Bootsy came in with two mugs of coffee. She set one down beside Emma and took the other one with her to the window seat. She curled up, sunlight making an aureole of her unbrushed hair, and sipped her coffee.

Emma wasn't finding what she needed. She checked the index listing under "fire," found cooking, found discovery of . . .

"Why are you in my library at dawn?" Bootsy said.

"I had some stuff I wanted to look up."

"Are you all right?"

"I'm fine. I made coffee," Emma said.

"I know. Emma, we were worried sick about you, you disappeared for two days, everybody was looking for you, you showed up again late last night, and Max said you were too exhausted for me even to see you, and now you're reading?"

"Because I smelled smoke."

"Smoke?"

"On Billy's fur. This morning. Is Dana awake?" Emma continued down the listing. Fire, use in hunting. She flipped back to the page.

"Dana's in Albany, trying to get an emergency executive order to protect the mammoths. Emma, it's a beautiful morning. Nothing's burning," Bootsy said.

Emma looked at her sister. She saw that she'd opened the window, letting in a phlox-scented morning breeze.

"I know. Not here," Emma said. She read the text, which was an explanation of how early man had staged vast hunts, and used fire to drive all the animals in an area into a confined space and then slaughter them. Often these would be migrating animals, so that large numbers of a species would be killed together. Often they were killed to the point of extinction.

Emma felt her stomach go suddenly cold, the room get fuzzy.

"Emma, I think I should call Max," Bootsy said.

Emma thought about the funnel-shaped ravine, and the line of dirt the men had been clearing.

Bootsy was next to her, making her sit down. "Does he know you're here?"

Emma had thought the purpose was agricultural, clearing a field. A funny way to do it. But not so funny if they were making a fire break to shield the camp from a fire they intended to set.

"Drink some coffee, Emma," Bootsy said. "You're cold, and your color's terrible. I think you really ought to be in bed."

Emma gulped the coffee Bootsy held to her mouth because Bootsy tipped the cup too far and it was either swallow hard or spill.

"That's better," said Bootsy.

And it was better. Emma could feel warmth returning, and the room wasn't so grey and grainy.

Bootsy patted Emma's hand. "I'm going to call Max," Bootsy said, and left the room.

Emma really was feeling much better. "Tell him to meet me at Rutledge's," she called after Bootsy. Then she slipped out the window.

chapter 30

Emma banged on Rutledge's door until he fi- nally opened it and stood there in a rumpled plaid bathrobe. Pudding darted past him out the door.

"Woman, don't you ever sleep?" he said. "What's wrong?"

"Rutledge, we've got a problem."

"Something else has happened? Since last night?"

"I think it's going to. Look, get some clothes on and come outside."

Rutledge withdrew, came back again. "Is somebody else dead?"

"No. Not that I know of. Rutledge, we have to talk."

Emma backed away, saw Rutledge nod and close the door. She turned and walked along the rocky promontory that jutted into the lake.

A grainy mist hung above the water, but was shredding quickly, tearing upward toward the sun. She could see the island, its rocky point in line with the rock where she stood, its cedar trees black with the morning sun behind them. The sky's intense blue told her the day would have its full share of summer heat.

Pudding rubbed against her ankles and she picked him up.

"Oof! You're a pudgy thing, aren't you? You'd make two of Billie."

He purred and held his chin out for her to scratch. She absent mindedly gave him attention, her thoughts straining toward the island. Were all the wisps of white moving across it just morning fog?

At the sound of an engine, Pudding flattened his ears and gripped Emma lightly with his claws. A boat came out of the mist.

"Hey, Emma! Seen any monsters besides the one you're holding?" Nelson called out from the power boat he was steering. Petey sat in the stern, frowning at the water.

"Not this morning," Emma said, deciding the pig wasn't worth mentioning.

Nelson slowed, rounding the point. "You shouldn't be out here without a weapon," he said, and Emma noticed the shiny gun barrel lying on the bottom of the boat near Petey's feet.

Rutledge came up beside her, bringing with him a faint smell of tobacco. He held a rifle loosely under one arm. "How's it going?" he called to the men in the boat.

"Quiet," Petey said.

"Nelson and Petey are our first patrol," Rutledge told Emma.

"Too much damn fog," Nelson said. "But the boat engine alone ought to discourage wild things from swimming this way. I'm going to continue along the shore," he shouted over the increased engine sound as he loosened the boat's throttle and sped off.

The noise spooked Pudding, who jumped down and ran for the underbrush.

"What's wrong, Emma?" Rutledge said.

"Billie came in this morning smelling of smoke. I think . . ."

"Smoke?" Rutledge looked at something over her shoulder and waved.

Emma turned and saw Max walking toward them, his shirt buttoned up wrong, his hair untidy.

"What's going on?" Max said. "Bootsy called me. Emma, are you all right?"

"Billie's fur smells of smoke," Emma said. "I think there must be a fire in that world she goes to. I think the people there set it to herd the animals together so they can kill them."

"You found this out at Bootsy's?" Max sounded totally confused.

"Not exactly. I went there to look up some things in Dana's books, because . . . Look, Max, that doesn't matter. The point is, I think they're herding the animals into that funnel-shaped ravine."

"Where they come through into our world," Rutledge said.

"If they can. It doesn't always work," Emma said. "But I think there are either going to be a lot of dead animals over there, or a lot of live ones here."

Rutledge peered toward the island and shook his head. "I can't make out anything. If we're looking for smoke, I'd better get the binoculars."

He went toward his house. Emma squinted at the island, shading her eyes with her hand. "Max, is anyone patrolling besides Nelson and Petey?"

"No, but I think we're pretty well set," Max said. "Walter's at the boat launch, Nelson's on the water, and Rutledge is watching from here. We should know if anything happens on the lake."

"But that's not enough people," Emma said.

"That's just the early warning line. If anything happens, we can call the fire company and have half the town here. We don't have the resources to keep a whole lot of people watching all the time."

"Something's going to happen today," Emma said. She sat on the rock, her legs stretched out in front of her.

"Are you going to sit there and wait for it?" Max asked, amusement in his tone.

"Yes."

"You're serious, aren't you?"

"Yes."

Rutledge came back with the binoculars and looked through them at the island. "Nothing," he said, and passed them to Emma. She looked, cleaned the lenses on her shirt tail, looked again. He was right.

"Emma's planning to sit right there on that rock all day," Max said.

"Probably a good idea," said Rutledge. "But not every minute. We can spell each other."

"I suppose that means I have to get my own breakfast again," Max said.

"While you're at it," Emma said, "why don't you bring out something for us?"

"Come on, Max," said Rutledge, "Let's see what we can find in my kitchen."

"Do you have any extra blankets, Rutledge?" Emma called after the two retreating figures. "This rock is pretty hard."

She was surprised when the plate of bacon and eggs they brought her was still warm. "You're a good cook, Rutledge," she said.

"Anything happening?" he asked.

"Nelson and Petey came through again, but that's all," Emma said.

"We heard them," Max said. He set a mug of coffee beside her and sipped his own. "I ought to get to work. But holler if anything happens."

"You won't hear me," Emma said.

"Yes, I will. I'll leave my studio door open."

Max left. Rutledge sat for a while, then said he had to make a run into town. "I'll bring sandwiches back with me."

Emma watched a family of ducks make their rounds of the lakeshore houses, stopping wherever people fed them. Who had been trained, the people or the ducks? Or to put it another way, who got the most out of the relationship?

The sun got higher, and shone into the island's ravine. From where she sat, the ravine looked like a stage set. She thought of her father dying there, and a picture of it came unbidden into her mind. She pushed the image away as too painful. But it had been part of an adventure, the way he died, and a larger adventure than just some random bear attack in the woods. He would have liked that. There was a tiny hook of comfort in the thought, and she accepted it.

Pudding came out to sun himself. The morning wore on, and heat shimmered in the air above the rock.

Petey rode by without Nelson, and Emma worried that people were already slacking off, but on the boat's next round Nelson was driving again.

By the time Rutledge got back, Emma needed a break from the sun. She went home, showered, collected her beach umbrella. Max carried it back for her, and they picnicked with Rutledge out on the rock.

The afternoon was similar to the morning, except Emma's shadow was in front instead of behind her.

At six o'clock she saw the first smoke.

Billie napped through midday, curled up in the nest of blankets the man had left on the bed. The woman always pulled them smooth, but he never did, and Billie preferred the contours he left behind.

When she woke, the house was quiet. And something was wrong.

Uneasy, she went downstairs to the kitchen. No one was around, but the door was slightly open and she pushed through onto the deck.

Billie opened her mouth to taste the air. It was scratchy with smoke, and she sneezed, then jumped onto the deck rail. Mouth shut, whiskers quivering, she looked across the lawn and lake to the island.

The big door was open, and smoke pushed through from otherside.

Billie's fur bristled with fear. She called to her people, looked for them on the lawn, the lake edge. At last she found them on her brother's rock. Crying out her warning, she ran to them.

chapter 31

When Emma saw the smoke, she shouted for Rutledge and Max.

It was white smoke, lit by the slanting rays of the late afternoon sun, and it billowed out of the ravine.

"Is it the lodge?" Rutledge asked, out of breath beside her.

"No," Emma said. "It's coming from the ravine."

"There's nothing to burn in the ravine. Too wet and marshy."

"The island's on fire!" Max called out, jogging toward them.

"I don't think so," Emma said. "Not our island."

"I'll call the firemen," Rutledge said, and went to his house.

Max stood beside Emma. "It must be the lodge. The trees haven't caught. Look: no fire in the branches."

"I don't think the fire's here, just the smoke. Billie!" Emma said as the cat came running toward her. She picked Billie up, and Billie purred briefly, but then tensed and looked at the island, her ears flattened, her nose twitching.

Emma looked, too. There were shapes coming toward them through the smoke.

Three mammoths emerged first, screaming. One of them had a spear embedded in its shoulder, and it pulled at the free end with its trunk. The spear came loose and the animal tossed it into the lake, screaming again. Blood ran from its shoulder, matting the dark fur with red. The others caressed the wounded mammoth with their trunks, apparently comforting it, then all three lumbered into the water, crowded from behind by a herd of giant deer.

The deer, their hooves clicking on the rock, leaped one after another into the lake and swam north in a group, only their heads and branching antlers visible above the surface, like flotsam trees after a storm. The largest male paused on the rock facing the low sun, the nine-foot span of his antlers catching the light, his eyes glowing amber even from this distance. He looked toward Emma, then jumped in and followed his herd. The mammoths followed, swimming toward the already-darkening northern woods.

"Max, they're going north!" Emma said, turning to him.

Max's expression was one of stunned amazement. He swallowed hard, and his hand twitched. "I'm going to get a sketchpad," he said, and ran toward his studio.

Emma returned her attention to the island, where frightened and wounded animals continued to pour out of the smoke. What had those people done? Was anything but fire left over there?

Suddenly dozens of squealing, piglike things swarmed onto the rock, over the rock, and were soon churning the water. Emma recognized them as the same kind of animal she had seen that morning.

Nelson's boat returned at full speed, splashing Emma and making Billie leap down and run for the woods. Emma looked at the bloody scratches on her arms and pressed the bottom of her shirt against them.

Max came back and stood beside her, sketching rapidly.

"There! There! That's it!" Petey shouted above the engine's noise.

What appeared to be a six-foot beaver was standing on the rock, sniffing the air. Petey pounded Nelson on the back, and since Nelson was steering, this made the boat swerve.

"Nelson! Herd the pigs!" Max shouted.

Nelson turned the boat around and cut off the pigs' route to the nearer shore. They squealed and swam frantically away from the boat's path.

"They're going to drown each other," Max said.

The siren sounded from town, and Rutledge joined Max and Emma. He looked at the scene in the lake. "Isn't that something?" Rutledge cupped his hands to his mouth. "Nelson, those pigs are drowning!"

Nelson slowed, returned to the pigs, and throttled the engine. Petey got out fishing nets on long poles, and the two of them tried to break up the worst of the congestion.

Emma gasped. "Look!" she said.

A sabertooth leaped onto the rock. The beaver moved hastily, tripped, and fell into the water. The cat's ears were flattened, its eyes scrunched up. It coughed several times, then took a deep breath and looked at the pigs, the boat, the people. It opened its mouth and hissed, flashing death white fangs, then, crowded from behind by emerging mammoths, it leaped into the water and swam.

"North," Emma said. "Rutledge, it's working."

The pigs seemed to be doing better. Petey had apparently dropped his net, because Emma saw him trying to retrieve it, and Nelson was just staring at the spot where the sabertooth had been, but they had managed to get some pigs headed in the right direction, and the others were following. Emma counted two still and floating bodies left behind in the general movement of snouts and ears.

Nelson turned to the people on shore. "Did I just see what I think I saw?"

"Behind you!" Max yelled.

A mammoth swam toward the boat. Nelson turned, saw it, grabbed the steering wheel. The boat lurched forward and Petey fended off the mammoth by whacking it with the handle of the net he'd just pulled from the water. The mammoth wrapped its trunk around the net and yanked it from Petey's hands, but the boat got away undamaged.

The mammoth continued toward the nearer shore. Nelson turned and cut across its path, sending waves over the animal, but it just raised its trunk higher and kept on swimming.

"We're getting this one to deal with," Rutledge said, checking his stun rifle.

The sound of a motor behind her made Emma turn to see a truck driving across Bootsy's lawn. It stopped on Rutledge's property and Walter climbed out, reached back in, took out a rifle. Emma tensed and jumped when he slammed the truck door. The fire engine arrived and parked on the road. Other cars and trucks drove up simultaneously. Men hurried from them toward the lake.

"I hope that's a stun rifle, Walter," Emma said. "Because that's the only kind we're using."

"No, it's not. It's a Winchester, and it fires real bullets, and you may be glad I'm here with it before this day is over."

"Are you looking to be remembered as the man who shot the last of an endangered species?"

"You still owe me for the Weatherby." He pushed past her and went closer to the shore, but kept his rifle down. The men from the cars converged on the lake and stood staring, many with their mouths open.

Animals kept coming: mammoths, deer, also smaller furry things that scurried into the water. Smoke had drifted across the lake, and Emma could smell it now, along with the stench of burnt fur and wet mammoth.

"Are we going to get any help here?" Nelson shouted from his boat, his tone filled with the exasperation of the overworked man who sees others idly watching him. "You didn't tell me there would be so many."

Emma could see he needed help: the press of numbers was sending animals swimming in all directions.

"There's two more boats coming," Rutledge yelled. "We'll herd the mammoth over to Howard's." He spoke to the men onshore, and three detached themselves from the group and positioned themselves around the mammoth as it emerged from the lake. Shaking water out of its fur, it splashed them, then looked around with a bewildered expression.

"See how tame it is? But why Howard's?" Emma asked.

"Sheep pasture," said Max. "It's fenced in. That's where the others are."

"And they're doing a job on Howard's tree branches, but I don't think he cares. Motel's full, and he's charging admission to see the mammoths," Walter said.

"I'm glad some people see the economic advantage instead of just some trophy to be killed," Emma said over the sound of the arriving powerboats.

"Woman, stop needling me," said Walter.

Max stepped between them. "That's enough. This isn't the time or place."

The lake was dotted with the heads of hundreds of animals swimming in confusion, their wakes intersecting behind them. Nelson shouted orders to the arriving boats, trying to coordinate his shore patrol. "Don't touch those pigs," he said. "They bite. Use nets or poles. And just fish out the cats and let them loose on board. They hide, we can deal with them later. The little cats. Any big ones come your way, call me: I've got a stun rifle."

The mammoth raised its trunk and let out a mournful cry, meant to carry, and Emma and nearly everyone else turned to look at it.

"My God, what's that?" Walter said.

Puzzled, Emma looked at him, saw he was looking at the island.

A ton or more of hair and muscle and bone stood on the island's projecting rock.

"It's a woolly rhinoceros," Emma said forcing the words out through her suddenly constricted throat.

The rhino lowered its head and snorted, its horn gilded by the setting sun. It looked toward them and stomped its hoof.

"This isn't good," Emma whispered to Max.

The mammoth wailed.

The rhino flattened its ears, snorted again. It stepped forward into the lake and swam toward the shore where the men, who had now seen it, were milling about excitedly.

"It can't see very well," Emma yelled. "If you don't move it has a harder time seeing you!"

But nobody paid attention.

Nelson's boat was at the far end of his patrol route. He turned, but another powerboat, a little blue one, intervened. The driver went in front of the rhino's path, turned quickly, and then again, sending a splashing wake across the protruding horn and head of the slowly swimming animal.

The rhino kept coming.

The boat tried again.

Emma noticed the rhino was suddenly higher in the water. "He's walking. He's go a foothold on the bottom. He'll . . ."

The driver of the boat completed one turn and started another.

". . . go faster," Emma said. "Max, the man in the boat doesn't see it's going faster."

Boat and rhino collided, and the boat flew apart in a flash of light.

Max dropped his sketchpad and held Emma close, hiding her face against his chest.

Emma pushed away so she could see. There were pieces of wood floating on the flat water. Then the tip of a horn emerged, sharklike, and the rhino stood up and continued toward shore.

The people scattered.

Walter raised his rifle.

"No!" Emma screamed.

"Max, keep her away from me!"

Max pulled Emma back. "This one's dangerous."

"Just don't attract its attention!" Emma shouted.

"Woman, you don't know nothing!" Walter said.

The rhino came onto the shore, and its shadow reached across the lawn. It sneezed twice and looked around.

The mammoth saw it and screamed again, alarm in its

tone this time. It turned and fled down the road, with the men detailed to herd it running hard to keep up.

Walter took aim.

"Walter, put that up!" Rutledge said. "You're not going get through his hide with that peashooter."

Walter fired.

The rhino twitched as though it had been stung by a bee.

The men stopped and looked back.

"I got him!" Walter said, and walked toward the rhino.

"Walter, you fool, you're just going to get him mad," said Rutledge.

Walter fired again. The rhino lowered its head and looked at him.

Emma felt sick. "Walter, stop it!" She shouted. She tried to run toward them, but Max held her back.

Walter knelt, fired.

The rhino charged, its hooves beating a loud rhythmn on the earth. Walter fired again, but the rhino kept coming, faster and faster, louder and louder.

Walter dropped the rifle and ran for his truck.

The rhino kept coming.

"Don't get inside! Keep the truck between you!" Emma said.

Walter got in, slammed the door.

The rhino slammed into the door. The truck rocked up off the ground, two wheels in the air, then righted itself.

The rhino backed up.

Walter looked relieved.

Emma shook her head. "He'd better get out of there."

Max held on to her. "He'll be all right. He's safe in the truck."

The rhino lowered its head and charged again. This time its horn pierced the truck's door, and Walter screamed.

The rhino pulled its horn free, shook its head, snorted. It trotted once around the truck, head up, in what looked like a victory lap, then took off down the road.

Emma broke free of Max and ran to the truck. Men were coming toward it from the far woods, but she got there first, with Max close behind. Together they pried open the mangled door.

Walter sat holding his leg. His pants were torn, and blood flowed from his thigh onto the seat.

"He's cut!" Max shouted. "Walter, are you all right? At least the rescue squad's here already."

"Yeah, he didn't get an artery. But I'm glad that door was between us."

Emma looked at Walter's face. She could see he was in pain, but his color was good. "Walter," she said, "considering it takes a lot to get some people to listen, and considering your gun's over there on the lawn somewhere, I'm going to take this opportunity to say one thing to you: I told you so."

Walter looked shocked, then amused. "Max, how do you live with her without killing her?" he said, as the rescue squad workers closed in. "And you still owe me for the Weatherby!"

chapter 32

Billie hid in the brush that grew close to shore and looked out at the lake.

The big doorway was full of smoke that corroded its sides, weakened it. Otherside animals came through in terror, screaming. Billie's fur bristled in sympathy.

The lake was a turmoil of boats and animals. Cries and gurgles came from the animals. People howled. The water slapped and sucked. A mammoth brayed, and Billie's ears twitched. There were animals everywhere. She checked the rock where her people had been, and there they stood, calmly watching it all, the man playing with his paper and stick, the woman not searching for cover. Didn't they know this was all wrong?

She made it to the edge of her lawn and sat there panting, looking across the open space. Smoke drifted in from the island and stung her nose. The sun shone low in the sky, and each grass blade cast a shadow. On the arbor's shady side, moonflowers twirled into bloom, and in the garden, a stunted doorway opened. Billie tensed, but no smoke came from it.

Almost home. She started across the lawn toward the house, looked up. All the windows blazed light. She jumped, hissed, turned. The sun blazed the same firey color as the windows, and she spit at it, too. Caught between the two lights, she ran for the doorway.

Billie hesitated, peered in. Otherside smelled of fire past, but it seemed quiet. A good place to hide until home calmed down. Billie jumped through.

The meadow was black. The thick layers of dried grass had burned, taking the new shoots with it. Without their cover, Billie felt exposed in this open place of dirt and rock. She looked up, checking for hawks, but saw only empty blue sky.

Billie jumped onto a rock. The tree line ahead seemed unaffected, but beyond it, smoke roiled up: not the calm thread of the cook fire, but a billowing turbulence that blotted out the lower sky until, rising, it dissipated into haze and then into nothing. Screams came from the same direction as the smoke, and she swiveled her ears, trying to locate the source more accurately.

The screams were coming from the ravine near the big doorway. That made sense, considering what she had seen on the home side. But why?

The noises upset her. She thought about going home right now, but when she turned, the little door she had come through had closed already. She didn't see any others, not on the rise that led to where her house would be on the home side, not on the meadow that would be the lake, not anywhere. That was even more frightening than the noise. She sat and cried, even though she knew there was no one who could solve this problem for her.

She had to find a door.

Billie walked toward the trees, picking her way across stubbly ground. Ashes rose unpleasantly every time she set a paw down, and she sneezed, but continued with watery eyes until she reached the forest.

She climbed the large oak, happy to have her claws in solid bark, happy the tree was unchanged. When she was high enough, she looked out over the countryside.

She had watched the great animals walking through, going farther and farther out onto the plain until they were lost in the distance. Now a curving line of fire blocked their passage, and to get away from it, they were running into the ravine, bumping against each other in their panic. A deer fell, and others stepped on it in their flight. It got partway up, was knocked down. It didn't move again. There were whinnies and screams and roars of fright, but most of the noise was coming from inside the ravine, not from near the fire.

Billie climbed down and crept closer to the ravine.

She smelled blood, and all the hairs along her spine stood up. She flattened her body, hugging the ground, and swiftly moved beneath a tree. She could hear cries of men now, under the screams. She climbed the tree trunk, pushing through dense evergreen branches until she was high enough to see what was happening.

The ravine was filled with animals, and the only ones not milling about in panic were the ones that were already dead. The fear smell that rose from them washed over Billie, and she clung to the tree, near panic herself. Herded by the fire, they crowded into the ravine. They slipped on blood as they tried to get through, tried to climb over fallen animals of their own and other species.

Men dotted the top of the ravine on either side, jumping up and down, moving jerkily above the melee in a frenzy of their own. They attacked the animals from above with sharpened sticks, pounded them with heavy branches weighted further with rocks. Blood flowed and animals screamed. The men screamed in pleasure, and hit again, and again, and again. They danced. The brown dog, whimpering, darted back and forth among them.

At the narrow end of the ravine, the big doorway stood open. Animals ran past the men and were escaping with the smoke.

Billie could find no lesser doorways. She would have to make a run for it. She took some comfort in the growing darkness, which would favor her over the men, but she was afraid to run past them. They seemed tireless, swinging their clubs which landed with unpleasant thuds and cracks.

The crowding was less: the fire had done its work, and was lapping at the wide end of the ravine. A mammoth went through the doorway, dragging a limping baby. A deer bolted. The ravine was emptying, except for the dead.

The men jumped into the ravine to set about finishing their work. The dog followed them and was hit by a blow from a club. It yelped, put its tail between its legs, and ran off.

Heat from the fire blasted the ravine and seared the old man's machine. Its outside shriveled. The doorway wavered.

She would have to go past the men. Billie leaped from the tree and ran, panting, toward the fading red light that could lead her home.

chapter 33

"**There are too many!**" Nelson shouted from his boat. Behind him, the driver of the blue boat sat wrapped in a blanket. "You didn't say there'd be so many. And some of them are wounded," Nelson continued.

Emma stood in the water and helped a tired deer ashore. The lake was a confusion of panicky, swimming animals, some going in circles, the stronger and more levelheaded making for the north shore. Men with boats tried to buoy up the exhausted and the wounded, bring them to shore, but given the size of most of the animals, and the sheer numbers, the task was out of control. Soon it would be dark.

"I called Encon," Rutledge said. "And the state police."

The firemen spread along the shore and helped the boatmen bring the wounded onto land. Emma's deer knelt, wet, its expression dazed, holding its head up with obvious effort.

"I think some of them are going into shock," Max said, and went to help the firemen get a six-foot beaver out of the lake.

271

Rutledge shook his head, but in sympathy, not disagreement.

Two Emergency Squad people carried Walter off on a stretcher. Others tried to put a compress on a limping mammoth who was bleeding from a shoulder wound. Pigs squealed and ran by a wolf who stood dazed, head bloodied, oblivious to them. Rutledge fired a tranquilizer dart into the wolf, who slowly fell over. The men rushed him, carrying bandages. Along the road, cars gathered.

"We've got to do something about light," said Rutledge, who was reloading and keeping an eye on another wolf swimming toward shore.

"I'll get those cars to shine their headlights out here," Emma said. She patted the deer reassuringly. It struggled to its feet and got out of the lake, only to collapse, panting, on the grass.

The wolf came out of the water, shook itself, then bristled and snarled at the nearby men. Rutledge took aim.

Bootsy rushed up to Emma. "What's going on? I was taking a nap, and . . . . Oh my god." Bootsy stared at the lake, her hand over her mouth.

Rutledge fired the dart into the wolf. This one jumped and yelped, then staggered to the ground.

"You need a veterinarian," Bootsy said. "Lots of them."

"You're right," Emma said, stepping out of the lake. The sun was setting. "Could you go home and call all the vets in the phone book? Try to get them to come?"

Bootsy nodded, but Emma didn't wait to see her go. She ran to the road and spoke to the driver of the first car she came to. "Sir, could we have your help please?"

"What's going on?"

"We have an emergency here. Some animals running

from a fire out on the lake. Could you turn your car and shine the headlights across the ground? It would sure help our workers."

When he nodded, she ran to the next car, and the next, down the line. Some left, but enough stayed to get the lawn illuminated. Just when she was feeling more hopeful, a pickup truck full of men carrying rifles sped by. The men were laughing and passing a bottle. She ran to Rutledge.

"A truckload of good old boys just went up the road in a pickup. Armed. I think they're going hunting," Emma said.

"Damn." Rutledge ran into his house. Emma followed as far as the doorway, and listened to Rutledge's angry voice and the crackling drone of the CB.

Max came up to her. "We're losing too many into the woods. We need . . ."

Emma put her finger on his lips. "Shh!"

". . . hunting party. Rhinoceros hunting, probably," Rutledge said. The CB squawked and Rutledge laughed. "Good, if they stay on the road. But watch out for that rhino. You should see what he did to Walter's truck. Opened the side right up. I've never seen an animal built more like a can opener."

"What's going on?" Max said.

"Hunters," said Emma.

"Just what we don't need, in the woods in the dark. Out-of-towners?" Max asked.

Rutledge finished on the CB and came to the doorway. "The police have a roadblock. Nobody's coming through hunting, not if they can help it."

"What about the rhino?" Emma asked.

"Evidently he likes the paved roadway. He's following

it north. He doesn't like garbage cans, and he's attacked a few, but so far people are staying out of his way."

"So we just have to worry about people with guns who are already here?" Max said.

Rutledge's smile faded. "That's about it."

"I was telling Emma, too many animals are coming ashore in the woods," Max said.

"They're afraid of fire," Emma said. "What if we build fires along the shore?"

"In the woods? With the dry weather we've had?" Rutledge said.

"How about headlights on the shore, like you have along the road?" said Max.

"I don't know. Might just hypnotize them, like jack-lighting deer," said Rutledge.

"What about fires on the water?" Emma said.

Max stared at her. "How are you going to do that?"

"Rowboats. We pile up brush in rowboats, tow them out a ways, throw in lighter fluid and a match."

"Yes," said Rutledge. "I'll pass the word."

"We'll go do ours," Max said.

Max and Emma hurried to their backyard, where the rowboat was tied.

"I'll run up to the house for firewood. It'll burn longer than brush," Max said.

Emma wondered how long it would be before the fire burned through the bottom of the wooden rowboat. The boat leaked a little, which posed a different problem. She looked around, grabbed the barbecue grille, sticky from the last time they'd used it, and set it in the bottom of the boat. That should raise the fire.

She was piling kindling into the boat when the house

lights came on, making sudden rectangles of light on the lawn. Max must have flipped the switch so they could see better.

Emma wondered where Billie was. The kitchen door was open. Billie had probably gone inside. Surely she wouldn't go to that other world, not with a fire over there. "Billie," she called.

Max dropped a stack of wood into the rowboat. "You start building the fire, I'll get more wood," he said.

"Did you see Billie inside?" she called after him.

"I didn't look."

Once the wood was stacked over the kindling, Max poured lighter fluid over it and set a match to it. The fire blazed up, and Emma used an oar to push the boat away from the dock. The boat rode low, because of the weight, and the flames reflected in the water. Along the shore floated other boats filled with fire.

Emma strained to see across the dark lake. A wet, furry head changed course to avoid a rowboat. A mammoth raised its trunk and did the same. "I think it's working," she said.

Max nodded. "They're moving farther away. Everything out there must be tired by now, but if you see anything swimming this way, don't take any chances: run for the house. I'm going back to help with the roundup."

"I'm coming, too," Emma said, annoyed. After all, she'd faced more of this than he had. She walked past him in the direction of Rutledge's. Max quickly caught up and, putting his arm around her, walked beside her.

Someone had made a bonfire on the rocky point below Rutledge's, and they seemed to be using it as a command point. She saw men run up to it, confer with Rutledge, run away. The boatmen were busy picking up animals farther from shore. The stars were out, but the fires from the rowboats outshone them on the lake.

Bootsy's calls must have been successful, because she was helping a couple of veterinarians sorting among the animals on the lawn. Rescue squad volunteers loaded a deer onto the back of a pickup truck and drove off.

"Where are they taking it?" Emma asked Rutledge.

"The healthy ones are going to the forest preserve, the injured ones back to the vet's. Some aren't going anywhere."

"But most of them are okay?"

"Most of them are okay."

Petey came up to the bonfire and stood warming himself. He was wet and the air had turned chilly. "Not much coming out of the water on this side anymore," he said.

"It's winding down," Rutledge said. "I'm going to organize a sweep through the woods, try to herd anything large toward the preserve. Want to come, Emma?"

"I will," Max said.

Emma looked at the island, lost now in darkness. Had it finished with them? "I think I'll hang around here. It was my idea to fire the boats. I ought to stick around and make sure none of them drift to shore and start a fire."

"Good idea," said Rutledge. He and Max walked along the shore, rounding up volunteers.

Petey grinned at Emma. "We showed them, didn't we?"

Emma laughed. "I guess we did."

"Well." He looked toward the gathering group of men. "I think I'll go see if they need my help," he said.

Not quite sure why she was staying, Emma stood alone by the fire. A branch cracked and sparks rose. She had a feeling of unfinished business. Would all the heat and smoke harm the maser? And where was Billie?

Emma went home and searched the house, but couldn't find Billie. She put on a sweater, then went back outside and sat on the dock.

She was tired. She hadn't noticed until she sat down. She leaned back on her hands, studying the lake. The rowboat fires burned and drifted. Powerboats whined in the distance.

A small head came toward her in the water, swimming slowly.

"Billie?" she said, getting up.

But the thing that came out wasn't a cat. It was some kind of rodent, and very tired. It pulled itself onto the shore and lay exhausted, defenseless. Emma looked at it carefully. Yes, it was like the animal Billie had left on her pillow. It didn't seem hurt.

Emma went back to the dock and sat down. After a while, the little animal scurried off toward the woods.

Emma wondered what changes they would be seeing in the local fauna over the next few years.

Nelson rode by slowly, checking the lake. He finished his patrol of the shore without having to stop for anything. As he turned and came back, a rowboat sank, its fire hissing into the water.

The moon rose. There seemed to be fewer men at Rutledge's, but she saw lights in the woods on the eastern shore.

"Emma?" It was Peggy's voice. Emma turned, saw Peggy coming toward her with a thermos. "I brought you some coffee."

"Thanks," Emma said, accepting a cup.

Peggy looked across the lake. "I saw wonderful things today. Wonderful things."

"No birds, though," said Emma.

"No. You'd think they'd be fleeing a fire, too, wouldn't you?"

"A natural fire, yes. A big one. But I guess it's hard to drive birds with fire. They can just fly away."

"You think this was done deliberately?" Peggy said. "I don't want to believe that."

"I think people did it."

Peggy sighed, wiped her hands on her shirt. "We have another chance now." She looked across the lake. "Wonderful things. Well, don't you stay up too late, dear."

"Just 'til the rowboats fizzle," Emma said. "How's Charles?"

"He's doing well. Dana was on the news, you know. A special bulletin."

"No, I didn't know."

"He's got some kind of emergency thing from the governor or the legislature, I didn't catch which. But the animals are all on the endangered list temporarily until this gets sorted out. So nobody can hunt them. And there's talk of sending teams from different zoos and universities. It'll be quite a boost for our economy."

Nelson zoomed by, waved. He seemed confident on the water. On dry land, he seemed afraid he might sink.

Emma and Peggy waved back.

"I think I've boosted Nelson's economy," Emma said. "Think of all the new rowboats he's going to sell."

Peggy smiled and went home, leaving the coffee.

The fire below Rutledge's went out, and Emma watched the speedboats return to the marina. Emma counted fewer rowboats, but four remained.

The moon cast a still light across the water. Occasionally something swam through its path, heading north.

There was a loud pop on the island. Something metallic skittered onto the rocks. The maser? Emma stood up and tried to see better, but it was too dark. There was nothing explosive in the maser.

Silence followed, and she sat down again. Had somebody in the past smashed the maser? Or could heat have made it explode?

The outside casing would burn or melt, but it would take a hot fire to melt the metal container or damage the ruby. It would need to be hotter than just a brushfire. And the liquid nitrogen inside the metal wasn't explosive.

Unless the heat made it expand and burst the container. Nitrogen is a gas at natural temperatures on this planet. Damn. That's probably what happened.

Maybe a physicist could look at the pieces and figure out how the machine had been constructed. If there was enough of it left, that is.

Emma waited for the remaining boats to sink or burn out, and she held the oar ready. But there was no harm in resting her head against the post.

A warm touch on her shoulder woke her and she whirled, oar in hand, whacking Max with the blade.

"Ouch!" he said, putting his hand to his head.

"I'm sorry. You startled me," Emma said. "Are you all right?"

"I was fine 'til I got home."

Emma looked around in the predawn light and mist. Their rowboat floated nearby, its sides charred, and farther out she saw another rowboat upended in shallow water. "So what's happening?"

Max yawned. "I just got back. I've been out all night. We chased those things all the way to the forest preserve, but the National Guard's here now, and they can do a sweep in daylight. I'm exhausted. And starving. I put coffee on when I passed through the house. Let's have breakfast and go to bed."

"Did you see Billie?"

"No, but I didn't look. Come on."

"I'll be up in a minute. You go on," Emma said.

Max put his arm around her. "She'll be all right. She's probably hiding somewhere."

"I think the maser could have exploded."

Max held her close, and she rested her head against his chest.

"It's probably for the best if it did," he said. "Come have breakfast."

"I want to look for Billie. Then I'll be in."

"She'll come when you get out the can opener," he said, and went into the house.

Emma remained on the dock. The lake was still, even the birds were still. What if Billie was caught in that other world when the maser exploded?

"Billie," Emma called. "Billie?"

She heard a meow, faint or distant, but she smiled to hear it. "Billie!"

The meow sounded louder, coming toward her, but . . . It was coming from the island.

"Oh, Billie." Emma looked through the mist, trying to see movement. There she was, looking at Emma and crying pitifully.

"All right, Billie," Emma called. "How am I going to get out there?" she muttered to herself, looking at the ruined boat.

They'd dropped the rope into the water, but the end was still tied. Emma pulled, and the boat floated toward her. She looked inside. The boat was charred, the bottom full of ashes, but it was still floating since it had been leaky in the first place. There was no way she could sit in the middle and row, so she climbed carefully into the bow and untied the rope. Then, using one oar, she paddled out canoe style.

Billie walked back and forth anxiously, crying. Emma secured the boat to the island and got out carefully. She climbed onto the rock and picked up her cat. Billie purred and clung to Emma's neck.

The sun came up. There were wrecks of rowboats along the shore, and Rutledge's point was charred. Broken branches extended from the woods to the water, and Emma saw a dead mammoth lying half out of the water. A deer and a few pigs floated nearby, but she had been afraid it would be far worse. On the rock in front of her, a scrap of metal and a shattered red crystal caught the light.

She stroked Billie and, wondering if the island was changed, turned to look at it.

A sabertooth cat lay at the entrance to the ravine and stared at her. The stun gun Emma had left behind was near the cat's tail. The remains of some animal lay nearby, partly eaten, and Emma hoped the cat was full. She remained absolutely still, as did Billie.

The cat got up slowly, stiffly. It sniffed the air.

Billie tensed.

The cat moved toward them, limping slightly in its hindquarters. Its fur was scuffed, and one ear had dried blood on it. The cat stopped in front of Billie and Emma and looked at them, the pupils of its eyes contracting in the bright morning light. It opened its mouth, and Emma felt its breath hot on her hands and arms. She didn't move. She didn't breathe.

Billie leaned forward and set one paw on the big cat's forehead. It closed its mouth and stood looking at Billie, letting the paw remain for a moment. A long moment. The longest moment of Emma's life.

Then it pulled its head slowly away, sneezed, and walked past them to the end of the rock. It turned once and looked back, raised its head and opened its mouth. Emma saw the gaping jaws, the white saberteeth against the sun. Then the cat closed its mouth, padded down the other side of the rock, into the water, and swam north.

Billie watched the sabertooth swim and was glad she didn't have to get in the nasty water. She had her person to carry her home.

She purred, rubbing her head against her person's chin and enjoying the hands that scratched behind her ears.

The woman took Billie to the boat and sat scrunched up in the front end. There was water in the bottom. She tried to set Billie down but, feeling safer up high, Billie climbed onto her shoulders.

The woman paddled away from the island. Billie clung to her shoulders and dug her claws in tighter. The woman grumbled and moved her arms more smoothly.

There were faint smells of otherside, and smells of ashes, but mostly the lake smelled like home. A bird flew teasingly close, then climbed into the sky.

They bumped against the dock, and Billie held on tighter. Her person yelled, pulled on Billie, but Billie kept her hold. The woman stopped pulling, stroked Billie's back, and walked toward the house.

Billie rode high above the ground, high above the nasty wet grass. She liked it up here, and licked her person's ear in appreciation. The feathery things were singing all around, and a smell of cooking meat came from the food room. She rode toward food and her soft bed, and she purred as loudly as she could. She was home.

When Annie and Mark and their five-year-old son, David, move into a grand old Victorian house surrounded by a jumble of gardens, they are not prepared for the terror that awaits them. Annie soon realizes something is changing little David, drawing him into an unnatural bond with the chaotic tendrils of vine and root.

Now strange things are happening in the garden, while terrible, violent events begin occurring in their once-peaceful town. As an unknown enemy stalks her family, Annie finds herself and her son drawn deeper and deeper into the dark and mysterious life of the garden. And what happens on this patch of land surrounding her home will send seeds of change blowing across the planet to sow a crop of transformation. . . or destruction.

WINIFRED ELZE

THE CHANGELING GARDEN

"For readers who like scares served up with a more subtle flavor than that of Anne Rice or Stephen King."
—*Library Journal*

THE CHANGELING GARDEN
Winifred Elze
_____ 96135-9 $5.99 U.S./$7.99 Can.

Publishers Book and Audio Mailing Service
P.O. Box 070059, Staten Island, NY 10307
Please send me the book(s) I have checked above. I am enclosing $_____ (please add $1.50 for the first book, and $.50 for each additional book to cover postage and handling. Send check or money order only—no CODs) or charge my VISA, MASTERCARD, DISCOVER or AMERICAN EXPRESS card.

Card Number_____

Expiration date_____Signature_____

Name_____

Address_____

City_____State/Zip _____
Please allow six weeks for delivery. Prices subject to change without notice. Payment in U.S. funds only. New York residents add applicable sales tax.   CHAN 7/97